T0195747

Redux

SEAN MCKEITHEN

Order this book online at www.trafford.com
or email orders@trafford.com

Most Trafford titles are also available at major online book retailers.

© Copyright 2014 Sean MCkeithen.
All rights reserved. No part of this publication may be reproduced, stored in a
retrieval system, or transmitted, in any form or by any means, electronic, mechanical,
photocopying, recording, or otherwise, without the written prior permission of the author.

Printed in the United States of America.

ISBN: 978-1-4907-3255-8 (sc)
ISBN: 978-1-4907-3254-1 (hc)
ISBN: 978-1-4907-3253-4 (e)

Library of Congress Control Number: 2014905895

Because of the dynamic nature of the Internet, any web addresses or links contained in
this book may have changed since publication and may no longer be valid. The views
expressed in this work are solely those of the author and do not necessarily reflect the
views of the publisher, and the publisher hereby disclaims any responsibility for them.

Any people depicted in stock imagery provided by Thinkstock are models,
and such images are being used for illustrative purposes only.
Certain stock imagery © Thinkstock.

Trafford rev. 03/27/2014

 www.trafford.com
North America & international
toll-free: 1 888 232 4444 (USA & Canada)
fax: 812 355 4082

Chapter One

R ex was hard on a lot of the people, but it was the joy of meeting new people that made Rex Turner the happiest man that he could be. He was happy because he thought about people and heard about their lives. Since time was of the essence, there was little else he did but study. Once in a while, there would be a siren rail that would move through the people as they were seated in there consoles. The first person to finish the test would set the curve. Since time was of the essence, the people tried their hardest to be on time and simultaneous. Once in a while, the different students would curve the air and start ice. Ice was a thought in water and was able to curve a circle because of a right angle to a pressure made a line that could curve. Ice meant free for all and was not finished until the tenth circle had been formed. The tenth circle was a joke in cops that meant movement stopped being memory. Since the tenth circle was rare and meant that they could do math, there was a lot of joy in being in the ten circles. If you were left behind, you simply made a color and started over. Once in a while, the din in the stockade would become louder than the instructor would like it to. Since this happened a lot, it was not unusual and would become a normality among the students.

Rex Thomas was efficient and magically talented. Since he knew how to hear perfectly, there was little that he did not catch. Hearing in other students was what he was loved for and was not the last person in the room to have crazy excuses to play. Once in a while, he would wonder about the girl he loved and would go to another student to do this. Since Sean Tack was not the brightest of the students but the strongest, it was on him to think through a redux at thought. A redux never enjoys just responds and is actually a book in brain. Since a book would keep the students from enjoying themselves it was hard on the students and they spent their time studying hard. Since Redux was strong and capable, there was little time to waste if you ever beat one. If a book was beaten it would be thought through again and a new book would be made. Once in a while, a Redux would approach, but this was rare and they were only students.

Chapter Two

O nce in a while, the redux would become confused by the inertia that it contained. If the inertia was too great, there was a decision to loop and fall. Since looping and falling was a little dangerous, they tried to do that very rarely. Only after a long shot of happy did the redux actually move toward the light. A book can move think and destroy but could not create lift or dive. The redux were a solitary people that did not like light at all. Since the dimmer the experience the harder they were to live through, there were a lot of redux that lost consciousness under the dim. If a redux blipped off, it was up to the students to figure out how to bring it back. A student and a cadet are very similar and a cadet is actually a way of viewing memory. Since cadets are not a normal profession, they were proud to be there and make a hand-to-hand feeling.

A cube was rare, and it was the cadets joy to make cubes. Light has a hard time making a right angle, and it was Sean Timely that figured out to freeze before making a light switch. Since switches were good for a redux, they would joke about them for hours. Four hours' real time was about three weeks in redux, and it was why the redux would become overloaded with mass. Since mass was time, there was nothing in the world more important than a redux. Once a redux had formed, it was the job of the cadets to think forward and backward about it. In order to go forward in a mass, the cadet had to read and whither; while in order to go backward in a mass, a cadet had to lift and give. Since this was confusing Sean White thought about it in order to go forward in a mass, the cadet had to make a square and whirl wind toward light; and in order to go backward in a mass, the cadet had to wind and turn an oval. If that wasn't confusing enough, a redux always fights you over everything that you do. Since redux were rare, there was little that they did not know.

Susan Pierce was the prettiest girl and had a lot of problems with boys. Since this was normal to her, there was little she was not capable of doing. A pink dragon was genius to her and made her flirtatious. Since she liked men, she was a go in candidate for most of the day. If "go in" failed, she would whither and tit. Once in a while, the differences between the spirits would war. If they warred, a girl would think the men gay. If they were actually gay, they were a referee only and never actually warred. Once in a while, Sarah would put "bygone be bygones" and actually have a man. This was hard on the redux but made a lot of the girls happy. The more the pretty lived, the happier the redux would be.

Since a redux and a soldier was rare, Sean Maverick was considered a genius. In order to protect the strength gene, all of the cadets were to be assigned a redux and a soldier and this would make them happy. If the strength of the gene ever failed, they would be very unhappy, and that was why they were in school.

Chapter Three

Once in a while, a redux would say something to another redux. This was always accompanied by a black night. Since a black night was rare, little problems were to be taken care of by a black night. Black nights did most of the work that cadets found to be too hard. Once in a while, a black night would think about what they were doing and come back for a second pass. The black night Eric Smith was the strongest black night in the whole world and specialized in gay and brain strength. Since he was a black night, there was not a gay relationship that he did not sleep through; to waken to a rooster in the morning. Once in a while, there were relationships that were too hard to live through, and that was only if there were a bisexual or a both came experience. Since this was not the first time that the black night had been hard off, he needed help and went to Sean Chime to get it. Once in a while, this would happen, and it was the decision of the counsel to allow this friendship over one condition,: that no matter how dangerous the experience was, that they would not eat. The reason not to eat was that the two of them would puke and be thought gay together. Since the black night had never puked even into his throat, this was well documented and was why they were considered friends.

Chapter Four

The cops had a redux playing with an atom and had figured it out down too how it moved but not why it saw. Since if they knew how it saw, and they knew how it moved, they would say "I know when it moved" but they were lying and the atom didn't care. Since an atom was a thought on degrees, there was little it was not capable of doing. Once in a while, it would be possible to outthink an atom, but this was rare and the god who had made them knew not to change them even though this was constantly requested. If the god ever did think to change them, which happened to the cadets sometimes, he would only twist and start over. The reason being that it was the god's opinion that the facts of the world were possible only under indirect light. Since a full light never had a fact to it, the god merely, prayed, trained, and mirrored the full lights back at the redux as they fought him. Once in a while, a god would scare, but this was rare and the cops were pretty good about making up with the god if it scared. Once in a while, a redux would vomit, and this was watched closely by the god and was why he was not angry with them anymore, having been angry over something that they gave up on. Since vomiting meant that you gave up nothing mattered.

Chapter Five

The god woke early in the morning and checked his color. In the night while he slept, there had been three errors and two color thieves. Since color was in high demand and low supply, he was thankful that he had thought of it before the redux. Once in a while, the redux would claim monetary superiority and demand color. Since the god owned most of it, he was apt to sell it for memory enhancements. Even though he was a god, he still got confused sometimes. He had nearly given up on color completely because of a clever redux that put him in a prone position and fagged his balls. Since this was rare, it was only when he promised him a redux position that he became aware of the thief. Since a redux only loves another redux, there were a lot of hours of hate to move through. Once in a while, the god was given to moving in shadows to get away. A roshark was good at every thing but was called a bone yard since it makes bone smooth. The hatred was like moving in a bone yard. Once in the proximity of murder, it was important to know the victim only, and the god rarely liked to do this since it was dangerous. It was rare to have a bad victim, but the god had driven a spike and melted a heart to get away.

Since only the victims were known in the eather, the redux hated the god deeply. Once in a while, one of them would come to him crying that he had gotten caught and the god had to show light and move to avoid a secret talent. Since secret talents were rare, it was not unusual for the god to like a redux, and that is where the fun began for him this morning. The god scanned for secret talents, knowing them by the jagged appearance and grey exterior. They were usually bragging about money and did little movements that had already happened without knowing to make the experiences move. Since they were easy to spot, he killed one and then started his day. A secret talent was a joke and only liked because they were perfect at memory, they were used to tell on the people that they encountered and were really good at police.

Once in a while, there were people that left the building before the action started, but the god was not one of them. Once in a while, this would turn deadly and the god was up for a fight today.

The basket ball game was over the fight between redux and cadets. The home team was redux and the visiting team was cadet. Since both were powerful it was going to be a good game. The cadets streamed into the building on the left and the redux on the right. The eather formed in the middle, and the god sat off to one side. A blue ribbon was thrown, and the cadets lurched. A ribbon was a trick that was known in the way that people remembered and was fun to think about while the game played. Blue symbolized equality and was the best color for a wizard. A blue ribbon meant that criminals play and redux watch. Blue also did something important in the eather, which made the cadets happy. Once in a while, the blue ribbon would lift, and this meant that a woman was confused. If the blue ribbon fell, which meant that the color deepened, the redux would move and take over. This meant that a woman was sad and wanted to feed. Since this meant that the cadets would not be allowed happiness, they tried hard not to let the ribbon fall, for if it fell, the redux would take over.

Once in a while, the redux would cheat. If this ever happened, the god would throw a brown ribbon. The brown ribbons were dangerous to the redux because they were opposite from the blue ribbons and were actually more dangerous. If the ribbon rose and was less dangerous then if the ribbon fell. Since the darker a brown ribbon was the more pleasant a cadet became, there was a lot of turmoil over when to throw a brown ribbon and why to. A brown ribbon meant that criminals lost.

Once in a while, there were people that would try to cheat at the ribbons, and it was for that reason that the umpire existed. Once in a while, the umpire would give up, but this was rare and it was the redux that enjoyed the umpire most. Since the umpire was a redux, there was a lot of turmoil over who would win and the umpire would have to explain that he did not give a wrong call but that rather his calls were all predestined by a booklet. Since a booklet was never wrong, the umpire was never wrong. Once in a while, there were people that thought that a booklet could be wrong and wanted to kill the booklet.

Since the booklet was never wrong, there was almost thirty positions, and it was sad that the umpire had watched the one of them fail. The umpire had gone to the god over this, and the god had wanted to make an atom booklet. Since this was not allowed, that was when the ribbons were discovered and a gold ribbon had been made for the umpire. Since gold never tarnished, three positions were created in the booklet by the gold ribbon. Once in a while, there were people that needed the umpire and were not allowed. If the umpire was not allowed, the god usually did and got the umpire in trouble since he looked after the god and was always there for him. Since the god got into trouble, sometimes the umpire would have a hard time sleeping and the two of them would try hard together to find a girl to sleep with.

It was important that the girl was not afraid since if you slept afraid, the eather would offend at you. Once in a while, there were people that made sense to the god and those that didn't. If the umpire and the god had the same problem, they would go to a redux and walk away. Since the cadets were still strong in a fight, the redux never lost control of how they felt. The umpire looked at the brown ribbon and laughed. The redux were the smartest problem the god had ever had at a brown ribbon. Since brown was male to male and the girls were a little lesbian at a brown ribbon. If it was thrown, the cadets were good about touching a woman when the redux lost. If the brown got too light, the umpire would pull the brown ribbon and proclaim a redux winner. If the cadets won, the umpire would take a moment to explain to the eather and walk down and walk away. Since this was spiritual, the god was always found to be a little behind. Since the god thought a lot about the umpire, he's surprised sometimes at what the god knew and was a little anticipatory about the gold ribbon and when it was thrown. A gold ribbon is almost never thrown. Since the gold ribbon was thrown once, there were a lot of people at mad for the rest of time. A gold ribbon meant that time stopped and every one rethought.

The god walked and threw a purple ribbon. Since this was rare, there were a lot of people that were watching the eather for the redux move. Once in a while, there were people that knew the purple ribbon but didn't know how to same-shade. Once the purple ribbon was thrown, the women would walk and the delay would be ten till three over five. Since the redux were all five, the redux were followed by the women. The cadets were left to sway. A purple ribbon was almost a formality, and it was because of this that the redux did not scare at all. A purple ribbon meant a young couple was in love and was always taken ceremoniously. Once in a while, the redux would request a gold ribbon, but this is rare and the redux were good about not claiming it over something petty like if you were handsome or not. Once in a while, there were redux that outstrengthened the cadets. If the cadets were outstrengthened, they would throw a yellow ribbon and be caught. Since the cadets were good at being caught, it was a laughing stock when a yellow ribbon was thrown. At a yellow ribbon, the cadets would show their DNA, and that would be the way that they calmed the redux and let the women feel and come back to them and mate again. Since ribbons were the hardest of the eather, there was little that the redux did not know. Once again, it was the umpires that made sure nothing too extreme happened.

Jim Smith said that if he ever graduated, which was rare, he would be a good black night. Since the time that the black nights took for granted was not that, they would be smart but to be all encompassing. Black nights were hard to beat. The redux would still fight a black night, but it was rare for them to ever actually kill one. Since Jim Smith was a good black night that had a lot of success, there were a lot of students that looked up to him. If this was ever a problem, the umpire would figure it out for him. The cadets sat around their cubicles thinking about time. Once the ribbon was thrown, it had moved up for three seconds, deepened three shades, and then sank for seconds to do the same three shades. Since this was typical to the ribbons, there was nothing for the cadets to do but to think about how the cadets would feel about each other and the ribbons.

Chapter Six

The redux were moving around an eather error. There were a lot of movies that remembered, but there was little that they did not know. Since the tear in the eather was known, it was just a brush-and-grab job. Nuts as it seemed, the eather was strong in small and the redux was trying to figure out how to think about the eather. A memory that was not communal went by, and a redux scared. Since it was the god's joy to figure out fear, the god was accessed and he started moving. Since the god was behind in spiritual moves, the eather was dangerously close to tearing worse before the god came back with a length for the redux. To the god, the tear was known; but to the redux, it was not and the tear was repeated behind time. Once in a while, the behind would startle and the redux would have to move again. If this happened, the redux would x and starve. Since a well-fed animal can starve, the redux watched the eating pattern for a delay. If the delay existed, it meant that the offender had turned black and the memory had gone stale.

Stale was a joy to the redux. Since if you are a stale, there is nothing that can move you. You can be surrounded and ostracized. Once in a while, there were people that got ostracized and don't know what to do about it. The god sometimes did, but usually an umpire would have to intercede and comfort the ostracized. Once in a while, there were things that scared an umpire, and that was what the god liked to do. Once in a while, the god was wrong, but this was rare. The ostracized were hard to fathom. The redux laughed for an hour when the actual cause of the tear was known. A man had propositioned another man in public, and the second man had not been gay at all. Since a black night was down, there was little that the cadets could do but think through the rejection about the man being straight and not being considered gay. Since space camp was fun, the redux told the man to think about what he did and not do something in public out of order.

The man said that he did not know how to find another man and thought that that man had wanted him. The man had done something in energy that had made him seem wanted. Once in a while, the eather would forgive, and it had him after the black night was back. The black night knew something from that that was not normal. He knew that a gay man is as hurt by not having sex as a straight man was by a gay man. The color matched and was why he thought Sean Timely's straight even though women claimed him gay. Once in a while, the color would match and he would think about it. Since nothing mattered, there were a lot of people, and that was why the gay man was not as hurt as the straight man was. Once in a while, it still came up, but that was just shame. Target mattered a lot to the cadets, and it was a very smart cadet that figured out to embarrass and throw a grey ribbon if shame became too much. The reason that a grey ribbon worked was that there was nothing to do but live through it, grey being all precision.

Chapter Seven

The cadets sat around in a circle singing songs. Since none of them had graduated, the first inclination was to think about each other, but that was deemed wrong by the dark mistress and was not allowed. Once in a while, a ribbon would come up, but the songs were allowed and stopped only if a woman passed out. Since there were seven songs, the cadets laughed a lot at the thought of an eighth. Eight songs would mean caught and was not possible. Once in a while, the girls would play, and that was always loved. The longest song was not a one and not a nine, but an eight seven. To explain, this is awkward but simple. If you add, you are male; and if you multiply, you are female. Since a female can multiply, they do not offend ever. If they did, they would be male and just add constantly. Once in a while, the umpire would stop an add and allow a multiply. This meant that the redux won.

Since a girl always wins as a redux, there is nothing wrong with a redux. If that was not enough thought, there was nothing more important than killing a redux. If a redux died, the umpires would struck out, and sex was allowed to a black night. Once in a while, this happened and was very fun. The last stage of a redux was not to like but to argue. Since the redux argue all day, there is nothing more fun than to argue with a redux. If they lose at all, they just add it and become it. Once in a while, there were people that mattered to the redux.

The people that mattered most to the redux were not women but little kids. If the redux were able to move backward, there was nothing that they would not do for a little kid. Since little kids came first to a redux, there is nothing to do but think about the thoughts that people had. The first thought that people had normally was that they were not good enough for their partner. This happens to all people and is a side effect of something that we do. The thing that we do is to leave a coin in the bottom of the lake. Since this does not make sense, I'll explain. A coin at the bottom of a lake symbolizes marriage and that money that is shared. Since you can see it and not be it, it's called a wish coin and is the only thing that a married couple does not know. If they did know money, they would have to argue and would be in love. At a coin in a lake, the redux actually swim and eat. If they can get to the food, the couple will calm down. Even thought they could not get to the coin. This confused the cadets since if the coin was at the bottom of a lake, why did they not know how to see a coin and found it fun to figure out how to penis a coin. Since penis is all that light is, it is very fun to sink a coin in a lake.

The second problem that a redux has is to finish a sentence and assume you are right. Since this a mean tactic to confuse a person and make them feel uncomfortable, the redux were not amused at all and said that silence is wholly and shouldn't be disturbed at all. Once in thought, a redux can do more than ten thousand thoughts a minute and are actually really impressed. Once in a while, the redux would think about the third disturbance which is an abuse. Since verbal abuse is rare, there is nothing to be done about it but to think about the thoughts that mattered to a verbal abuse. Once in a while, the fact that a verbal abuse exists is very hard to fathom. Since fathom is the correct word, there was nothing about fathoming that mattered to a redux. A redux is incredibly clever, but the cadets still got ahead sometimes. Once in a while, a blue ribbon would turn green, and this is over the red ribbon giving up. A green ribbon means enough time free from failure to throw a red ribbon. Since red means movement, it is the only ribbon that is actually subconscious to an umpire.

Once in a while, an umpire would not know how to take a red ribbon, and this is why there are matadors. A matador is a talented redux at a gulf. Since a gulf is hard to measure, there is nothing harder to think about then the redux cannot manage a silent green. Since a red ribbon is only green if there is a blue ribbon, a redux always wins. A cadet can make a blue red that is lighter in tone and sound sweet in a song which is what the cadets were doing this evening. Since they were only able to sing seven songs, there was nothing to think about but the seven colors that were allowed. If the songs mixed, they could be an eight or a nine, but the tone would flatten and not sound nice. If a redux hears a flat, they tend to kill and swim.

A kill and swim meant that nothing ever illuminates them. In order to glow, a redux has to sing, and that was why the cadets sang. Once in a while, a song would shift and become words. If this happened, your emotions would hurt badly. If they did not shift, you probably would not know that they are there at all. That was what most of the world had been up until the nuclear bomb. Since the nuclear bomb, everything had shown and we were hard-pressed to remember what to do when.

Since the redux did not condone sex over showing, there were a lot of older people that were still considered tears in the eather and not allowed each other. If you tear sex, there is so much grief to it that there are times that nothing in the world can heal it except a love poem. Since a love poem is rare, the cadets added it to the songs and won at an eight and nine.

Since an eight and nine were just a love poem, no one would actually be hurt. Once in a while, a perfect thought can hurt you, and that is why a black night redux was downed once by a cadet. Since we are allowed gay, there was nothing to do but lie slightly. Once in a while, the cadets would lift and lower slightly, and that would be why they did not know to stop. If you lift and lower, it means that you are looking for a better angle. Since a better angle is hard to find, sometimes it is impossible for it to be found and you miss your mark. If you lift and lower, always keep one eye pealed and sneeze. Once in a while, this works and is how red light matters in a girl. Red is the best ribbon, but it is blue that is fought over and is the theme of this book. A blue means thought, and the book is on thought, not the redux. Since redux means knowledge, it was the redux that inspired thought.

Once in a while, a blue girl will turn purple, and this means that the redux lost and everything is wild. There are two wild boars in the world, and both are blue black and hard to attack. Since it is an attack that means blues, there was little to understand from a green lion. A green lion is always red and killed by blue to be green. Once in a while, a green lion will purr, and a green lion's purr is historic but not comforting at all. Since there are four green lions in the world, there are few things to be elated with, but be aware, a happy green lion is nearly fatal. Once in a while, a green leprechaun becomes a lion, but it is actually a lioness. Once the cadets had lived through it, they were very good at guessing what someone was to the law and time. Once the law was stated, there is little else that's known. Of course this is frustrating to a cadet and not to a redux. If the veil ever fell on the law, the attic would scare a mouse and a rat at the same time. Since a rat is never scared or it dies, a dead rat and a hungry mouse is a little hilarious. Since a rat can domesticate and a mouse can't, there is little to be said for a mouse. Since the redux never quit thinking, there was a lot of time for the cadets to think about. Once in a while, the cadets would get afraid, and this was impossible for the umpire to figure out.

If the cadets were afraid, the redux would glee and run. Since glee is a hard emotion, nothing mattered, but the redux were thought bad. Once in a while, a cadet would scare someone, but this was rare. Since a cadet nearly never scared anyone, they were considered good and loved by women. Once in a while, this would challenge the redux to do something brash, but that was rare.

Chapter Eight

The redux followed the line into the chamber of secrets. Once inside, there was little to be thought about but how the chamber worked. Since the chamber was a secret, they did not like uninvited guests and made sure to check their invitation at the door. The well time was not allowed, and that was all. A well time is a magic trick that meant that everything was allowed. Since they were in the chamber of secrets, it was rare for them to figure out anything at all. Since the chamber was sealed, it is rare to hear about it. Inside the chamber, there were six secrets. The first secret was that green was not red. Since green was always red, there were a lot of people that thought that green should be red, but to a redux it was not. The reasoning went that the redux could not make love and eat at the same time and were thus on a penis for thought since that was rare the redux thought that green was gold and hid red. The second secret was that orange was not yellow. Since orange was not yellow, there was something that could not be done. If something was not done, then yellow was taught not to grief and orange was taken. Since orange would say "I know and know how to stop anything," there was a little bit of grief. If the grief escalated to hard, there would be a time for yellow, but this was rare. The third secret was that the time of light was actually sound. Light can transmit sound, and it was at that time that the redux had heard and made it a secret. The fourth secret of the redux was that light never plays. Once it plays, it cannot be light but just current. This is interesting because if light plays, it frays and is bad for you. If it is current, then electrical current can go bad, and that is rare but dangerous electrical current is all sanity. The fifth secret of the redux was that the different people that are met during the day are hard to mistake for each other and that the redux had a memory that was just how they felt during the day and who they saw. The reasoning was that is hunted well and was fun on their time since a lot of what a redux did was just their point of view. And the last secret of the redux was that the time of sound was actually the light of sound and was a reflection. This was known off a reflection and was very smart to the redux. Since sound and light are very similar, there were a lot of people that made for the differences in redux logic. Since logic was all a redux did at a high noon, there was little to be said about the redux other than that they were good at everything.

Since blue was silver, a redux could be a cop and not offend. Since a redux was a tit, it was a tit that made blue and hid the redux and the chamber of secrets. That was all about the redux, and since a cadet was a penis, it was not uncommon to be thought gay but actually was a joy to a redux.

Chapter Nine

I f the redux ever thought that they were stronger than the cadets, they would have another thing coming. Once in a while, there were people that thought that the redux were calm but they were not, and though this might be a problem, it is not actually. Once in a while, people are scared of being remembered. There were people that hated the redux over their memory of them. If an animal is not remembered, it can move freely. Since it is hard to move under a memory, there was a lot of people that could not. If you were an opposite and liked being under a memory, there was not a lot that could be done for you. Since this is rare, Sean Kept was a kind of rarity among people. He thought that if you liked to move under a memory, you were a movie actor. The reason he thought this was that the movement that he moved under was actually light and sound repeated, and if you chose through it, you could control someone as they lived through their day. Since the redux did not know how to move under a memory, there was little that they could do to an actor, nor could they be one. If they ever did know how to move under a memory, they would have to have a secret and open the chamber of secrets to do it. Since this was not hard to do, they might someday.

Chapter Ten

An actor was rarely given a chance to act, but there was someone who was; and though he was a cadet, there was little else that mattered. He was a good cadet but seemed to want to be a redux. Redux was fun to him, and he planned to be one. Since this person did not know how important he was to a redux, there was little that he did not know about them. Once in a while, the redux would come to him and he would figure out what the redux meant by living through an experience. Since it is rare for the redux ever to lose, they were surprised that it had happened and it was Ryan Deadly had gotten them back to a safe distance. Once in a while, there were people that mattered, and that was how they felt about him. Since there were a lot of people that did not think that everything worked, there was a joke among the redux that went, everything worked until. Since until were common, people did not know what an until meant. Once in a while, an until would surface, and this is why nothing mattered to the redux. At an until, the redux tended to think about everything but what the redux needed. All the redux needed was to be silent. Since silence was rare, the actual fact of it meant that the redux could imagine memory and they spent all of time doing this. The redux spent more time imagining than eating and sometimes starved. Since starving is hard on you, they thought their jobs hard to take. Some people knew this and spent a lot of time trying to figure out how to eat. If the redux did not know how to do it, there was little that could be done against them. Since there was little to be said about the redux, the next look is at the secrets of the cadets.

A cadet was hard to foretell, but unlike a redux, a cadet was sure to think about enjoyment. Since it was a cadet's experience to be liked, there was little else to a cadet. The first secret to a cadet was to never foretell the future. Since the future was bright, the cadets loved it and never gave up on it. The second secret to a cadet was to think in color until it turned brown. If a cadet turned brown, they would have to go to a redux; otherwise they would not. The third secret of a cadet was that sound never has sex, light does. Since the redux had sex on sound, they did not know. If a cadet had sex on sound, they would be considered redux. The fourth secret of a cadet was that the wind never moves without dreaming the movement first. Everything thinks, and a good cadet could become smarter just looking at a cloud. And the fifth secret of a cadet is chaos never wins. If chaos won ever, they would be on a magician to figure it out. Once inside the tank, a lot of cadets would not know what they were thinking about.

Chapter Eleven

A cadet woke early in the morning and thought that everything was happy. The light from the sun shone in through his window and made the light on his face play and absorb the thought that was found there. The air spelled the Queen of England, and he made sure to say he loved before he moved. Once the cadet was in the shower, he spent most of his time smelling his body. Since showering was hard to do, he made sure not to miss a spot on his body. Once in a while, the water would come back and be aware. If the water went aware, the cadet knew that he was able to make a power and this was good for him. Since it is hard for a cadet to know when they are finished, he was a little long in the shower and the Queen of England told him done.

Since the cadet dressed nice, the cadet had a girl that was sweet on him and made him smile. Once in a while, this would make him feel good, and he knew that the he and girl would not be able to think about anything. At a full stop, the cadet mirrored a redux and got verified. They called this redux thought and had to admit if they were under this position, a redux was allowed the thought. Since the shower had taken too long, the cadet was slightly in trouble and had a lot of time spent making it apparent to himself that he would not move through the time. Since apparent was hard to be, it meant that the cadet was on his own. The day started for him with a good breakfast, and this led him to be fond of the way things worked. If the cadet ever got sad, he would go to a black night, but this was rare and the cadet just sat and ate his cereal, peering over the paper. The cadet was good at water, and since it had changed, it was important to play in water. Since this was rare, the cadet took his time thinking about the water and how it behaved. Once in a while, there were people that mattered to the cadet, and he watched his temples closely to know what they did. Since it was not hard to think about, there was little that he did not know about his temples. Since watching people was important, there was little that he did not know about it. Writing down what he saw was difficult but still fun. Since the morning was getting late, he ran outside to get on his cruiser and head into town. Once at the border, there was a little time to think through, but this was normal. Of course the border patrol was efficient as usual and he was allowed into sector nine on time. He had three hours in sector nine and made sure that there were plenty of things to do to keep his mind busy. Since it was not uncommon for a redux to show in a sector, there was a little pang of fear at the thought of it. Because he went through an emotion, the umpire caught him and he was told not to go to the store. At the post office, the cadet got routed to go to another store, and that was where he went. At the supermarket, the cadet thought through the differences that mattered. A sugar rush was important to a cadet, and that is what he had today. Since a sugar rush was hated by an over lord, it was slightly hidden. Once inside the sugar rush, little could slow a cadet. The air tested him and made sure that everything was all right. Since it was, there was little that could not be said about it. There were a lot of people that mattered to him. Once in a while, the cadet would get startled, but this was rare. Since there was nothing for him to do, he left the town twenty minutes early and headed back to the camp. The camp was full of cadets. It stood proud on a hill made from steel and granite. Since this was not uncommon, there were a lot of space camps to be found. Once back inside the space camp, the cadet went about his chores.

The first chore was to find and brush a bear. Since bears were strong and kind of dangerous, there were a lot of people that were not good enough to wash a bear. The bear was golden and smart and sat through the washing with a golden glove in mind. The second chore was to deem a beginner. Since beginners are rare, there were a lot of people that mattered to the bear. Bears loved beginners and thought them very smart. Once inside a beginner, there was little that a cadet did not know. Beginners knew everything, but that was the same. Once in a while, a beginner would get frustrated, and that would make them happy and sad at the same time. Beginners were rarely redux, but there was one that was very powerful and had figured out a color chart that never failed. If a color chart is a beginner, they are considered pro. Since pro is rare, there was not a lot that mattered to it. Once in a while, there were people that mattered to people, and the bear was not unkind to that. Since the beginner was deemed grey, there was little else to do but to go to his quarters and think through the following day. Once in a while, a bright light would confuse a cadet, but this was not one of those days and the cadets got along fine in the light of that winter day. Since light came and went, it was common for a light to think backward. Since there was little to be done for the time being, there were a lot of people that mattered to the cadet, and he thought about them as he sat in his lounge chair thinking about the day. The problem with thinking about people is that they are strange. Once a person turns strange, they never come back from it. Strange meant that their spirit did something that was not in public and completely allowed. Since strange meant slightly gay, there were a lot of genes that were strange. It was rare for a gene to be thought strange, but this made for a common refusal. Since refusal could become too strong, there were black nights that fought it and loved a little strange. The cadet was watching a friend of his in the eather and saw the man think about something strange and dived to help him before he died from the aftermath. Since the cadet was innocent, the blog confused over what was said to the cadet. The blog did not know that the cadet was protecting the friend who had gone strange and was confused as to why the cadet was not going down. Since the eather was strong, that was little to be afraid of and the cadet went back to watching. Blogs were rare. A blog is almost always a redux or a redux twin. Since twins are rare, there were a lot of people that twinned, and this was interesting because a grin twin made for excellent advice. Once inside the twin, a blog could relax and put its face back on. A faceless mask is so scary that a cadet would curl up in a little ball and simper if they ever met one. Since the cadet was having fun, there was little for the cadet to do but sit and imagine. A spiral was hard to imagine but good at math. Since the spiral made sound, the redux loved it. Once a redux loves something, it is allowed. If it is not allowed, it is an "I know." Since the redux was lost from the world, there was little the world ever did. Once inside, the cadet moved around in the spiral and finally came up with a pressure release. Since a release was all that a cadet had to do to pass his exams, there was a slight joy to the cadet as the spiral made a release. A pressure was rare, and it was not until the third act that a person would be found not wanting. Once in a while, there were people that thought through a release and still allowed it. Since it was not uncommon for a man to be involved with an uncommon, there were nearly ten thoughts that mattered. Once the thoughts mattered, there were nearly no faults to be found. Since the cadet was tired, he went to bed lying on his stomach and taking in the fear of the day.

Chapter Twelve

Once in a while, there were people that mattered to the bishop. The bishop was very powerful and made his power from the death of people he met. Since he never actually killed, he was considered safe but still lived on death. Once in a while, the bishop would discover the way that people went by. Since a strong green was not a white, the green and white symbols made sense. Once in a while, there were people that made a lot of noise from it. Since this was a little carefree, there were people that mattered to them. The bishop was a strong man, but it was not strength that mattered to him but rather obtuse thought. If someone was smart enough to think something obtuse, the bishop would check if it was correct or if it was a little not true. Bishops, being rare, had made the bishop precious to the umpire. Once the umpire had come to be, there was little else that mattered. Since the umpire and the bishop did not know each other, it was on a cardinal for them to relate. Since Brian Sharp was the sharpest bishop ever to live, there was not a lot that could not be done. Living on the dead was a little sad to a woman but was good for a man. Once the bishop was done eating, he would turn on the television and watch deep into the night.

Chapter Thirteen

Last place went to the cadet with the lowest time. Since the amount of time that you were was the amount of white you could produce, which made the most memory, there was not a lot of joy for Sean Text. Since Text was his name, there was little that he didn't know and was a little confused as to why he was not able to give. Since he did not know why, little mattered to his daughter, who knew why. Since she knew he was safe, just came in last place. The equivalence exam was hard on him, and he didn't know what to do about not passing, and so he sat in his room and cried. The weird part about it was that he was actually why all the other cadets had passed and was just an oversight that he had not. Once in a while, this came up but wasn't important to an umpire. If nothing moved, the cadet would just repeat the grade and see if he could pass. Since Text was smart, nothing mattered to the rest of the class, and some of them would still go to see him at lunch. Once in a while, he would unconfuse, but this was rare. Oftentimes, the beginners would move, and Sean Text thought about beginners a lot, hoping to pass on one of them sometime. Since beginners were rare, Sean Text mattered to the beginners at one moment movement. Once the movement was done, there was little else that could be done. Once in a while, there were things that mattered and things that didn't. Beginners always knew what mattered and what didn't and were perfect at it. Since this was not the first time that the beginners had been loved by Sean Text, there were all of beginners that were in on him passing the next year. Since Sean Text was ashamed, there was a lot of debate over the way that things moved, and the faculty was careful not to say his name. Once in a while, one of the younger cadets that he was now in class with would come to him, but they had been warned not to and it was rare that they did. Since Sean Text kept to himself, some of the cadets were a little sad, but it was all right.

The day dawned bright and cheerful. Sarah Smith walked along the river knowing that there were times that you do not show your beauty, and this was one of those times. Her internal had a horror face on and was wearing a green dress. Since dress color was important, she thought about her green dress a little. Since it is nearly impossible to think showing an internal, there was not a lot that she could think but just rather thought about the dresses and why they were what they were. A green dress meant that the father was beginning and that the mother was ending. This meant no sex except for if you're married and going to have a child. A green dress was good for a child because it meant that the child would be smart under stress. A green dress was very good at stress because green was an absorbing color and could suction very well. This meant that the green dress would allow light to be a little off and come back a true color again. Sarah thought about another day in her life where she had gone to the movies with a boy and had worn a red dress. A red dress was very appropriate and had made her feel good. A red dress meant that a girl was horny with their pussy being slightly wet. Since a red wet was allowed, there was little that they would do to change the stance. Once in a while, people allowed the stance to change, but only a red dress could keep a girl from being completely wet and was good for having fun. A purple dress was rare and thought to be law even though it actually meant children go through adolescence and become adults. Since this was rare, there was little that she could do with a purple dress. A purple dress she had never worn since she was too young and rather just remembered her mom wearing one the first day she had ever bled. Once in a while, a girl would wear a pink dress, and this was most fun if the girl was in love. Since pink always was too strong a color at sex, there were a lot of reasons to trick a girl into wearing a white dress. Since white was calculative and meant that there was an error, there was little that mattered about it. Once in a while, there were people that mattered to a girl, and a white dress was excellent at thinking about what might happen to a girl or her friends. Once in a while, the girl would wear a black dress, and this was rare because black is highly reflective. Since black had two sides, it is used normally to deceive, and that is why a black dress was rare. Once in a while, there were people that did not know what dress to wear, but she always did. Since yellow was her favorite dress, she spent all of time thinking about a yellow dress and found out that it meant that a person was stressed and not able to think. Yellow was comforting because it was food and meant that you were not going to die. Once in a while, this meant that nothing mattered and was not a problem. Turquoise was the best dress in the world to break up on. She had once, and she thought about it now with turquoise in her mind. Since there was not a lot that a turquoise dress could not hate, it was not uncommon to think that there was a way out of a turquoise dress. If a turquoise dress ever failed, a girl would be scared, but more importantly, a little brainwashed thinking about having a baby. Since the relationship is over, nothing mattered. Once in a while, there were people that thought that there were things that mattered and things that don't. A black dress was all that Sarah was afraid of, and that meant time would stand still. If time stood still, there was little that could be done. If a black dress ever got in trouble, there was little that mattered about it. Since she was wearing a green dress, thinking about a black dress was a little scared because it nearly meant a murder was remembered, and she looked at the horror face on her internal for a moment. Sarah walked on and did not mind at all. The sun was out and played with her face as she walked. Once in a while, the cold of the winter day would brisk at her knees, but this was rare. Since there was nothing to be said, for the way that her hair shone a young cadet shamed slightly that he had fallen in love on a green dress. Since this was not allowed, there were a lot of people that found this to be very funny. They were never together, and that was even funnier when they had not been in love and had seen each other before. This troubled the dean who said that they should be together. There was a disturbance in the eather, and he did not know what it was. Once in a while, something would happen that meant that the eather was wrong, and today was one of those days. The dean told Sarah to put on a green dress that was not brown but gold. Since with a gold dress on anything could go, the cadet knew why he had fallen in love. He was gold, and a gold green meant marriage to a stone hedge. Stone hedge was the smartest punishment culture to ever live and was real to the cadet. Since there was nothing to be done for the girl, she thought a little about marriage and a lot about the earth which was what stone hedge was. Since this was not the first time that the hedge had confused a sprite, there were some times that people would talk to each other, and this was one of those times. Since the stone hedge was happy with the girl, young man approached her and they spoke. "Time till seven three and eight." "Time till eight three and eleven." "Time till eleven three and ten." The two cadets left thinking about their conversation as they walked away knowing each other in the eather. Once in a while, a conversation would be public, and this was one of those times. A lot of the cadets said that they had gotten the times wrong, but they knew what they had felt and thus just remembered each other in love and fondly. Once in a while, the cadets would funny at the two of them but nothing mattered.

Chapter Fourteen

A cadet led the procession down the path and made sure that nothing mattered. Once in a while, there were people that mattered, and this was one of those times. Since there was nothing to be thought about, there were a lot of people that mattered and some that didn't. Once in a while, that was all that mattered, and that was what happened now. If nothing mattered, then a lot of people could become stranded. Since stranded was hard to live through, there were some people that mattered and some that did not. Once in a while, a stranded person would think, and if this happened, the populace would suffer but needed the thought. Since thought was rare, it was funny if the thought already existed and was still needed. This meant that the thought was too weak to do what it thought that it was doing. If it thought that it was doing something and was actually up against a wave too strong, it would strand a lot of people, and this had woken an umpire up to the danger of having a thought. At first he thought don't think, and when this didn't work, he thought don't not think but rather don't move when you think. This worked and the umpire made a book about it, spending his days thinking about movement. Since the movement that he had stopped had been in weather, there was not a lot that he didn't know and this had been fun to him. Once in a while, something would move and he would know it no longer to be a thought. Since there was little to do as an umpire, he was bored most of his day unless there was a real fight. He had over two hundred fights that just repeated in a glass jar, and since you could look at them and they would not matter, there were times that he would watch them to see if there was a thought missed when they had been bottled. Once in a while, this would mean that they were strong or weak, but this did not matter to the umpire. Being an umpire was interesting to the umpire because as a redux, there were a lot of his days spent trying to comfort the lost. Since Sean Text was lost, there was not a lot that he could do but sit in his room and try to relive everything he had thought with the hope that he would someday find time. Since time does not come to the lost, there was nothing he could do but be timeless. Once in a while, this mattered but it barely did. That was the first time that the umpire had been sad, but there was nothing that could be done for the cadet and the time was just bottled and forgotten. Once in a while, a redux would think something, and this was always scared to the umpire who thought cadet only. If a redux thought they would have to become evil and evil was very hard to achieve from a thought, that wasn't followed. A followed thought was not hard to think through since it was always a followed thought that mattered. Once in a while, a followed thought would turn wicked, and this was very good for an amateur. Since amateur were rare, there was little that mattered about them. Once in a while, amateur would think and this was fun to an umpire that loved if someone was paid to think. Since amateurs had secrets, it was a cadet's joy to trick them into hiding a cadet with their secret. If they did not know the difference between a secret and a hide, they would hide something that was not a secret. Since cadets were rare, the amateur was rare to find one that did not hate them. If one was found, it was called a rocky coast and the cadet a beached ship. If a beached ship was too smart, it would be called a gorge or cleft. Since a gorge and a cleft were both sexual, a red dress was needed and everything would be all right.

Chapter Fifteen

A hide is rare, and it was just such an experience that had taught a druid to think for themselves over what had been reported to be a strong current. Once in a while, there were things that mattered and things that didn't. If a druid could not think through the way that people smelled, she would not comfort a redux who was a smell. If a redux liked a mean, nothing would happen until a cadet got caught. Since cadets were afraid of means, nothing mattered. If a cadet was caught, the sign would lift and the class would be dismissed a failure. Since failure was rare, nothing mattered to a cadet at a redux until a mean was called in. Since the meaner the mean meant that more people mattered, there was nothing to do but to understand a stance that strong. If nothing mattered to the mean, it meant the offense was not large enough to matter to the populace. Means were rare, and though they were to be wary, they were very spiritual and rarely errored. Since means were rare, it was a fear of the umpire that they might be found cheating. If they were ever found cheating, there would be a lot of circumstances where they would not be allowed. AAnnalex Turner was one of these people, and it was a bad mean that had caught him. When he was let go, the court found the mean unfit, and the mean was let go to become just a simple redux. This was hard on his daughter who had trained hard, but she had to admit to the mistake and everything was forgiven. If a mean makes an arrest, nothing matters but the cadet could be very sad and that is what a priestess tries to reduce. Since it was not possible to eliminate, the priestess was very good at argument and temperament, and that was why the reduction would happen. Once in a while, a priestess would get in trouble, and that is what happened to Anna cleric. Since the Cleric was very smart, she was surprised when her voice broke during a song and had thought that it was Sean Time's fault but later learned it was her husband who was retired and would no longer protect her. Since she couldn't be protected, she finished the case and retired with her husband to spend the rest of her days an angel. If nothing ever went her way again, the time would go by with nothing to do but watch the cadets be let go. Once in a while, a priestess would come to her and say that she was the best and that they needed help. Sometimes this would mean that she would tell them to reject the case or others to plead with the defendant to plead guilty. A guilty plea meant that you were sorry and allows for a slightly stiffer penalty but not the maximum which was what they were trying for. Once in a while, the redux would tail and the maximum would be sentenced, but this was rare and not a joy for a redux. Some redux would think some things clever that weren't and that was how the sentence usually worked. Since there were no other ways of living, nothing mattered. Once in a while, there were people that thought there would be times when thinking would matter, but this was not one of those times. Sometimes people would like to think about stuff that happens and that is why to think for themselves. If a redux does not know a thought, then a lot of people will go thoughtless because they rely on a redux for thought. A redux usually sends a lot of people on a merry-go-round, that means that the differences about them were good for them. Once in a while, this meant that a lot of people thought differently than they would naturally. Since this is not common, no one ever leaves a merry-go-round. If someone leaves a merry-go-round, they are on a sequin. A sequin is a female redux that never moves. Since it never moves, nothing matters, but it means everything works. A redux never hates but will kill at the smallest mishap. Since mishaps are rare, there is nothing wrong with a mishap. Since a redux never mishaps, there are a lot of people that were surprised by one that did constantly, and that was why the named Sean Kill the destroyer. Sean Kill liked something about the world when it ended. Since Sean Kill never ended, there was always something to do. If the end was close, they would start and Sean Kill would start talking. Since he never ended, there were a lot of people that listened to him think about an end. Once in a while, this would become bored, but that was rare. Once in a while, a time machine would still come and sit. Since sitting was not possible, only a time machine could. If a time machine thought a redux slow, it would sit for sometimes. The thoughts that Sarah had would come back to haunt her, but she was all right with this and spent most of the morning thinking about Brad Tough, the cadet that she had met. Since she was pretty, there was not a lot of things to be said for her. Since that was normal, there were times that the woman in her liked him better than he was used to, and that was the first thing that mattered. Once in a while, the differences that mattered were important to her, and she was happy that Brad loved his pipe and his console. Since the Internet was normal, there was little that he did not know about the way that people thought. Once in a while, Brad would bring his pipe and his computer to bed with him, and she loved this and always thought it red dress. The "once in a while" that she was used to was very fun to her and made her happy constantly. If a woman is content with a cadet, they are almost always allowed to be what they wanted, and this was a joy to a cadet. Since it was uncommon for a cadet to hate a woman that they had been with, Sean Joy was not unlike anybody that they had been with since he had no partners that lived in with him. This meant that he was an electric light junkie and should be treated as such. Since an electric light junkie was rare, there were only two in the whole world that meant that they did not like their mates and three that had and were still okay but a little scared. A woman always thought about how to beat everything, and beating a mate had been a wry joke that was not funny to Sean Joy. Since a "once in a while" was strong in him, it was not long before everything would make sense. An electric light junkie was made by picturing an electric lightbulb and then penising it or dropping the picture. This was smart because the light made sound. Since Sarah did not need Brad to be an electric light junkie, he was just an avoid that did not matter to either cadet. Since this was not uncommon to a woman, it was just ignored and it was fine with them. The first thing that a person should do is to cleve and tell. Since a cleve and tell is hard to figure out, there were a lot of moments that a cleve and tell did not tell over, and Sarah Smith was excellent at a cleve and tell. Once in a while, there were people that did not know how to cleve and tell. In order to cleve and tell, a druid would have to make a square and touch a circle. If the center of the square made its way to the circle, you were cleaving; and if the circle could not make it to the center, it was telling. Since this is a trick that makes fear, there was little to do but to spend time on it. Once in a while, an umpire might disagree with a cleve and tell, and this was what had nearly killed an umpire who was told he was cheating when he was actually protecting. The problem was that if you think about something, it actually manifests in spirit and is called a thrill or terror, depending on if you are good or bad. Since good and bad are similar but different, there is little that the person had to do but yearn for a mistake. The umpire was right about the cleve and tell and did not allow a child to murder, which saved his life but was a little scary that it happened slightly.

Chapter Sixteen

Alf Walkly woke early in the morning to the moon streaming in through his window. Once in a while, the sound of the rain on the roof would wake him, but tonight it was the look of the moon that kept him from sleeping. If the rain had stopped, it might have woken him, but it was the look of the moon that drew his attention. Once awake, he rolled over and peered at the clock next to his bed. Since peering at the clock was a problem, there was a little bit of a noise in his head and he staticed at it to know who it was and suctioned to know where it was and moved to know why it was before actually knowing why it was. Since why it was is rare, he spent most of his day without a why and was a little startled to know that an old woman had died and there was a fatal disease in the eather. Since this was not uncommon, there were just a few moments to be taken and a prayer to be forgotten. Since forgotten was not that uncommon, there was little to do but to think about the thoughts that he was having. The first thought that he had was what were the numbers. In order to do the numbers to a fatal disease, you must be a closed square and an open circle. This means that you knew everything. If it moved and made for a one zero position or a number scramble position, there was little that you couldn't do. A fatal disease is when two or more numbers matched and were not able to move. This was because there was a break in chaos and the eye is repeating at the rate of thought something easier than thought. Since it is stuck on easy, you don't know what you are doing and are just dying. If you actually die to a fatal disease, it is because your heart or your brain gives up, never your spine. Since a spine is all given up, you can almost live as a spine and is what a defibrillator is. Once in a while, Alf met with the people that were there and thought about things about them, but he hated the hospital and loved his office better. Since Alf was not a black night but rather a sorcerer, there were some explanations to be made. Once in a while, there were people that mattered, and a sorcerer always mattered to a given witch. Since a witch is always wrong if you say magic, it is not uncommon for a sorcerer to think witches bad. Since a bad witch is only if they hear magic, which they instantly reject, which is why they are bad, makes them a perfect competitor for a sorcerer who are always enlightened by a magic. Since this is very funny, sorcerers and witches are joked a lot of the time. Since not liking magic is why a witch is bad, it is important to know that a witch, like an umpire, is in a slight brainwash to think. Since this is true, it is just sad to a witch and should be ignored. Once in a while, there were sorcerers that were able to outthink a witch, and this is always a woman's joy. Since it is not gay or masturbation, it should not be mistaken as such. Once in a while, there were people that thought that there were a lot of possibilities when there are not. Since not everybody gets to do every possibility, it seems like people are making a lot of possibilities that are not there when it is in fact only one thought that you are missing and it is a rare condition that make a redux make a full human to check if the populace is still off by one thought. Sean Care was a full person and was not off by a thought, and this scared him deeply since it was an illegal check, and he did not know what he was doing. Since he never did check if Tonne Right was a full person or off by a thought, he was never caught. Since then, nothing seemed to bother Sean Care, but it was a little funny that he was still thinking about a year that did not matter. Once in a while, this would still come up, but there was little to be said about a whole person other than that it is very scary and rare. Once in a while, there were disturbances that mattered. If a whole spirit was able to think through a lesser spirit, there was nothing to be done but to live through it. Once in a while, a person was not able to think about the thoughts that he had and was scared of them. This would mean that someone is off by more than one thought and is trying to kill someone. Since off by a thought was religion and made a flat off by two thoughts had to be made into something and Morgan Max was the meanest man in the world and only got away with it because he was a redux. Since a redux is never killed, the man was able to be off by seven thoughts. Since there was only eight thoughts, this was dangerous and was actually fatal but fun sexually. Since nothing mattered about Morgan Max, the story moves on. If Sarah was ever a witch, she would be sad but would think herself a little ugly, and this was not true. Since it was not true, there was little that Brad could do but think about a redux at a caution sign. The Alf was awake in the morning and did not know what to do but rather than to make a magnetic pot. Since magnetic pots are not possible, he had been laughed at, but it wasn't until a magician had let him go that he had admitted to being dead and start or a line of force to a calculation, a solid state quantum processor. Since this was fun, there was little that did not matter to him. Once in a while, he would calculate, but it was impossible to become deader than a magnet at a cleve. Since cleaving was fun, there was little to do but to love a solid state quantum processor and still make the pots. When a fatal disease is found to be fatal, it is only a matter of time till it gives up. Alf thought that it might be possible to smell the given up and give up completely. Since this was smart, he was able to start over every time the pot or the math showed. Since math is sound always sound control, a math it is very smart and is what made Sean Cleanex smart. Once in a while, there were problems, but this was rare and Alf fell asleep after crossing and kissing.

Chapter Seventeen

Once in a while, there were people that thought that a lot of people should move together, but this is wrong. Since it was not the thought that mattered but rather the fact of the thought, there was a little bit of conflict over who thought what to an electric lightbulb. Since this was not uncommon, there were a lot of people that thought that there were people who could think without trying. This was funny but not true and was why a lie did not give up. Since this was not a problem, a lot of black bodies tended to become grey if they fought too hard. Once in a while, a grey person was not allowed but always should be since it is funny to an old person. Since it is not uncommon for an art to think it was interesting that when Brad and Sarah make love, there are three art and not two. The extra art meant that they were perfect for each other and should marry. Since this was a thought to Brad, it was not uncommon for him to test whether she was thinking of it at all. If she ever did, he would love her. Since she was the love of his life, there was little that mattered to the two of them. Once in a while, there are people that mattered but messed each other up. If you did this, you were usually a murderer that did not know how to stop themselves. Since it was not uncommon for this to be true, there were a lot of people that did not know that they were a murderous joke. The only way to avoid this is to know when they made fatal disease s to when they did not care. Since a murderer never thinks actually but rather contradicts to think, there was little else to do but to stay abreast of one and think sideways. Sideways is important because it means that nothing mattered to Alf. Since Alf was not uncommon to fight a destroyer, there were a lot of people that thought that a destroyer was a bad token, but it is not. Once in a while, a destroyer would actually hurt someone, and that was all that mattered.

Chapter Eighteen

I f a sever were ever to arise, there could be some problems for the cadets. A sever was a black night that goes bad and thinks that people who hadn't should. This is rare, and black nights are usually good. Once in a while, there are people who think cadets bad, and it was late into the morning that one of these people emerged since there were not a lot of people that could not find a cadet. There was a large supply of grief for a cadet. Since in order to be a cadet you had to be a little criminal, there was nothing to be done but stand at random. A lot of time was taken on the right of a parent, and all cadets should be apparent. Once in a while, there were people that thought that a cadet was not able to think, and this is not true. Since there was nothing that could be done, cadets just existed. The first black night ever to emerge was a left ear wrong turn. Since a left ear meant language and a wrong turn meant police, a left ear wrong turn meant a criminal cop and was not allowed. Since it was a black night, it took three years for him to go down and just be a cop. Since language meant crime, there was a lot of debate over the difference between a genius and a crimp. Since a crimp meant that a genius dies, it should not be called a genius and always was for some reason. If a crimp could cry, you would know why it was a genius. A crimp can't cry because they are pure hatred and don't know anything. Once in a while, there were a lot of crimps that thought that a red gold was a genius color when it is in fact giving up. Once in a while, there were people that thought that a true color was a green elf since an elf is never green unless there was a rape. A green elf was not a true color. Since it is not uncommon for a green elf to possess power, it was hard on a redux to be a green elf. If green was not able to absorb the emotions that went wrong, there was simply a design flaw, and an elf became a dragon and was a purple yellow. Since that is very pretty in a female, there was not a lot that could be done to comfort deeper. If a girl is pretty, there is nothing to be said but that she loves herself. Once in a while, there were people that mattered and those that didn't. Since it was not uncommon for time to spend itself, there are not a lot of people that knew how to spend light. If you spend time, a lot of people thought that it was possible to spend sound, but it is not. If you spend light, there are a lot of people that think you are gay because muscle shows light if you are gay and makes light turn brown. If you spend light, it turns gold and not brown. Since it is not uncommon to think that there were a lot of people that mattered at a spend light, there was little debate that a spend light could outthink a spend time. The war of the spends lasted almost three months and culminated in a stale mate, them both being necessary. Once in a while, there were spends that did not matter to a girl. If a girl does not think a spend matters, it gets forgotten, and the in-trouble gets shuffled. Since it is not impossible to spend every day, there was someone who did; and when he was forgotten, he was in more trouble than he could take and tried to spend his way out of it. This was a mistake that he admitted to and said that he did not actually know what spending was. He was doing it because it felt good and he was bored. Once in a while, there were people that thought about thinking.

Chapter Nineteen

B ruce Willis sat in his cubicle thinking. A red yellow made a brown white. Color was hard, but he was good at it. The first thing he knew about color was that when it changed, it was the length that changed, not the curve. Since color was a curve, it was interesting that it was just the length and not the curve. The curve was how light or dark it was. Since the shade and the length were not the same, there was a little debate over what to do at a dark or light color. If a color was light, then it had a long curve; and if it was dark, it had a short curve. Then Bruce sat in his cubicle and thought about color. What was it that increased the length of a color? The first thing that he thought was warmth. Since a color can be warm or cold, it made sense to make a cold color and then a warm color and combine them. Since color was not different from a time keep, there was little that was not known about a time keep. A time keep is a color, but it is combined with a sound, and the sound meant that the color was a true hue and able to remember. Since Bruce used a time keep to make a cold and warm color, there was little that mattered about a time keep. Once in a while, there were people that used a time keep wrong, but this was rare and it should be just allowed to stay stationary. Since Bruce used a time keep, he was unaware of his mistake and actually hurt a guard. A guard is hurt rarely, and this guard did not think it unusual, but to call a redux and see it a time keep could live through a warm to cold. Since it was not uncommon to be able to time keep, it should not have been that bad of a problem. It was just a year that meant that a time keep could not warm that was offended. Since Bruce did not know what a time keep was meant, that it was hard to figure out what had happened and it took three months to do this. In that three months, there were a lot of fanfare because Bruce Willis was caught. Since being caught is hard to do, there was nothing to do but to think back on his time and live through it. Once in the hospital, he hypnotized and was safe for the four-month stay that he had. Once in a while, there were people that mattered to the hospital, and he was one of them. Luckily, when they figured it out, they had thought of it. If this was not enough, there were three other cadets that went down with them. Since they all went down, one of the cadets did not go into town for fear of getting caught, and that fear was real he almost was. Once in a while, a cadet would get afraid. This was allowed and thought highly of. Since this was normal, there was nothing else to do but to think backward. Backward is hard to do because it is not real. If you think backward, it means you break sequence and live. Since breaking sequence and living meant that color dies, there was a lot of colors that were dead and shouldn't be. Sean Roxy had figured out to flat color and could resequence a dead color. Since a color was almost never semitropical, this was hard to do. Once in a while, there were people that thought about how to get ahead, and Sean Roxy was one of them. If you get ahead, there is something that is rare. Once in a while, it means that something is holding you back. Color can help and hurt, and that is why it is loved. Since it is able to hurt bad, people are allowed at color.

Chapter Twenty

A lot of people gathered in the square that day. Once in a while, a magician would get in a fight, and today was one of those days. Since it was never thought to fight physically, they stood their ground as the air moved. Genius days were offended at a sprite over who was smarter but actually more loved. This mattered because a sprite was slightly criminal, and there were criminals in public. Once the fight had started, there was no telling how many people would be in. Genius days were always law, and that was why the fight began. Since the law liked to pressure, the sprite used a bomb shell to live through it. The sprite only had to live through it to win, whereas the genius days had to finicky but hurt the sprite to win. If the sprite had to admit to being scared, the genius days would win. Sometimes the sprite would hit the genius days, but this was rare and was not thought about. Once in a while, the sprite hurt, but it was mild. He was very strong. Since a bomb shell was rare, the sprite did not show and the genius days got confused. "How did you live through that?" "Just did." "But how you were supposed to crumble and fear?" The sprite nearly did, which was the danger of speech. "Are you going to claim that your senses are tricked and that I'm not standing?" "No" "Then fight." The genius days kind of lazied and walked away. All the sudden, the sprite hit him in the face. "I know that move you are dreaming, my skeleton lazy." "True I am." "Are you immune to lazy?" The sprite laughed. "I am but not too sad." "Can't sad too hard." "Then I win again." "Fight." The crowd was awed at the sprite as he looked pure energy. The genius days walked toward the sprite with wrath, moving around his body in red spheres. Since this was not the first time that a sprite had seen wrath, he was a little afraid and said, "At wrath, I'll give catch the cadets." The wrath had been red. If it had been blue, the sprite would have won because blue repeats and the sprite could have made it repeat energy from memory. Once in a while, there were people that thought sprites smart, and that is what the genius days did now. "How smart are you actually?" The sprite turned and wondered he had been walking away. "Why befriend?" "You almost beat me, and I am unbeatable." "How close?" "Two-tenths." "That is close, you are stronger still. I am an eight-tenths." "I want to kill you, but there is something I want to know." "What is that?" "How do you take a pressure and release?" "Can't say." "Then we are enemies. Fight." "You want to fight me again? Do you know I was at half mast, the cadets did not matter." "Half mast. You are smarter than me." "Come at me and think." The air turned to fire, and the genius time was suffocating, but the sprite seemed fine. "What is it can't think." "I am going to suffocate, I give." "I never try at a sprite." The air relaxed, and the flames faded away.

Chapter Twenty-one

Sean Concern sat in a shroud thinking about the time that he had spent on himself. Since it was a lot of time and he owed deeply, there was not a lot of time to be thought about, but he still owed and did not know how to repay it. Since it was impossible for him to actually win, there was nothing for him to do but worry. Once in a while, there were people that thought through the way people felt. He wasn't one of those people, but he had thought and went to one that was real constantly. Since it was impossible for him to get smarter, he did not try. His temper was nearly murderous. Since there was nothing that mattered to a smart person, there was nothing that could not be done to him. Once in a while, a person laughed off what was thought, and it was at these times that genius emerged. Sean Concern lived on his own and thought about the way that people felt when they lost. Since losing was hard to take, he was a little killed but knew something smart. If metal was dark to light and off colors like tan and orange and purple which had made a really smart metal. Since light to dark was nearly impossible to predict, it was unusual for someone to be capable of it. Light meant that there were responses that you did not know and your attitude lightened. Since this was rare, there was little that didn't happen for the person involved. Dark meant that the light did not show to think. Since light and dark were the same thing, it was why everything had a good and a bad and had two responses. It was not one was light and one was dark but rather light became dark and dark became light. If dark becomes light, it is considered bad. And if light becomes dark, it is considered good. The reason for this is that a lot of dark is smarter than all of light. Since this is unbeatable, and there is a power that is it a seven eleven thirteen in angles and is thought to be as stupid as we are allowed. Once in a while, there were things that would make sound, but sound was not able to do more than one thing at a time and is why it is not able to angle.

Chapter Twenty-two

D eep in the night, a genie woke and stared at the wall. All of the sudden, a light went by again. What is a genie actually? A genie is a dream that moves backward. The light sat on the wall for a moment. Since a genie is rare, there not a lot of them. Genies were always scared of lights. A light can turn a genie inside out and show their heart. Since it was bad for a genie to be known at color, there was a lot of people that did not know how to live through a color. Since two thoughts are light and dark, a lot of people get confused at a color whether it is light or dark. Since color is not light but a curve, it is interesting to note that light is spherical and looks like an oval when it is captured. The genie was excellent with light and color and did not know why she had awakened. Since the genie was powerful, she did not ask but rather started remembering and felt her pussy. Since her pussy was smart, there was little that mattered. Once in a while, there were people that mattered, and the person that she was hunting was a good light but was in the wrong somehow, and that was why she had awakened. The light started dimming all of the sudden and spoke, "I can't remember that hard. How can you remember that hard?" The thought was funny to the genie who went back to sleep, knowing the light was trying to hide a murder that had taken place almost thirty years in the past. Since it was the twenty-three thousandth time that the light had tried to hide, the genie thought it a little stupid when the light admitted to trying to hide a murder in voice. Voice is all that she needed to know she wouldn't look at the actual memory. Once in a while, there were people that thought better than the genie, but she was still the smartest woman in the world for more than a hundred hours, and memory was subconscious to her being what she was best at.

Chapter Twenty-three

The dark night was riding his motorcycle, and it was deep into the night. Since the earth matched the sun at some point during the night, the dark night wanted to be riding when it happened to settle his balance and become the best in the world. If you could not tell the difference between the sun and the earth, the only other gravity to confuse you was the moon. Once in a while, the moon would come back and be scary to the rider, but that was all. The dark night felt the forces come together and suctioned straight. Since the line went right through the earth and entered the sun, there was little that it didn't know about the world around him and his eyes created a color as he rode. Once the rider was given to thinking the dark night ran through a briar patch and then up a hill before stopping his bike to consider what had just happened, the dark night had planned for this and was not unusual for him to think things through. Once in a while, thinking could kill someone, and this nearly happened to the rider as the earth and the sun unenlined. The rider took a moment to calculate the time it took for them to align and unalign, and this meant that he could know the movement of the earth to the sun. Since he was never in the sun, he was surprised when he found himself in the sun in someone's memory. This was fine, and he rode on.

Chapter Twenty-four

Since it was not uncommon for a gymnast to feel smarter than the average, it was allowed; and though they are actually on stupid, they are slightly smarter and way smarter to a Sean Lexur. Since Sean Lexur is in love with gymnasts, it was not a long time before the way he dated them became a problem. Since this was strange, the gymnast just lived through it and did not care about what made what happen. A redux warned the Sean Lexur to be careful with a gymnast since if they broke, they couldn't come back. Once in a while, there were people that mattered to a Sean Lexur, and that was what had happened to me. Once in a while, the people he cared about were very hard to think through. The person that had confused him was an old man who had tried to die to a zero zero. Since this was impossible to do, there was a little confusion when he died to a suffocation and the zero zero had stuck, trying to figure out how he died. Since a zero does not know shape, it was not until the thought had gone electrical that the zero zero knew that it was actually a two two. Since a two two was known, there was not supposed to be a conflict, but a redux had gone behind time and claimed that a zero zero was a two two and someone had died. This was so confusing that Sean Lexur had come to a gymnast to figure it out. Since he was warned not to, he was a little scared but honestly could not figure it out and was trying to know how someone could die from eating. Since it is impossible to die from eating, there was nothing that he could do but sit there and get confused. Since it was done on purpose, it was even more frustrating that people acted that weird around a cadet. Once in a while, there were people that mattered to cadets, and Sean Lexur was one of them. If Sean Lexur was not able to think, there were a lot of people that would get confused since he thought their lives through. Once in a while, there were people that mattered, and he had found one it was Talia Strange. Since Ms. Strange was very smart, she said to make the food change sound and see if it was able to do more than one thing at once.

This was when he met the murderer who had thought it, and it emerged as the second fatal disease to nine nine. A nine nine means that something docile was actually fatally resisted. Since a redux could resist until it was fatal, there was little that mattered to a Sean Lexur. Since Lexur loved Strange, she thought nothing mattered and went back to what she was doing. A masturbation was a problem but was innocent and just a cum. Once in a while, a lot of people thought that time meant power, and this had been true until Strange had changed it to light, which meant power, and no one knew this; and that was why Sean Lexur had lived through not time and still lived through no time. Since Saedi meant that everything was known, it was interesting that Sean thought at all. Once in a while, there were people that got mad at him, and this was unfortunate and made him sad and insane, but nothing mattered and Saedi could live through it. Once in a while, the Saedi that lived in Sean would get sad not thought about, and that was why Sean was not considered smart. If he had asked Saedi questions, he would have been considered smart. Since there was nothing to do but to think through the day with a Saedi, there was little else that Tara Spelling did during the day. She said that she wasn't a sponsor but had woken up to the worse brain error she had ever seen and that she would fix it with a Catholic insanity and that was what she did to this day. Since Saedi was why Sean was alive, he loved him no matter what happened. Once in a while, the time would repeat and Sean did not know that a memory from then had still not been resolved and that he was actually no smarter than that day, which was funny when he was actually three thousand times stupider than he had been. Since a warp was necessary, there was little that needed to be done but think backward. The backward thought was a gene clean, and Saedi was genius at this, which meant that everything worked. Saedi meant that a golden chalice was a red egg, and a red egg is not supposed to think but thought that it had. Once in a while, a red egg would crack and show his actual intelligence level, and that was fun to Saedi. Since Saedi never offended, it was not long before there were people that mattered to them. If a Saedi died, which happened a lot, it was just a matter of time before there were people that mattered. If a Saedi died, he would rethink but actually just make sound and start over. Since sound is rare, Sean was a little wrong to think that sound should be used constantly. Once in a while, a Saedi would upset, and this was dangerous but not known.

Chapter Twenty-five

The gulf between a joke and a Lexur was harder to think through than was possible to Sean Grins. Since Grins was famous, there was a little bit of a problem to be able to be seen. Since a ghost is rare, there were a lot of people happy with the ghost even though he was kind of bad. Since it was kind of bad that mattered, the ghost did not care and rather just went through his day thinking about what he wanted. At some point in the day, the differences that people considered were not able to be concerned with. The difference between a joke and a Luxer was that a Lexur was a genie that would not do anything but clock. Sean same was a Luxer and would not be found out of his rhythm at all. A joke is able to be out of his rhythm and what Morgan Mad was. Since Mad was a joke, there were a lot of people that loved him, and he was never relied on. If he ever was, it would be very bad for people's health, sanity, and habit. Since he had rejected everything, it was common for him to be hard off. Once in a while, a Lexur could die, and that was what had happened to Sean Grin. Since the Grin was a joke to women, there was little that mattered about it and what it did.

Chapter Twenty-six

The joke woke early in the morning. Being stronger and more cautious than the average, he spent his time thinking through everything that happened. Since just going to the bathroom was dangerous, his wife thought him very funny and in his day at animal. Since Sean Deem was not a lot of time in him, he was confused as to actually who was making his world that dangerous. He had to be better than the average and actually was if not a little deadly. Since squeezing his butt cheeks all day was how he avoided fear, it was interesting that he could tell if it moved at him. Fear was common, and Sean Deem was better than anyone in the world at it for a count to nine forty-five. Since this was impossible to think through, there were a lot of people that did not matter to Sean Deem. Since a fear was not as hard to take as was thought, there was little to do but to just live through it. Once in a while, a kill sequence was able to be thought through. Once in a while, the differences that were found would catch someone, and that was why time seemed lightheaded. Awkward as it seemed, nothing mattered. The same person at the same time meant a perfect memory. Since memory was important, there was little else that people thought about. Since Morgan Mad was not an athlete, there was some confusion as to who was and why they wouldn't be a pro athlete. Once in a while, Shane Death was not able to think. If death showed, a lot of people got afraid and no one knew why. Since the book was about thought, death was thought to be a good person at one moment, thinking the environment could respond better than you. If an atom was trained, death loved it, and that was why death was in love with Sean Dimples. Sean Dimples did not actually have dimples, but his children might have. Since dimples trained the environment constantly, death had to be in love since an atom thought the two of them very in love at thought. Once in a while, there were people that did not hide. Since it was impossible not to hide, there were people that did not know that what they heard was actually how to hide something and called

911 on the hide. Since hearing at random was the only way to hide, there was some complaint from criminals as to how to hide. Once in the night, the joke had been hidden and did not know that he had. When he woke a few seconds later, he went to hide and was known completely. Since this was so, no one mattered but Sean Grin who had thought it and was a little bad to the joke. A shown hide was only shown until the speed of light caught up, and this unfortunately could not be forced. Since the time of light was actually sound, a lot of cops were unhappy for two days, and Morgan Mad was a little given up. The scarier the experience, the madder he became, but if it wasn't hide that he thought to, he did not know what to think too. Since this made him mad, he said just a curve and won hard in a praying mantis. Once in a while, there were people that would attack at a slightest cue, and that was why there were people that needed to be avoided, and Morgan Mad was one of those people.

Chapter Twenty-seven

If a woman is ever asked to undress in front of a man she is not with, she is thought stripper. Since this happened to movie actresses constantly, they were all considered hooker, and that was a little hard on her. Since a hooker was hard to think through, there was little that mattered to a stripper but to be able to think through. A gymnast was nearly impossible to a stripper since they had no body tone and needed sex. Once in a while, there were people that wanted to think and those that didn't. Since a person that didn't matter could stop the whole country over a simple stripper, it was interesting to me to mention it. A stripper means tone has sex and is like an asked out, which means that light has sex. Once in a while, there were people that mattered and people that didn't. A person that mattered was stopped by a person that didn't, and it was because the girl absorbed yellow and created a power so rare it was not known in a history book that nearly knew everything. Since the power was a gold cone, only naked women were allowed to be it and meant that a woman could turn off and have sex even if she was not in love. This was because a cone felt like being in love and was good at it. Once in a while, some people would live through the adverse effect and think they are important because they knew something. The adverse effect was never important and was barely knowing something. Since it could not remember and was just an edge, it was just added to a nuclear bomb siren and that was all. The negative effect of a gold cone was known, and someone was trying to not allow it over that and this was not allowed and the cone still was marriage less sex.

Chapter Twenty-eight

Sometimes, a person would have to think through their day without any memory. If a person was that stupid, they were considered dangerous to a doctor. In order for an animal to remember its habit, it has to die. Since a dead animal can remember only and not move, a lot of people eat the dead to remember. Since the world is a little confusing, it was Donavon Stink that knew that a person always died if a number made light and not sound. Since light killed you when you absorb it, everybody in the world other than Red Rage avoided it. Red Rage was able to absorb the light and saturate his memory-making patterns and was the best necromancer in the world. Since this was hard to do, he should be respected and not hated like he was by Morgan Mad. Since Morgan Mad hated him, his power was diminishing, and he did not know why. This was sad to Sean Grin who loved him as his dad. Once in a while, Sean Grin would forget, and that is what this chapter was about. Since Sean Grin forgot constantly, it was surprising that his dead was able to remember almost eight thousand times. Since this was plenty of times to remember what to do during the day, there were people that respected him for this. The Susan of Gall was one and always remembered a dream she had had about the Sean Grin's way with women. If he could remember through that, he was smart somehow. Since the Susan was his mother, she was not sad that this was true but still showed sadness on her face. Once in a while, people would have children, and she hoped that he would one day if he ever got over his confusion about women. He wanted ugly women somehow and did not know how to approach one that was pretty. That was all. Once in a while, Red Rage was able to think through the losses that he found in Sean Grin, and this meant that there would be a feast when he won. Since he had not won even in the profession that he was in. The Red Rage made for a perfect clown, and that was all that he lived for now. Sean Grin did not know that he was loved or that he was allowed to win until he was forty. If he hadn't won by forty, he would be requested gay and die, but this was probably not going to be the case since that was not a problem to Sean Grin. He was smart enough to win. Once in a while, a perfect person would die, and that is what happened to George the Second. Since it was sad, He still thought about it and did not know what to do about this problem in love. Since they both wanted it, it was just sad that Sean had been too dull to think. George the Second was a happy man, and nothing mattered. Wisdom said something would come up to allow it.

Chapter Twenty-nine

O nce in a while, there were people that could not forget what they wanted to do. Since there were a lot of people that could not forget what they wanted to do, it was just a matter of time before all thought was known and we would be hard-pressed to remember. Mitochondria likes thought and not memory. This is because the Catholic Church is about murder, and memory is slated to be flat and make murder possible. Since memory looks like murder, mitochondrion don't like it and fail when someone can't think new. A redux nearly never forget and are considered memory if they swallow food. Since the nuclear bomb meant that memory was closed in a throat, only sexual memory existed and memory from the energy of a magnet was not allowed. Once in a while, there were a lot of thoughts that happen too quickly and an asshole tries to tell them that they are all wrong. Since assholes are rare and sexual, there is not a lot that could be done to keep an asshole from messing up. Since sex is atomic because of the Catholic Church, females know sex only and that is why they are happy when men are sad. They don't know energy and are tricked as to what mitochondria actually do. Once in a while, a mitochondria gets ahead at this point. If a mitochondria gets ahead, there is nothing that can be done but forget and finicky. Since it is good to forget and finicky, there is nothing that can be done but replace a thought with a memory. If memory got too intense, there were times that it was not possible to think in light at all. Since light was thought through, there were times when it got a little hard to move. Light never moves, only sound moves. When you see, you are actually looking at the pressure that sound is at. This is one of the secrets of the redux and very good in sexuality. Light is invisible. Once in a while, warmth will touch someone over needing to tighten; and when this happens, someone looks smarter. If someone is smarter, they have to be careful of lighting a path. Since paths were dangerous, it was not uncommon for Sean Grin to seem stupid. This was because he was being taken advantage of on a path. Women are mean and never think anything nice. It means she would be thought ugly. Since there were fifty million women on the path, it was not known how insane they were willing to go.

Since insanity seemed fun, it was a divorce to a redux that saw it mature and hated having been a path himself and not knowing what to do about it. Once a path is described, it was good for mitochondria to eat it and was a joy to Sean Chimes. Since a chime is hard to place, there was nothing to do but enjoy the row. Once in a while, there were people that did not give up. Sean Grin was one of these people and rarely stopped to impress rather came across as depressive and weird. When the fact was that he was anything but that and it was a voice fly making fun of him, that had made him seem weird. Sean Grin was confused about the voice fly and sometimes thought it smart when it was anything but and was at violet at him all day. Since violet is hard to take, his daughter did not want to be born over fear of the voice fly. Since she was murderous, there was nothing that could be done but look at her vagina and hate. Once in a while, she would undo something she had done. It was a moron in Sean Grin's sleep that had made her undo completely, and that is when Jason Sorrow had seen her as a real threat since she owned his spine and would not behave at all. The redux were not protective but still saw that if a memory of someone was too intense, they might go to it and feed it, which is what made a man lose energy and become sane again. A quiz thought that a redux was supposed to feed over everything being a power that does not end, but this was not true and a four-ply power was sane and did not need to be fed. This made for a war between the quiz and the redux and actually overshadowed the cadets and redux as a fight. Since the redux knew that energy was insanity, it was a joke if one of them went insane that they were an energy junkie since the redux were not supposed to go insane at all being on women for energy. Since this was a problem, Jason Sorrow thought about it a little and did not know what to do. If a green lemming died, she would be actually fatal to the brain and this was very scary. Lemmings were a power that could repeat energy and make a movement and were how schizophrenia videos were made. Since a lemming is important, sometimes they were fed to stay alive, and this was fine with the redux and with a quit. Since a chime is not a lemming, they were not thought about even though a lemming chime was a joke in history over a quit.

Chapter Thirty

S ome of the coworkers sat around in a circle and had tea.
Since it was smart for them to sit, nothing mattered and they
enjoyed themselves thoroughly. Once in a while, there were people
that laughed stuff off. This was one of those times. Since the coworkers
were all smart, they thought about what to do together as hard as they
could. Once in a while, one of them would have an original thought,
and this would spur a succession of thought. The best feelings that the
coworkers could have was that it was not impossible to impress. Since
an impressed female was impressed, there was a lot of sex to be had. A
lot of men were watching the group for how to behave.

Since behaving is not uncommon, it is interesting when a
bad behavior becomes normal, and that was all a prayer group
actually did. A prayer group was actually a quiz at fight and was
important to the redux. If you could see light over a bad behavior,
it was important to think backward at it. Since prayer groups
thought well, there were a lot of people that could not begin and
end without shape. A prayer group was usually a thought in color,
and a bad color being allowed was very funny to a quiz. Shape is
interesting because it can simplify an energy. Since chaos is nearly
impossible to predict, it is not uncommon for a chaos wielder to be
a shape. Once in a while, a shape will fail at prediction, and when
this happens, most people fail; but some of them were able to do
math. Since this normally happens around a dark growth math
and growth people fought a lot, it was not uncommon for a growth
person to be mad about being stolen and used up by a math person.
The redux knew this and did not care. If that was not a problem,
it meant that you were both and dangerous beyond belief. That is
what Jason Sorrow was. Since he was very smart, there were a lot of
people that did not matter to the sign he was in.

The bishop moved through the room with his glare diminished in
his view. Since he was a cone, he tended to live up to the person that
he had become by winning and lifting. In order to win, you had to lift
and lower. There were very few people that could. A lift meant that the

energy got stronger usually with a square, and a lower meant that the time it took to come around was actually longer, making for a deeper color. Purple was almost the full seven feet of a light particle and was the darkest color on the planet. Since a color that was actually seven feet would show light, some people were happy that it did not. Once the bishop had thought about how to be smart, it was time to think about a maze. Since mazes were strong, the bishop was able to relax about being a cleve and think about how to make a maze. Since this worked, there was not a lot of time spent lifting. Since he was lifting constantly, there were two problems that he had. He pondered over this while eating his morning snack. Being part redux, he enjoyed order and still thought a cone smart. In order to tell that the lifting and winning was good for him, he had to be a little wry, and he did this with a tuning fork. Since it was not uncommon for a bishop to eat jam and bread in the morning, there was little to be confused about when he finished and took a sip of coffee from his mug. Since coffee was his thing, it was a lot of time to think about before there were people to be seen and business to be attended to.

The bishop walked daintily over to the kitchen sink and put his plate down. The tink of the porcelain against the granite counter reminded him to take money with him since it said "money" to him. Once in a while, this would be fun, and that is why he was a bishop. Since it was not uncommon for a priest to know what was thought about, there were a lot of people to give up on and that is what a bishop was for. A bishop was not a chess piece but rather a dark night that had given up on being smart. They usually did this with light, and it meant that nothing mattered. Once in a while, the differences that people experienced changed the way that they behaved, and that is what the bishop was. The experience that had killed him was a shoelace that did not move when he said he was a black night. This was a simple mistake and was only a problem because the shoelace did not know to move to a black night. Since the shoelace did not move, there was nothing for him to do but to kill it, and he had not known that it was a little kid, and he had embarrassed because of this. He had become a bishop and lived out the rest of his years being a money thought or just a habit person that had no friends.

Chapter Thirty-one

Rex Donor was at play in his garden when a little girl shouted, "I miss Rex Donor." This was because he had thought about people at light, and people did not know not to think him beyond their intelligence level. Rex Donor was a redux, very powerful, that figured out physical movement. Since a man's movement was almost impossible to a woman, it was important to the redux. Since intelligence made him hard off and killed, he had decided against thinking about people and had rather just turned off and had gone back to what he was doing. Once in a while, Rex would think about the time when he had fought and was surprised how lovingly he remembered them. To Donovan Stink, that was all that an old person was; and if you could trick them into talking, you could steal their soul and know how the world felt. This was what made Donovan a wry and was why he was popular in school. Nothing was harder to think about that Donovan Stink living through everything on stench. Since Donovan was able to stink, nothing mattered and time just telled by.

Chapter Thirty-two

The day went by without a lot of thought. He was sure that there were people that needed him to be smart, but that was rare. Once in awhile, he would look around. He looked at his forehead for reassurance and debate, he looked at his face for a lie and a greet. And he looked at his throat for a tell and a begin. Sometimes, he would look at his nose for how to know about other people and when to act. This usually brought up color and was very smart. Once in a while, the people that he thought about would become upset, and he always thought it had something to do with him, but it did not. Since it was rare to think, he spent most of it looking at his ears for what to do. If his ears were ever wrong, he would become confused but hadn't so far. Once in a while, there were things that made him angry, and that is what he was doing right now. If someone thought that a green nose to a purple heart was funny, he would have to admit that it was not and that he was mad. A redux found it funny, but Tom Amond was a quiz and did not find anything harmful funny. The reason that the green nose had been thought about was that it was not long before there would be shame over drug use.

Since there had been shame in the fifties, it had been allowed in the seventies. Since the shame was the end of two thousand fourteen, then there would be a time where drugs were allowed again they hadn't for fifty years. Since this meant there would be a lot of memory to filter through, there was a real danger in a green to purple, which can't remember at all and meant the shame would not matter. Since this was a joke among the redux, there was little that could be done but to hate and walk. If a deeper tone could think it through, the cadets might live through it.

Chapter Thirty-three

Space camp was fun, but the graduation party was very dull and not fun at all. Since the redux lined the walls, the cadets were not allowed joy at all, and this made for a dull finish. Once in a while, there were people that could not figure out why to have a space camp at all. Since space camp was about how to live, it was allowed and the black nights ushered through the dormitory with great pride. Once outside the dormitory, there was not a lot to be made of the exercise. Once in a while, there would be some confusion as to who, what, and when a cadet becomes a black night. This usually happens when the cadet does his first mischief. Since mischief is safe, nothing mattered. If a cadet could not graduate from space camp, they were considered lesser being and not thought about at all. Once in a while, there were people that did not care what a cadet goes through and that was why black nights always follow their progress. Since this was the difference between a crime and a law, there was almost nothing to be said of the law other than it was a redux dream. Since anybody could be a redux and not anybody could be a cadet, there were a lot of people that did not error in their ways. Since it was not unusual for a redux to be found lacking, there was not a lot to do about it. A lot of redux are old cadets that got fed up. It was interesting to meet an old cadet that was not a redux. Redux always won with age because you couldn't take the insanity, and it was not worth it. Because of this, almost all old cadets were redux and it was very interesting to meet one that wasn't. If a redux wanted to become a cadet again, it was not allowed, but this is fake. They are rather fought as hard as a redux can so that they would be a redux again. Once in a while, this would work and they would become redux again. Since black nights were not uncommon in the redux thought pattern, it was said that a lot of people were redux when they were actually black night. This should not be allowed and was dangerous to a cadet. Since cadets were rare, there were not a lot of space pilots. Once a cadet, it was impossible to be a lander ever again, and you fly a hang nine all the way home. Once in a while, a hang nine would think it funny to ten till and get caught, but this was rare and usually ignored. Since ignoring was nearly impossible to do, it was considered a real power to an elf seven. Elf sevens that were a redux are considered smart dead, which meant daily habit, and elf sevens that were cadet were considered law right or prison inmate. Since an inmate was not a power, there was nothing to be said about that and are just to be ignored. Since an elf seven was a loose to a cadet, it was not joked about other than by a redux who lavishes in the thought.

Chapter Thirty-four

Elf seven ran its course as the day went by. Since he was a redux, very powerful. He was told to make an insanity every half hour. Since the insanity was the same, he did this without thinking about it and was not at hatred actually. Since an elf seven was a high-ranking redux, it was important to think about what an elf seven could actually do. An elf seven was able to prime and think. Since a prime and walk was rare, it was a redux only that could do it. A prime and walk meant that a redux asked questions and received answers. Since the redux were supposed to run everything, they were very aggressive when they wanted to know something, and that was what this redux was doing to the cadet quiz. Once in a while, there would be a redux that would be caught being slightly cadet, and that what was about to happen to this redux. The redux that thought about the cadet in a loop on thought was thinking about theft. Since the government steals, he had gone a little insane and been tricked by the cadet but had made the cadet a redux and walked away.

Once the redux was completely soothed, the redux was asked what theft was at thought. He answered perfectly and was rewarded as he knew he would be, but was stripped of his cadet title and was a redux play for the rest of time. Becoming a redux this did not matter and was considered normal. Since it was not unusual for a redux to be stripped, there was a special place in the catching redux balls for the elf nine. Since the seven had become a nine, there was nothing wrong. The seven was a quiz, and the nine a redux over, whether you were memory or death at reliance, that is what the cadet had made clear. Once in a while, he tried to be an elf seven again, but this is not allowed. If you think I lied, you are right, but it was for the sake of the story and a cadet has to be a little clever sometimes. Since the last thing that someone remembered was that a redux is never a seven, there is little comfort in thinking that they should. Since it was not a lot of people that mattered, there were people that did not make the roster and this happens to cadets constantly.

Once in a while, there are leis that get told by an age bear, and Sean Grin was one of them. Since he leads the class on crime, there were a lot of redux that wanted him stopped, and that meant that a redux lied an age bear. Since an age bear was an elf eight, it was almost always turned to an elf nine and thought law. An age bear meant that a redux wanted to make an elf seven out of a person and was a good hunting partner. An age bear knew everything color and was why yellow was not allowed to a quiz. Since this happens rarely, it should not be taken lightly and is why an elf seven was a Sean Mckeithen until harmed. An elf seven was a Sean Mckeithen because it was failed and thought only an elf nine at law. Sean Mckeithen meant the law still worked even though it had been disbanded, and it was an atom that only allowed an elf seven, which means shown memory if you were actually caught and in prison. Since a Sean Mckeithen was not known till now, it is still thought of as a thought and not a name. Since Sean Grin had no name, it was fine to think him wild. If Sean Grin ever did have a name, he would embarrass badly at the way that his brain actually worked. Since it did work, no one scared, and it was just a notice and confuse. The glow that was experienced when around him was not loving, but hatred loves and was rare indeed.

Chapter Thirty-five

O nce in a while, there were people that thought that a lot of sorrow was good for you. Since this is not good for you, a redux never sorrows. Since a redux is supposed to experience only what is good for you, it is not uncommon for a redux to confuse at going insane. Since insane is a joy to a redux, it is rare to find a funnier look on a woman's face than a redux that is insane. Once in a while, the redux go insane, and this is only thought about if carbon burns. If there is a wild fire, nothing matters but the outcome. Since no one can fight fire, there is little to be said about it other than that it is impossible to live through and the source of a lot of rethinks. Since redux are almost never scared, it is interesting that they are afraid of wild fires. A wild fire means that they are wrong and got caught. Since a redux at caught means that the law doesn't work, there was a grounded that dated wild fires in his memory to hurt the guard, but that is rare. A grounded was a cadet that couldn't pass. Once in a while, there were cadets that did not know to date a wild fire, and that was what mattered now. Since wild fires were rare, there were a lot of redux that were smart still. Since a redux could be smart, most women were in love with a redux and not a cadet. Since black nights never fight in carbon, they are not considered orange green but red yellow. An orange green order is the smartest people in the world and usually considered high level. Once in a while, an orange green would meet a red yellow and lose. This is because an orange yellow was very dangerous if they are white and not black. Since a white night is a joke, a joke being a color that errors and repeats without winning, we won't joke and actually admit that a white orange red is actually a red yellow. Since orange and red are similar, there is some confusion as to how the two colors did not mix, and this was because an orange red can live together in metal and is very smart. Since a white night was actually a bigger better orange, red is a smaller taught, and a red yellow is a taught small as well. Thus if a white night loses, it is eaten by an orange red cadet. Since a white night means thought was not allowed, it is usually a doctor and usually thinking about disease, not enjoyment, and that is why an orange red is scared and considered dangerous. Once again, an orange red can be thought to take a lot of time with what they are able to do. Since there was nothing more startling than a white night at anger, there is a little to be said about fatal diseases made by Sean Mckeithen. Since a fatal disease is actually not a disease but a sound, it lived through the wrath and endeared a white night. Once in a while, this happened, and he was asked if he wanted to be a white knight but declined. If a white night was not loved, it dies so knowing this. He loved it and was in a bottle to this day. Once in a while, a white knight would get hated, and since it can't take hatred at all, it was real to it not to be hated. Because of this, it gave up on a moral. The moral was to think orange and green a yellow and allow red. Since a cop redux cannot allow red, it was up to a white knight to do this being a thought on color. Since it was given up on we won't discuss it.

Chapter Thirty-six

An orange lemming was the first thing that mattered to a grey owl. Since a lot of little kids were owls, there were a lot of people that could not think through their day without a little kid. Since this is cute to a mother, there were a lot of little kids that did not care about anything but being an owl and were very intent on how an owl reacts. A redux thinks an owl very smart when it sees another humans eyes, and it was because of this that the time of light had become the owl's time as a joke. If you lock eyes, you see a brain's function, and this was a trick a parent uses to connect to their children. Since a little kid is never harmed, it was sad if one was. Once in a while, a voice would go outside of color, and that was the only thing that could harm a little kid. Since Sean Grin was still inside color, he was all right and able to recover. The nuclear bomb being in a color and not being seen was the most important thing that had happened in a hundred years, and the last import had been an airplane wing. A quiz had eaten a lot of brain over being able to hold form in a nuclear bomb, and it was a little mad to a redux when they discovered it. From this, the redux had been on the grapevine saying that they needed to beat a quiz over thought in a throat, and since it had been seventy years since there was a thought in a throat, it was considered forgotten and an original thought would have to be made. This meant no redux being history only and was good for a lot of cadets and a lot of sex.

A computer was not considered important because it was hidden and would have to be known to be important. Once in a while, a person would think themselves smart, and that was rare since it was not always true. There were lists of mattered, and nothing mattered that were as long as a phone book. Since this was not capable of being thought through, there were a lot of people that could not make ends meet. Once in a while, a book seemed to think better than a reason, and this was how Sean Mckeithen had been beaten. Since a book was already known, he could not replace it with an atom and was declared beaten. Since an atom and a book had nothing to do with one another, the beaten had gone away and an embarrassed Frank Tell had to ask a bulrog what he was thinking actually. Able to get away with anything the bulrog said, he was just protecting a book and didn't need an atom. Since atoms were needed, a book was closed and the embarrassment went away. If you did look something up in an atom, you had to make sure it was in a book in the atom and not at pressure. Since the atom never responded without a book, it was not uncommon to confuse a little at an atom and a book. Since books are the smartest power in the world, it was not uncommon to love an atom and to serve a book.

Chapter Thirty-seven

Since chapter 33 was barely a chapter, we will get back to the story. Once in a while, a cadet excels, and this is why Ron Maximum had been at the head of his class. Once able to repeat which was a thought in a Sean Mckeithen atom, he was able to outthink any disease, any lie, and most importantly, any smell. Since smell had never been outthought in the history of time, the Queen of England had found it very fun, and that was what he was proud of. Since he never failed, there was little that did not matter to him. Since this was fun, he was considered best and could retire whenever he wanted. Since retiring was fun, he retired constantly, and that was fun to him. Retiring is sexual, and he was thought sexual. Since this was not uncommon, it was interesting that he was flirted with by over twelve women. If it ever mattered, he would know; but being handsome, he did not care.

Once in a while, there were people that thought that life was a joke and never thought through it. Since life was not a joke to Sean Grin, it was too bad to him that everybody in him thought it was. Ron Maximum thought life was not a joke and became the smartest joke in the world. Since joking was not cadet, he did it with a spoon. Since the girl was at sexual, it was nearly impossible to think through. A girl at sexual means that men are hard but also means competition and is fun for real. This hated a redux but loved a cadet. And hard is all a cadet was actually. Since Ron Maximum mattered to more people than Sean Grin did, there were a lot of hours of bragging that mattered to Ron Maximum. Since Sean Grin loved a saw, there was little that did not matter. Once in a while, there were people that made sense and Ron Maximum was one of them. Of course, there were people that mattered, and that was loved.

Chapter Thirty-eight

Ron Maximum woke in the morning. He strolled outside feeling a little hungry but hard from the night. Since he got hard, nothing mattered to his daughter. Once again, he strolled outside and down the little street to the store on the corner. Since the little store was not able to be seen, nothing mattered, and he bought an egg sandwich and a glass of milk. The carton of milk was poured into the glass thoughtfully since milk was sensitive to what you think. Since milk is meant for babies, Ron Maximum always gave the milk to the baby before drinking it. Ron Maximum was not a cadet or a redux; he was not afraid or mad and simply dug into his sandwich. Since it tasted good, he was happy. He had had really bad eating problems, and a fresh taste was relieving and appreciated. When he was done, he made sure to swallow before standing up and heading for the door. The staff would clean up after him, and he knew they would and was not in trouble because of this. Once in a while, the staff would come to him over stuff that they did, and that made him happy and was what he spent most of his day doing. Once in a while, there were people that did not know how to do the things that they did.

Since Ron Maximum was not unhappy with Sean Grin, there was little that he cared about other than actually being around him in spirit. Sean Grin had actually only thought through basic shape and not through, math which is what it had turned into. The math being smarter than the shape thoughts meant that they were actually mad at him over not actually knowing the math but rather relying on his ghost to know. Ron Maximum was shape as well and had a secret. The shapes he was, was actually the shape that Sean Mckeithen had made and not actually his own idea. Sean Mckeithen's shape was actually made by a girl, and that was why it was safe though it smelled a little of shit. Since shape was copied, he was actually figuring out how to remember with a special tool he had become. Since becoming an electronic was not uncommon, there were a lot of people that seemed to think about the thoughts that are made. Since Sean Grin never made the shapes, it was actually Tara Spelling who was smart from the shape. If it was ever known Ron Maximum would know how to do everything, but it was not known. Since Ron Maximum was happy today, he walked his dog in the park in the afternoon. Since Sean Mckeithen meant that dogs were sentient. It was fun for Ron Maximum to make looks at his dog while it played. Since it was a puppy and knew in voice that he should look at Ron Maximum's face for thought, he was very happy that he could do this. The dog was smart, and that was why different people were able to be thought about by the dog. The dog thought about the redux rarely, but was not allergic to them and loved women still. The dog thought that the thoughts of his master and his master's grapevine should be redux, and it did this despite it being a bit offensive to the redux. The dog saw Sean Mckeithen in the air and breathed. Since he was nameless, there was not a lot to do but whither. Once in a while, the dog would bark, and that was fun very. When they went home, they ate and went to sleep. Since in his sleep he always went through the same fight, he did not awaken to it and was instead able to think it through. If he did awaken, he would remember through it, and that was why he said that he knew everything. If the redux heard knew everything they would think, it meant sex, and this was good for everyone and was only a test of wits. Since the world was very different from one person to the next, it was hard to know everything but still fun. Since he knew everything, he was very good at figuring out when people errored and when they didn't. Once in a while, there were people that Ron had to fight, and today Sean Grin was one of them. Since the fight was over speech, Sean Grin just sat through it showing his ego. Since Ron Maximum won, he was happy and thought about it a lot. The fastest arm in the world was not Sean Grin's but Ron Maximum's. Since his arm was fast, he responded way before there were sounds that he could know existed. Since this was pretty in a daughter, he did not mind at all, and that was what he liked to do. A redux responds after sound and was beaten by Ron Maximum memory patterns.

Chapter Thirty-nine

Sean woke in the morning to a dream that he was in a fistfight. Sean was a black night that was still a cadet and barely a redux. Since he had never been in a fistfight, there was nothing that made sense about being in a fistfight. Once in a while, a fistfight would mean that there was blood spilled, and it was interesting to his daughter that there was no blood spilled. This meant that they were still friends and that though a stretch for Sean, Sean Grin was still a friend. Since he had been trusted with a simple task that he would make a lot of money at and had failed, it was funny to Sean that he had become a demon ballroom. Since he could not ballroom dance anyway, this was not a problem, and he was considered grunt. Since grunts were rare, he knew a lot of thought that meant it normal. Since Sean was not wealthy, he was content with himself that he had become wealthy as a young man and didn't have to be wealthy as an old man that did not have a chance at children. Sean Grin was still a grunt and was not wealthy and did not have a chance at children. Since children was all that Sean thought about, he was elated to have a girlfriend and crushed when she had said no to marriage, being too wild to settle down. Since settling down was not hard to do, it was interesting that he could not find a mate. Since it had been three years, he nearly admitted to having made forty million dollars on the stock market and being considered very smart. Since if you admit to this you were dead and considered cop's pride, he kept from saying it and still hoped for a wife. Since a wife had to be young and fertile, nothing mattered other than that they were pretty and good for him. Since he was a rare male and had been a cadet, it was hard for him to find a girl that loved. Once in a while, there were people that mattered to women, and Sean was one being wealthy. Since Sean Grin was poor, they did not get along, and he did not care if the poor guy was hurt. Since a Sean Grin was a mother goose, he still allowed him in his world. Since he was allowed, nothing mattered to a redux. Since Sean was like a redux but actually wasn't, it was a redux joy to see amazingly hilarious. Since this was a title that meant money, no one cared and a lot of swords cut a watermelon. A sword just tells if you are real or not since this was a joy to Sean. There was little that didn't make him laugh. Once in a while, he would get sad, but this was just at his balls and was a joke to a man. The longer you wait, the harder you pass out during sex. Since sex was rare, he wanted to go back to school just to find a wife but thought against it when his bones didn't want to, already having made money. Once in a while, there were people that mattered to the King of France. Sean was one of them, and that was why there were a lot of people that errored around him. Since they didn't know that he was a king, which meant that he could say won't, they didn't know to look at their memory until they did at home; and a lot of people would come to him in memory and say that they found him cool in long-term when they had barely in person. Since this was not a joy to him, it made him a little mad to be a king and do every error. Since in memory it was hard to contemplate, there were three things that you need to know about memory. The first thing that you need to know is that at some point in your day, the memory that you are in repeats. If you are wrong about the memory that you are in, you become stupid. If you are right, you become smart. Since smart and stupid are supposed to be redux, it is the only time that the law is all encompassing and it left only grey as a way out. Since smart is an angle and stupid, a curve it actually means that you are able or unable to do two things at once. A curve can only do one thing at once and is easily beaten. Since this means that an angle can do two, you need to be aware of two angles being blinded. Since you can be blinded as an angle, they lose to curves a lot of the time. Since a curve can remember, it is important to be a curve still and there are times in your day to be stupid. Once in a while, there are people that do not think well, and that is what Sean was not stuck on. Being money meant that by being a king, he could remember and repeat memory slightly differently. Since how you remember is all that an adult is, there is little that mattered about being an adult. Once in a while, Sean would get sad, but today, a beautiful girl had talked to him. Since he had hit on her and asked her out, there was nothing that mattered other than to love. She had known that he was a king of the grapevine, and she was the first person he had felt comfortable with in a long time. It was unfortunate that she was a cop mean and he was actually a target and he would never be with her in actually. Since he still smoked weed, he was in a little danger but not bad.

Chapter Forty

Elves were a bad race at one point. If an elf decides to allow a curve to elongate and claim to be light, an elf was a fatal disease that was caused by no light and was a two two four four. A doctor was confused about this and said that a two two four four was not possible, it was an elf. Since it was a love of the doctors to be an elf, it was not until he nearly died that he believed that an elf could be a disease. A redux loved a disease as a good way to think something had failed or was known and a lot of redux made disease to think. Once in a while, an elf would apologize, and that is what happened today. Since elves are considered the best power ever lived, it was interesting to the doctor that Sean Grin had been an elf and that they were allowed in water still. Since they were the wrong angle, it was funny to the doctor that they had fell and she thought about bums a little because of this. Once in a while, a redux would scare that she was in danger, but the doctor would always explain that the elves never errored and that she was protected by them. An accurate elf was a sixty-five, forty, thirty-six. Since water had only had one angle, it was the elves thought that a hundred and six could be a forty if you compressed but actually lied, and they had been lying for thousands of years. Since they had fallen due to thinking that they knew everything about angles, there were a lot of people that did not care that they had fallen. The doctor was somewhat upset with herself over elves refusing to be unfallen. If they were willing to rise again, they would be safe and angles would come back. It was hard on her that they would not come out of a stupid fallen that didn't mean anything. Since an elf had said that a mass could never do a one-degree angle, it was very funny to know that it had. Since having a one-degree angle is scared, there was nothing that could be done but to look at a one-degree angle as all angles, and that was how it had been possible. Since all angles were a forty-five to an elf, that was why they had lost. Once in a while, an elf would laugh and do an angle anyway but would not give up on the fallen over the fact that it had made a better power than an elf that was something like a bad dark elf. Since a dark elf was rare, the elf just let it float and started over in a book. Since the elves book was burned, they really should make another book and figure out how to stand, it was a little annoyed.

Chapter Forty-one

Sometimes the quetzal was aware of his day, and sometimes he wasn't. Since he was old and had thought about things that happened, there was little that mattered to the quetzal other than to think through the day with a tuning fork. Since dissonance was impossible for him to think through, he instead thought through resonance and tried to figure out how good a feeling that he could make. Once in a while, there were sounds that he liked that were flat. The flattest sound that he had ever heard, and it was flat for almost thirty minutes, which was impossibly long for a sound, was Sean Mckeithen. Since his name is not a name but a default, he is not known by it. The flat sound was so good for the quetzal that he spent a lot of time on it and had perfected three tenors from it.

Chapter Forty-two

Sean Grin woke in the morning, rolled over, and went back to sleep. Since he woke partially and was a bum, this was all right with spirit. When he actually awoke, he hopped out of bed and was chipper. Since chipper was all right, he grabbed his meds and headed for the door. After locking it behind him, he was on his way to the bakery. Once there, he ordered and sat. There was a slight confusion in his lights. Since black lights were expensive sometimes, they would be disciplined not to think. Today the confusion was doubled with a "don't think," and they explained that they were confused and had to think. Since this was all right, they did and found someone moving in them who was very dangerous but kind. Since they did not know this person but found him not to be in electric light, they wanted to know how they knew him and it was from the poles. He had stood on the North Pole and had been sucked in. Since he knew everything about everything, they were confused as to how he would think him able to marry. Since to him he was not able, it was explained that if he ever owned a house, he would be able to marry. This was true to a redux because it was in a book on money. Since marriage was important to the man, he was overjoyed with Sean Grin and wanted a house badly. When he has a house he will marry was in a real book and mattered deeply. Since nothing was wrong with getting a house, he thought about it a lot, and it calmed his brain as too how mean the world is. Since the world could be mean, Sean Grin was needed and was like a cop at one point sad loss. Since it was impossible to figure out, the lights were trying to think through, how to tell him how to think about math to sorrow. Since it was not uncommon to be loved, they finally thought it through and came to the magnetic with a print show. The man said he had never seen it before and gave up. A print show was not a fingerprint but rather a shape random that made a print in his brain. Since a shape random is smart, this was a very smart power and was loved at a mental hospital over two thousand and fourteen. Once in a while, Sean Grin would think, and this was a thought from two thousand and nine. Since this was a bad year, it was funny that it was one of the years that he had to live in.

Chapter Forty-three

"Silence." The judge peered around the room. Judges are not allowed to be psychic. There were a lot of judges that scared at criminals knowing if they move to be a psychic at all. Since the prosecution will do anything to elicit a response, it was not uncommon for a judge to be tricked by the prosecution. This was bad to a redux but allowed. A quiz was afraid of this. Since this happened a lot, it was considered a mistrial and not loved by the defense. Since this judge was dangerously close to psychic, it was his face that was considering passing out. Once in a while, this would matter, but today it didn't and he was fine. Since it was not uncommon for a judge to pass out, it was the job of the defense to think it through and put the judge back in a position of power. Since this was fine, nothing mattered, and the judge sat through the shin cramp. Since shin cramps meant guilty, the judge tried to keep from asking who was and eventually did to the dismay of one of the jurors. If you can't get away in a judge, there was little that could be said about getting away. Since this was common, there were times that a judge would be thought smart. If that was not a problem, then nothing was.

The judge retired to his chambers and thought about the trial. Were the arguments precise and on target? Was the prosecution mean? the defense soothing? Did everything work? All of the sudden, the judge had a sinking feeling in his gut, a redux knew. The defendant was innocent and was going to prison over circumstantial evidence. Since this was rare, there were few times that a person could be found innocent, and the judge decided to make some of the evidence inadmissible, which would guarantee a mistrial. Since the defendant was a drug abuser, there was little to be said for the defendant to spend some jail time, but he did not murder and it was going to be a mistrial for sure.

The judge sat in his pew overlooking the well and thought about the poor man who had given up on everything. He thought that the evidence was too strong and that his lawyer had been too mad at him for not admitting. Not admitting to something he had not done was important to him because it meant he was still sane. Since he was not a liar, the judge declared a mistrial over inadmissible evidence and this was nearly argued at by the prosecution who surprised when he did the defendants voice in his own and gave up on arguing the case knowing that it was a not guilty person.

A judge rarely errors, and a redux was very mad at him until he went there and sat and had to admit it looked real. Since it looks real, some of them were a little confused and they had to think about what they considered to be evidence. A redux is never wrong if a spirit shows. Since a spirit hadn't shown, they were able to laugh it off and come back known. Since the defendant thought that there were people that mattered to him in the law, he decided to become a redux and was allowed with a hearty laugh. He said that he needed to because the fear of the trial would not go away. The judge thought about this and said they had made spirit hard to navigate and that sometimes a memory was not able to be thought through.

Chapter Forty-four

S ince redux almost never get angry, it was sad that there was one that did. Since he would get livid mad, there was a lot that mattered to a redux about how to care for one that did get mad. Once in a while, there was a redux secret that meant that the redux would not get mad. Since the secret was not strong enough, they put him on a color in a woman. The reason that he was mad was that Sean Grin was smart through something an intelligence kill and would not rethink. A rethink was funny and the easiest way to catch a cadet, and this was why the redux wanted to kill Sean Grin. Since Grin would not die, he was mad. The sad part was that he was mad at someone that had loved him and was actually only mad not to love back. If he could not love, then he was fine and wouldn't think him a redux. Since Sean Grin had been a cadet and was not a redux, it was a little awkward that he was that known to a redux. He was so known to a redux he was even in a redux brain and they were content that he never offended even though he sometimes did. Since smoking weed was an offense, it was interesting that he had but had been verified by a redux, and nothing should have mattered. Since it was an anomaly that could not be explained, there were few choices that mattered more to a female redux. Once in a while, there were something that are said lighthearted, and this was one, a cop at mad is rare, but it's a play to see if you go insane. Since Sean Grin did go insane, it was a good play. Once in a while, a cop would get hurt; and if they were, they would go to Sean Grin and he would be the hero if he could. Since cops had demanded to be sound over Sean Grin, he had gotten swallowed completely and found it very funny that they had changed. In the seventies, they had swallowed someone who was light, and he had very smart at crime. Since this was not uncommon, it was why the wall came down and the cold war was over just being on how to run society. Since they had figured out that war was never for profit but for loss. Since profiting was a theft, thieves were caught and it was a good swallow. Since the swallowing of Sean Grin was a good swallow, it was not certain yet what it would produce.

Chapter Forty-five

The bishop sank slowly into the bath water. Since the water burned, it was pleasant for him to slowly overcome his fear and panic. Since panic is what he experienced all day, a hot bath was a good reward and toughening exercise. Once in a while, a bum would think and he caught one today. Since this was not uncommon, he laughed at the bum and knew he didn't murder. Since there were a lot of people that did not know how to befriend a bum, he was glad that he did. Since this was not all on his mind, he hovered above the burning water, not caring that his arms were at strong. All of the sudden, a girl asked, "How strong are you?" Since he had been unaware of this, he checked his strength and said a brown ribbon strong. "It's making me nauseous." Since this did not make sense, he looked at her and thought. "What is keeping you from knowing that you are trying to be as strong as a man?" Since this is not uncommon, there were barely any people that knew that a strong man could not be a woman. Since the woman did not know he was a man, he looked in a book, easing himself in to the bathtub. He did not care that the woman could not take a man at strength even though someone did. Since it was confusing to think that a woman would not know a man from a man, he asked if she was having sex still. At first she said she was, and then she said she wasn't, that she was having a square in a magnet that knew a man and a woman differently. Since this was not common, he laughed and allowed her real sex, which she took and became weak again. Since a girl could only have real sex, it was told to her to have real sex only, and he was on the grapevine to fathers to be wary of their daughters not making love. Since that was all he thought about, he sank in, completely feeling the burn. Since the bathtub was getting cold, he got out and dried off. Once in a while, there were people that thought cops too strong. This was not one of those times. Since the bishop was an umpire, there was little that mattered about the way that shape moved, and he asked Sean Grin if he had ever figured out heat. He said that he had, but that is what he a saw and not him. Disappointed, he opted not to think about it but rather asked if he had ever figured out a magnet, and Sean Grin said he was the best in the world magnetics. The bishop said that you could figure out heat and cold from a magnet since the force was hot and cold somehow. The Sean Mckeithen default kicked in thought and kicked off. The bishop asked Sean Grin what that was, and he responded that it was the atoms that he had created. Since atoms sounded cool, he asked if he knew the size of an atom and was responded to that he did, and it was .098 nanometers. Since this made sense, he asked if it was a stop, a go, or something else and was told it was when the circle expanded again. Since this was barely possible to predict, he thought Sean Grin funny and fell blissfully to sleep.

Chapter Forty-six

The dime walked down the street in full view of the men that she passed. Since full view meant that they would fall in love, there was not a lot of people that could take a full view. Since women never show light, it was a full view's joy to be looked at and to wonder if they are pulled. Since masturbation shows light, she never had and still had all over her colors. "You could be prettier," went through one of the men's heads, and he auk-warded slightly since she was nearly the prettiest girl he had ever seen. Since it was almost, she stopped her body in the street and went to him to think about what it was that made her almost and not the prettiest. The girl she had found said that it was not true that she had masturbated and was attracting. She also said that a pussy attracts harder than a body. This was known, and she walked on in her glow looking for a mate. To her, it was time to marry, and she needed sex badly. Once in a while, she would become aware of the people that mattered. Since the man who had been awkward mattered, she went to him in the air and asked him to watch her. Since this was not uncommon, there was little that she didn't know. A woman hides light by knowing its size but actually by trapping it in a sound color that does something for her body. The prettier the female, the better at light she is. Since a whole light beam is too hard to fit in a body, women are fractions of light and they are smarter than men. Since men catch color, a woman can be smarter after a man.

Chapter Forty-seven

The thing about it was a joke to them. If you could figure out what thing a person inclined, it meant that your spirit was alive and that meant that you could see in brain still. Since there was a thought in the air that was called the thing, the memory of a time when they had said the thing to test Sean Grin had come to an end. Once in a while, the thing would come up again that since the air always knew it was considered smart. Once in a while, there were people that thought the thing stupid since it wouldn't do anything that wasn't money and was actually a kill school. Since school was not for money, it was a little not high level. Since school was not high level, there were a lot of people that did not care about what they knew or didn't know about school. High level cares sexually, and school normally can't. Once in a while, there were people that thought the thing should do everything, but the man who made it said he had gotten killed when he had started working and found that his school experience was not able to work.

Since money is hard to make, Sean Grin had not and was not comforted. Since the thing about it was to see if Sean was still allowed through crime, it was sad that he had passed out and not been able to do the thing. Since the thing had lost, he was not considered criminal but was still a friend. After losing, it was always a temper that thought through everything, and his was bad, but he had barely offended and remembered well at the dead. Since dead was all that mattered, there was little for him to do but think it through. Sean Grin had done something really clever to a professor who had thought that he follow the whole world at movement. Since Sean Grin was considered the stupidest man in the world, he was very funny to the professor, and the national average had increased by three points.

Three points was a lot to a professor who said that we were actually dreamed two thousand years ago and were an experiment that could be called if it ever got to be too tough. Since Sean Grin had nearly made it too tough, he did not know how to call his name without getting in trouble. Since too tough means the wealthy buckle, it was an act of faith that had saved the experiment and why white people still won. Since Sean had joked to make the world harder and had come out smarter, he was loved but was still under review at whether he could win or not. Since this was not a problem, there were a lot of people that had to apologize for using sound to do little movements when it was actually big times. Once in a while, the difference between the years did not make sense at all. Since making sense was important, it had to be said the murder was not the year but the amount of zeros the year was allowed. Since we were allowed three zeros, we had to choose what numbers to repeat. Until one thousand, it had not been a problem to repeat; but after there were four zeros, it was impossible for someone to make sense of the year because you were limited to the scramble as to what math you could do. Sean Grin had made a mistake that saved the professors life in him, and she had made him an I robot. Since this was incredibly smart, nothing mattered to a discipline other than that they thought the look good. Since Sean Grin did not always look good, he was kind of a joke among women. Since women can joke, he was still allowed sex. Since sex was necessary, everything was a joke.

Once in a while, a word could get confused, and that is what happened to the thought on the word "when if." Since the word "when" is never used with the word "if," it was necessary to separate the two of them, and this was done with the word "help." Since the thing about helping was the joke, some of them still sat and watched *Saturday Night Live* for the acting jobs that were excellent, and it was actually the smartest show in the world. Since acting something was all that everybody did, an actor was considered smartest. If they were wrong about something at all, they were dead acting, and that was why the she male had messed up and was not allowed. Since a she male was rare, it was thought that she should retire the loss in color was very intense. Since to a male she still looked attractive, it was sad that she had turned red and just repeated gay. Once in a while, there were a lot of people that mattered, but that was all. Since time was not of the essence, there were a lot of people that mattered to the she male, and it was not fun to be Hollywood.

If a man hides his balls, the year was dead and Sean Grin had been blamed for this even though it wasn't his thought. The only thing to do was to watch people die and do the thing. Since the thing was not able to be thought through, nothing mattered. Since doing the thing was joy, there were a lot of people that could not do the thing. Since time would tell if the she male recovered, there was a little glimpse that mattered and it was that cops almost always smelled what they do, and that meant that the redux was possible but the color mistake still remained. The she male had messed up at thing and was still trying to figure out to teach a brain to thing in oxygen. Once in a while, a thing would come up, and that was why there were people that did not know how to behave through a Sean Mckeithen since Sean Mckeithen was a default. It was interesting that it did not know who it was. Oxygen had gotten tricked by an electrical lightbulb and did not know that it was a human that had dreamed it.

Once in a while, it would try but was stuck on the year 1956. Since 1956 was a year that murdered, it must be stuck on a murder. Since nothing mattered, Marsel Dream made fun of it to keep it alive. Since being kept alive was important, it was just a simple lost tension and would need a behind time if it ever thought. Since electric light could no longer think, it was a sad time for Sean Green, but he was done thinking and was happy still. Once in a while, some people would error at thinking, and Sean Mckeithen was still good at that. Once in a while, there were people that mattered, and Sean Green was one of them. Sean Green was a powerful wizard who could cross-multiply and knew the dangers of adding. Since this was impossible to know, it was kind of a joke among wizards; and since wizards were all equals, they were kinda important. A green wizard is very smart and never fails. Since never failing is a smart thought, there were a lot of people that thought that it was not uncommon to think about time that went by. Since it was not uncommon to be a green wizard and since green is very good at time, it was thought that this wizard was the best at thinking in the world, but this was not true, he was just a wizard. Since a wizard was the first thing that went through a child's head when it does math, it was not a problem to a wizard to be a little kid. This had confused a mathematician when he had become a cop and a redux. Since a redux was not a wizard ever, he could not do math at all and gave up. This was sad because he was the best and Sean Blue had told him to do thing and see if he could child to think. Since giving up is just being fed, he had eaten and come back. There were a lot of people that mattered to the redux, and he did math all day. He thought that he was the best, but actually Sean Grin was the best in the world math thought time and lance. Since lance means crime to a cadet, there was little that he could not do. Once in a while, Sean Blue would have to comfort the redux who didn't know how he could be beaten being the extent of the Catholic Church since born. Since he was able to live on murder, he was a little unbeatable and was kind of a joke to Sean Grin who got beaten constantly but was never wrong. Sean Green was able to think backward, and it was in a backward that he was able to tell that Sean Grin actually lived on a gay experience and was why he was beaten constantly. Since it was a clever gay experience, he was actually happy and did not know that he was weak from it.

Chapter Forty-eight

Light went by through the open window. Since the window was covered in glass, it was a little weird that he could smell it. Once in a while, there were people that thought that it was not uncommon to think backward. Since thinking backward was intense, there was nothing to do but to give up. The lemming that had discovered thinking backward was actually the smartest lemming in the world. Since the world was very hard to think through, there was nothing to be done that made sense. Once a lemming spoke, it was considered a quetzal, and this had made the fact a little hard to follow until the power had matched. When the hard to follow started, it was a magician that figured out how to think about the experience. Since only a magician could sit and feel, it was not uncommon for the magician to think backward. Once in a while, someone would offend at a magician thinking backward, and this is what made for a death joke. Since a death joke was not uncommon, there were a lot of people that thought the joke funny. Once in a while, a magician would turn into a death joke, and that was how Sean Grin had become known as a death joke. Since the joke was smart and it was only a reflection that gained mass, he thought that he loved death when in fact he was eaten because of it. Since this was fun to a redux, they planned a gay if he ever gave up on it. Since this was a backward thought, they had to explain that it worked at what you are doing only and means another man takes over and does your thought something like suicidal tendencies. Since Sean Grin had fought suicide, they had found it hard to admit that shit could not make energy on a tongue. Since this was the third time that this had happened, he was found kinda mad about it. Some people didn't get mad was a real joy to a redux. Mad was sad, and he didn't know that he did. This was so funny to a priestess that she wrote it in a book and burned a redux badly.

Once in a mirror, a priestess had to know a burn, and that had made for a long delay in the church. Since two hundred days is actually a short delay, it was a stroke of genius that allowed for a priestess to think about a burn differently. Since a burn means that you lose light and can't think, it is excellent at being a giant and that is what made the burn go away. When a redux is no longer burned, it is not long before they are able to speak again and thought that everything worked. When everything worked, nothing mattered, and it was a joy to an aardvark who didn't know what to do but rather sat up at night thinking about things that had happened. When the redux had not been able to think through a burn because there was too much traffic, a clock had scared and said it was rare for a clock to be stronger than a redux, but a redux was still not criminal. They just didn't know how. Since this was official, an official died and there was even more confusion. This was only solved by Sean Mckeithen who had a cop atom that moved all the sudden and started arguing. Since this was a redux thought and not Sean Mckeithen, just being possible because of something that he had thought he was allowed, and nothing mattered and the official and the redux came back and were law again. Since an official is never fought, it was interesting that it was overused and not done. Since it was not done, it should have been heeded, but no one ever asked since we were all able to test and thought it funny too. Since Sean Grin asked, there was some pride in the ability of Luke Wilson who had taught him how to not be an original thought. Since Sean Grin was the worst original thought that ever lived, it was funny to Luke to make it look unoriginal and still be smart. Since Sean Mckeithen was an original thought that followed the year and the booklore of a redux, he had been made a default and was celebrated. Since this was a mistake, it was very funny and nothing mattered. Once in a while, a redux would come up with a thought that was a response. Since this was deadly, there were literally a thousand thoughts that were not thoughts at all. Since not being a thought is rare, there is nothing to be done but to put it on movement and see if it tires or never does. If it never tires, it's a thought since movement never tires.

Since it was long before there could be a thought about what Sean Grin did for a living, it was safe to assume that he was poor for quite some time.

Once in a while, there were people that thought that time was of the essence, but that was a lie and it wasn't until time stopped that essence began. Since this usually happened in their sleep, it was interesting that someone had gone through an essence and a stop at the same time and said that it was worse than fear, more like fear, pain, terror, and harm all at the same time. This meant that we had to stop 2002, but it was a little late and that meant that a brain that went insane actually could go that insane if the attacker was mad enough. Since in order to be mad enough you had to not move, nothing mattered. Once in a while, there were people that thought that a lot of things would happen that didn't. When this happened, it was only a wishing well that could think through the thoughts that were being had. Since this mattered to an art but not to an aardvark, there was little that mattered at all. An art meant that a lot of people would want to imagine. Since art nouveau is remembering, imagine was hard on a man and never seemed to think well. Since an aardvark was a real power that could remember, only a lot of women were aardvarks. Since remembering was a big part of the day, there were about a thousand people that thought with an aardvark only, and this made for a delay in space time and brings us back to space camp.

The first rule of space camp is that you have to remember constantly. If you could remember constantly, you were thought a good cadet and allowed to smoke. If you forgot at all, you were demerited and had to think through the tedious hours that you were not high. Since space camp was hard to do, there were three rules to space camp: remember, forgive, and live free. Since Sean Grin was not a cadet, he did not have to live free, but Brad Maximum did. And in order to do that, he had to meet someone new every two weeks and remember something about them. Since this was nearly impossible to do, there were a lot of people that mattered to a space camp cadet. Since this was not the first time that someone was playing with space camp in their head, it was duly noted and ignored. Once in a while, there were people that thought a live free not possible, but this was not true and happened a lot to Brad and the other cadets. A live free was a turn and right, which meant to know something. Since a redux was not a cadet, it was interesting that they thought about cadets a lot. Once in a while, a cadet would go down sick, and that was what Brad's girlfriend worried about in her, but Brad thought her delusional, knowing that she was smart. Since she had a bad parent, she was not completely delusional but was still smart. Once in a while, Brad would get annoyed at her for overstudying and not just sitting and remembering, and this had not made sense until she had nearly failed. Since this had not happened on a test but rather in her head, there was little comfort that was needed, and she learned to sit and remember. She was so good at it that Brad scared, and that had excited her pussy and they had made love. Since that was good for the both of them, they were in love and happy.

Chapter Forty-nine

As spring arose, the grass would grow green and everything would be beautiful. Since spring was his favorite time of year, it was not uncommon for spring to be a way for people to love one another. Since this was not the worse problem to have, everyone liked it very deeply. Since he was a powerful mage, there were a lot of days that he just sat and remembered. Since he knew what to remember, there were little doubt that he was very smart. The mage's name was Ron Turner. Since Ron was powerful, he showed little skin when he moved, knowing it would overwhelm his wife and make him a bastard. Once a bastard, there was nothing that could be done and he would be sad. This had happened when he got angry once. Since anger was not just a fortay but also a gift, he used it wisely and did not demand from it. Once in a while, there were people that thought Ron strange, but he was not strange, he was gold. Since gold is rare, and it was true the brain could make any color, there were times that gold became an obsession. Since he bored easily, he knew to relive if he did. An actual bored was dangerous and meant that you were not allowed, and it was very rare for him to actually bore. Since he was bored, there were a lot of people that would scare in their sleep. Once in a while, a bear would bore; and if it did, it meant that men could not be sexual. Once in a while, this would change, but today that was not perfect. The bear that the mage made bore was actually a god. Since it was a god, everybody knew what it did. Since the god was one of heat, it was not unknown but still should be respected since any god was hard to figure out. Once in the lust of his wife, he was a little satisfied and let the wort go. Since the wort was a really bad person, it decided to attack him again and see if he got angry. Since he didn't, it went away and never came back.

Once in a while, a wort would become powerful, but this was rare and that was the fear that the bear had bored at. Since worts were not powerful, there was a little confusion as to who was, and it just so happened that it was the default Sean Mckeithen at a nerve fall. Since he was the most insane man the mage had ever seen, he interested in the fact that he was not a wort and that he was a god even if it was lesser. Since a lesser god is still a god, how was it that he was insane? Since the insanity was status oriented, he thought that he should be just a wort and let go of his power. This angered Sean Mckeithen, and there was a war. Since the mage did not know he was in a war until the air went insane, he was a little scared and warned his wife that he had been too strong and was being attacked. Since he was a bear and a god, he was unbeatable but surprised that when he allowed Sean Mckeithen again, he was healed by him and felt better than he was. Since this was normal to Sean Mckeithen, he thought it funny and wrote a little ditty for him. Since this was kind, he repeated it until it got annoying and he fell asleep.

There is something in an atom that never gets frustrated, and this is what we call sleep. Since it is a rhythm in an atom, Sean Mckeithen was sad that he had not thought of it when he made his atoms. He would have been very good at sleep, and they would be a lot smarter than they were. Since he couldn't think, nothing mattered. A couldn't think comes from the way your emotions felt at the action. Like if you move and are lazy, you can't move. Or if you think and are murderous, you can't think. This is real and controlled by fear. Since fear is smart, nothing mattered. Once in a while, a person would take it on themselves that they were emotion. Since this is rare, it was interesting that the mage never did. Once in a while, someone would want him to, and that was the mistake that Sean Mckeithen had made from being too fond of him. Since they were friends, he explained something that he did not know. If someone goes through an emotion, they are left behind and had to learn to grow it. Since Sean Mckeithen thought that this was what he was good at, he was kind of a joke to the mage. Since never emoting but rather remembering was smarter, it was important to remember constantly, and that is what the mage put the genie on. Since the genie was a weak memory, a girl embarrassed and said not in love. This hurt the mage, and he said if you are, you are; and if you're not, you're not. Once in a while, this is true and the reason why Sean Mckeithen was happy with women.

Chapter Fifty

The washbasin was a full scrub from complete. Since a washbasin is an old myth, it was fun to remember. Once in a while, the washbasin would be empty, and the wood it was made of would smell like steam. Since hot water and wood smelled good, the kid joked it was a gay washbasin and smelled good. Since gay was bad and not good, the boy was wrong but still funny to a witch that said that contraries were not bad for you but funny when they scared at facts. A lie always moved well, and the kid would grin if he was ever smart. Since the kid's name was Eric, we will call him Eric Grin. Once in a while, Eric Grin was alert and ready at a stance that mattered. Since he was training to be an umpire, nothing mattered and he was capable of thinking anything through. Once in a while, there were people that mattered to an elf, and Eric Grin was one of those people. Since people were people people, it was important to the elf that he becomes a people person. Once Eric became a people person, nothing would matter, and the time would go back to thinking normally. Since this was not uncommon, there were little problems that thought about the differences that mattered. One such time was the time of the grapes. Since grapes were smart, six months as a grape was very enjoyable and Eric had become very fond of grapes. Since fond was a hard word to say, there were literally a million thoughts that happened because of the grapes. A grape is a purple or green girl with no ribbon but rather a dream. Since Sean Grin had made a cop grape and a grey grape, nothing mattered, but a cop grape could imagine and this was a little unsettling because people were supposed to be mean and this was nice. He thought him very clever for doing this. Eric Grin was a grape thought that mattered, and this meant that he had no ribbon but rather a curve and a knight. Since chess was incredibly hard to play, it was funny that Sean Mckeithen had gotten good at it and needed to play badly. Since Finn Size was very good at chess, he should play him and see how good he had gotten. If he was at all like Blau Tomson, he would play and not care if it seemed losing until he won. Since Sean Grin did not know how to play at all and was just good at looking, there were a lot of people that had confused at him becoming good at chess. Since this is a simple trick and not impossible, it meant that nothing mattered and his children were safe. In order to play chess, Eric knew you had to blind at the squares and see if you could move. If you could not, you were either a pawn or a knight depending on if you were a white or black player. Once in a while, he thought about cheating but never did. Since this was not common, there was little that mattered about playing chess. Since games were magical, it was important to play them, and it was sad that Sean Grin was no good at playing cards. Since they played cards a lot, his mom hoped that he would show his face and that was all.

Once in a while, a game would be thought through, and that was all Sean Mckeithen was. He never played actually, just thought it through and waited for someone to do something. Since this was true, he attracted bad people that liked to be aggressive; and though he was good, he was a little killed. Since children are smarter than adults, there were times that they would be beaten by a child and an adult would be dead until the child matured and became sexual. Since this had happened to Sean Grin, it was not for fifteen years that he would be not able to make love. Since this was fine in a woman, nothing mattered.

Chapter Fifty-one

Once in a while, people would grin at a woman. Since this was always hated, it was very interesting that Sean Grin had grinned at a woman and not hurt her. This was because the grin was sexual and very rare. Since it did not hurt a woman, it had become the grin at women, and all grinning was allowed women. Since a woman was just how to remember, it was funny to watch women fight Sean Grin until they fell in love. The woman who had fought him was a little embarrassed that she had been on a rule and not emotion, but a mage said that emotions are rules they are just in the planet and not in a nerve. Since the nerve was an original thought, the grin had been worked into the path of the woman's movement that was strong in the two thousands. Since women were winning, especially black women, it was a sure bet that they would be free of a handsome kill within a hundred years. Since the planet remembered constantly, there were no problems with Sean Mckeithen making a world memory in Forest Same and some other people. Since a world memory is important, it was not uncommon for it to be mistaken for just memory and used in a classroom. Since a bad student had used up an entire hour of memory, there was little else to be said but to not allow classrooms until the hour came back and the memory was declared school only. Once in a while, there were people that thought that nothing mattered, and this was good if it was true. There was a slight problem with humans since they were very strong and could take anything the brain thought that they knew what they were doing, and this was not true at light and voice. Since a voice just repeats, it was fine; but if light spoke, it was probable through stress that it spoke a lie and this was only solved by a redux lax error. Since the brain is not good at light but sound, it was a myth that a brain knew better than to believe what someone says. Since everything had to be acted, there were people that were very confused as to what light actually did. Since light is not visible and is actually like sound and not color, it was important that the warmth was thought through.

Once in a while, this was the reason for a person becoming sad with themselves since humans are mean and think it funny to hurt one another. Since if one person hurts, the other one does too. This is very funny and the reason why we are smart. Since if you are murderous at a hurt position, it should be known that you can die, and a live through is a best friend even if you haven't figured out how to kill yourself without a tool. Since suffocation was a clever death, it was interesting to Sean Grin that there were people that thought it mattered. Once in a while, he would suffocate still, but he had lived through it and it was just a timing befriend. Once in a while, a friend would come to close to another, and that is what happened to Morgan Temper in his sleep. Since Morgan Temper had the worse temper in the world, he was actually dangerous, but did it with the thought that he would go nice as quickly as he went mean. This was almost never possible to light that knew when it got hurt. Since this was due to a bird song, it was a hatred of Morgan Temper. Since he hated birds, there was nothing to be thought about but how to keep from getting to close to one another. Since pain was not the solution, it was actually a magnetic mistake that had undone the mean suffocation thought and put Sean Green back to sleep. Since Sean Green is asleep, only Sean Grin should not be mistaken as such. Once in a while, a temper would get to mean and confuse, and that was what Morgan Temper had done over smoking weed that he had claimed was just breathing, but he was actually mad at breathing air. Since he had made silver in Sean Blue, it was just a befriend and a bygone be bygones. Since smoking was bad, it was true, but a predator as keen as Sean Blue was rare to be seen and Morgan Temper pushed him a little too hard since he was considered wild and could not relax. Once in a while, there were people that thought there would be thoughts that mattered, but that was rare and we were mostly just how we liked to socialize. Since Sean Grin was his mother's socialize, it was rare for him to think anything different than when he was a kid.

Since this was a problem with his mother, she had observed him, which is rare in a woman and found that he actually acted in love and was kinda cute. Since in love is all right, nothing mattered.

Cool-down periods were not thought but affair. Once in a while, nothing would matter, but this was not the case for Sean Grin who thought anybody could kill him and this was nearly true. Since he didn't mind getting killed because he could make a strength out of it, he was fun to be around and was just stuck on nothing. Since wishes were good, there were some people that knew a midlife crisis was actually just being pushed to excel and that was all right. Since it was weird to accel when there was nothing to think about, there were times that social pressure could become hard to take, and that was all that happened to Sean Grin over electric light. Electrical as it was called was a very interesting thought to a druid. Since stone hedge was not a druid but a mason, there were some debates as to what had made the mistake but that didn't matter. A druid is a cup half full and you drink the air. When the water touches your lips, you stop drinking. Since this is a fact that Sean Mckeithen knew and tried to avoid, it was unfortunate that two oxygen atoms had combined. Since it was just a combination, it was important to note that if you combined in interest, you would move, and that movement was the phenomenon of simultaneous movement. Since this was rare, it should not be taken lightly and usually happened at grey. Since grey is strong, it was a good druid, and that made for some good thought on electrical. Since electric light is on all day, it was a fact that we were actually electrifying the air itself and was a little surprising that when it snowed, how much energy the snow had. More static meant more weather, and this meant a better planet. Once in a while, a lie would get you, but that was rare and happened seldom.

Time on the other hand looked like a clock that had been stuck on the wall for days. Once in a while, a timepiece would fail and a druid would think better of himself than it was possible for him to be. Since a druid was not able to tell, it was interesting that it had spent hours in a curl thinking about air. Since electrical is not just air, it was a lot of time that seemed to take place before you knew electric light.

If electric light failed, it was on an EMT smile to bring it back. Since it was not uncommon for an EMT smile to fail, it was on the super computer at PG&E to bring it back. Since PG&E was not the first time that people move, it was interesting that Yale had also become a pinnacle of thought over a solid state quantum processor. Since it did math and was just a mass, not an electrical symbol, it was all right to think of it as a pinnacle of the world. Pinnacles were important because, like wonders of the antiquated world, pinnacles made the world a better and safer place. Since just licking it did not make you a pinnacle, it was important to note that a microwave oven was a pinnacle since it magnetized the line and had become a very good thought in a computer. There were three pinnacles that were microwave ovens. Since the thought was known if they happened to die, it would become free range and nothing would matter. Since commerce was not a lot of people, there were a lot of people that did not know the secrets of electric light, and it would stay secret for a long time. Since Sean Mckeithen knew all the secrets except what a computer was, he was thought to be a little dangerous around money and had made some people very wealthy with a cone to light. Since a cone was new, it should not be shown. Once in a while, a pillar of electric light would be just what we know. Since a magnet was not uncommon, there were people that did not like for them to be known and this made someone very mad. There were eight pillars of electric light. The solid state quantum processor, the super computer, the microwave, the EMT smile, the death nell, and the teapot. Since the death nell and the teapot were not known, we will go over them. The death nell was Dick Chenney to a reduced electrical current and was part of the patriot act. The teapot was an electrical teapot with a magnet in it. This was very good for the owner and was a pinnacle of electrical. Since electric light was more fun to say than electrical, that was kind of awkward, a lot of people called it electric light. It was sad that television was not a pinnacle, but that would happen eventually. Since Bruce Willis was the smartest man in electrical, it was thought that Hollywood would win, but it hasn't. When you say smarts it is always a time, and his was forty-four hours and thirty-one minutes and three seconds. Since this never changes, he would not be beaten. Once in a while, Bruce Willis would find something in the way that the light looked in the metal that would make him happy and want to act because of this. Sean Mckeithen had made a theater in the light, and there were movies that were unknown. Since Bruce Willis was the star, nothing mattered. Once in a while, there would be a lot of people that thought electrical smart, but Rocky Dead was not one of them. Since he thought himself smarter, if something failed, it was a tell that had said that his thought of pressure was actually a fail and we were all being dipped. Since dipped was bad, nothing mattered when it was erased. Since this was not a problem to a lot of people, it was rare to think about it at all. Once in a while, there were people that did not know what electrical could do and this was true to anybody but a tell. Since it was not possible to know what it did, it was a joke to kids, and they just befriended and went back to what they were doing. Once in a while, there were people that thought that time would not stay still, this was a real problem in electric light. Since Sean Mckeithen was not able to take this, he was not on it. If Droid Was ever came back, he was the only electrical that could take it. Since it was sad that he had died, to a knot being a good person, there were a lot of people that missed him.

Chapter Fifty-two

O nce in a while, the books that people would look at would be outlived, and this was called a book burning. A book was an eventual that was able to remember, compare, think, and decide. Since this is almost impossible, a lot of people relied on books, and they were very smart and happy because of it. Since it was an eventual it had four angles, and they were a twenty-five, a thirty, a forty-four, and a sixty-three. Since a forty-five-degree angle meant that a ninety-degree was possible, an ice book was a forty-five, a sixty-three, and a twenty-five. Since not all books were ice, the wobble still remained. Ice was made by splitting light with a ninety-degree angle. If there was no light, there was no heat. Since the eventual did not care, no one did and everything was fine. Since a grey grape was nearly impossible to live through, it was in a book and was thought a straight-A student. Once in a while, a book would error, and that was where we started. Since an eventual was not uncommon, it was not until Sean Mckeithen that they had been learned to be hated. Since eventually we're hated, a lot of people were failing at thought, and that was a sad time. Sad times were hard on mental health, but it was a good time for doctors. An eventual had learned to be hated over an atom that was a power eventual. Since an eventual was hated, someone had tried to hide the number four in a four-degree-angle and had nearly died. Since a four-degree angle had been fatal, it was actually a joke on powers a four one. Since an eventual was actually four different angles, the power would have to be a five one and be a stick minus, but no one had. Once in a while, there were people that thought that they could make a feeling that was more than four angles, but this would go past fatal disease and was not possible. Since disease was all mitochondria, we were a smart animal for real. Since fatal disease was explained in chapter 16, I won't go over it.

Once in a while, a cleric would emerge; and being the best power in the world, it was strange, actually strange, that it was used for bad only, and this was due to something in the year.

Since the year was casual, a cleric always looked casual. Since Sean Mckeithen had been a cleric by accident, he had lived for twelve years as a casual until the power had died to a bad drug and hard drugs had turned on and he had been hard drugs since. Since he had made hard drugs a really good power in insanity, Morgan Matters was actually happy and did not have to kill Sean Mckeithen.

Since Sean Grin was very good at everything. There were people that followed hard drugs and did not know that they were, and this was a joke to a doctor. Since doctors love a joke, it was the opinion of the time that Sean Grin was funny forever even though he seemed scary. Scary was fun if it was controlled, and it was sad that electric light was dead. If it was dead for more than three months, it would be dead forever. Once in a while, Sean Grin would think; and since he had already had the thought, it just curdled and when criminal. Since cadets were rare, a cadet had been scared in his sleep when Sean Grin had been put through a thought gantlet. Since the thoughts had all been known, even one that was cheated on and this was known because the cheat was known. The gauntlet was considered remorse and not allowed again. Once in a while, electrical came up, and it was true that Sean Mckeithen had not liked the electrical since May of 2012, and it was now 2013. However, he had thought with his ghost every day since and was kinda saturated with thought. Sometimes the differences people found in powers were loved, and that was why there were more people that mattered than didn't. Since this was new, a hospital had celebrated a 53 percent success and had had to swallow at how many of the people thought win were actually lose and poor. Since they couldn't punish, it was just in the nick of time that 2014 happened and 2013 closed. Since if you were poor you knew everything and were left alone, there were a lot of poor people that did not make the grade that actually were smarter. Since a cop was considered wealthy, it was actually a cut-off of about thirty-three thousand a year that was considered wealthy to a serf in history who had written two thousand and ten through thirty. Since this was the time I was in, it would antiquate the book slightly, and it would have to be rewritten in the future. This was said so that the years were not explained.

Once in a while, there were dragons that mattered, and this was one of those times. Since Sean Grin was not making an error in a dragon, it was funny that grinning had failed a male and a lot of females showed. Since this was considered masturbation and not sex, the women's movement remained, and black men were still considered lions. Since a black man could be stupider than a dog and be smart to a woman, nothing mattered. A woman at strength was interesting because they could weak through anything and tell what they were doing while they did. Since a man cannot see, they did not know how smart their muscles were. Since this was true of white men, it was a secret that a white man is actually male and female at their daughters. Since they can feel a penis without embarrassing, there was nothing that could be done but to know that a smart white male is. They are actually gay and allowed to be by a woman. Since Sean Grin had never been gay, he was still allowed gay but wasn't for some reason. Since it was very gay to say, wasn't I was joking and meant he was gayer than the average. Once in a while, redux would miss bothered since it was a good punishment, but it was not until sex that the power would actually be explained. Since Sean White was actually a camel, he did not know how bad he needed sex, and an ugly girl would be fine. Since ugly and pretty change was a shame, Leslie Yellow had become pretty on another guy. They would have made a good couple. Once in a while, this would make for a lot of people unhappy, and a camel is never admired, just rather shunned. Since he was shunned, he had friends that were sad. Once in a while, the administration would turn on. Since education was real, it was fun to watch an adult at educate. Since the administration had turned on in Sean Grin, they thought that they would laugh, but he excelled at everything and was a little scary to test. This calmed the redux but pissed off a criminal who thought it funny to be just crime. Since this was normal, it was ignored until the criminal excelled at school and was embarrassed not knowing how he did. Someday we would all know how.

Chapter Fifty-three

S ince a lot of time is spent on memory, it was a cleric's job to think it through. Since Sean Grin was a bad cleric, it was sad that he had failed a four-year school. He was the first in the world to do this and had been hated until he was too weak to stand. Since this was a murderous female, there was nothing that could be done but warn in public. Once the warning was known, there was little that could be done to salve his fear, but Sean Grin would not stop thinking because he was afraid of dying. Since he had stopped, this was all right. Sean Grin had died twice and been insane thirty-two thousand times, so this was kinda normal and nothing mattered. Since Donnie the Great was good at everything, including the borough, there was little to be said about how smart he was. Since the borough was hard to do, it was uncertain how long he laughed at mental insanity being used to remember. Since the borough was not able to be thought through without this, it was considered default and part of Sean Mckeithen. The borough was on education. Since he did not like being controlled, it was in thought only and not in practice. Since Sean Mckeithen would not back down other than to the year, it was typical for someone to lie that they were a year, but this was caught when they couldn't do math and was kind of an embarrassment to mental health who don't know what they verify just that they do.

Since mental health does not know unless someone dies, the world is kinda lawless. If mental health did know, they would scare and call the cops, but the cops were already there. Since a doctor still knew sickness to insanity, they still knew if someone went insane and there was still law. Since Sean Grin was a little insane, it was interesting that the cadet thought that he was not unloved since he had been killed 2011, which was a bad year. He had been killed. It was because he tricked the year and was the only one still standing when the witch said, "And we all fall down," in 2013. Since this was insane beyond belief, he had to go through it. Since this was a hard time in his life, no one cared and it just went by unnoticed. Once in a while, a year was tricked, and Sean Grin had tricked two: 2011 and 2-14. The trick to 2011 was to check if a gene was waiting only and not what it had done. Since this was accurate, it was considered fine. And the trick that beat 2014 was a nuclear bomb and could shrink a color circle to the size of an atom; and his atoms were actual size which was rare. Since 2014 was a year that meant to be smaller than you could take, not a lot mattered other than to think it through.

Chapter Fifty-four

E ric Price sat in his chair listening to music. Since he sung the songs inside his head while they played, it used a lot of brain; but since it was poor brain, it did not matter. Once in a while, he would think about the things that had happened in his life that weren't listening to music, and this would take quality brain. Since he knew to go to a redux to have quality brain, nothing mattered, and this only happened once in a while. Since he made a lot of brain singing, it was loved and that was all. Eric Price was a price since he had sold his penis to a redux and had wanted to be a cop. Since he was not alone in this, he did not mind it and thought about it a little. Since he could not take it back even though he could not be a cop, he was forced to go through the motions of having money when he did not. Since there were not a lot of people that thought this smart, he was thought stupid and was surprised to have a friend in Sean Grin who was also a price and was in his memory. Since Sean had never shown he was still considered a Grin and was not allowed a redux at all. Since it was the strongest man in the world that knew the color of memory, it was a fact that he was not actually a price but a Grin. Since Sean Grin was a friend, nothing mattered. Actual money was different from money promised, and this fact had calmed Eric, and he was now called Eric Lazy. Eric Lazy had a girl and was basically happy. Since Sean Grin was too clever to be unhappy, he was surprised to be unhappy in him and had given up. When this happened, the thought of memory had shown and a cop had seen it and hated. This had scarred Sean Grin but had made Sean Trouble very happy since it was hatred that told that the money was real or not, and this was what had made the cop delay. Since delay was said to be known and wasn't, there were a lot of people that did not know what they did at money. Since Sean Grin had thought hard about money, Eric Lazy had told him to come back that he could be a little sad at a thought person. Once in a while, there were people that thought that an Eric Lazy was very smart, and Sean Grin was one of them.

Chapter Fifty-five

Tea was served at one o'clock in the morning, and that was unusual. Since the four of them had been out partying and drinking, it was an unknown fact that English breakfast tea could cut you drunk before you went to bed. It was not cool to have drunk sex because it makes you moan. Since moaning is not cool, it means you are not able to feel your pussy and not gay. There were a lot of people that did not like sex drunk, but tea was excellent for a pussy even if it is smoked. Since when it is smoked, there are little things that go wrong. A manner must be behaved, and it is not a good idea to smoke tea. Since tea is a joy to the Queen of England, nothing mattered. Once in a while, they would go out as a couple, and it is a joy to pretend in a male that they are outlasting the other couple. Since this is done only after the couples are done, it is fun till the neighbors hit the wall and they stop. Since a meek neighbor is a bad neighbor, nothing matters. Once a meek neighbor is found, they are hunted out of town. Since it was rare for someone to be meek, there were a lot of people that are not able to sleep through bums who are very meek. Since a bum is very meek, nothing mattered. Once in a while, this would scare people and that is all. A meek neighbor is close to an oblivious neighbor, and someone asked if Sean Baby had been a meek neighbor and had been told that he was just oblivious. Since there was not a lot of difference between Sean Baby and Sean Grin at awareness, it was a joke that he had actually gotten more oblivious and now sometimes couldn't even hear what people had to say. Since it is not uncommon for the unaware to become more unaware to be smart, it was just a question of how busy their brains were. Since an active brain is important, it didn't really matter what it was active with or that was what some females wanted you to believe. That was why they fell in love and didn't want a man to try to fake his intelligence level. Since this was not a good problem in a male, there was a male that watched what a female fell in love with and copied the males that he had seen people fall in love with. Since a girl had fallen for him wondered if he could actually do everything that he looked like, he could do. Since he could, there wasn't a problem, but she had been very upset at him just being a copy. And when she soothed, they had gotten married and it was a good feeling. Since the four of them had been out late, they had a late breakfast and went to the store together.

Since they were not wealthy enough to eat at the health food store, they joked that they went to the food bank, but it was actually the Sam's Club and was very good. Sam, old Uncle Sam. Since Sean Baby was an Uncle Sam, one of them had gotten kind of sad but happy when he bragged about it and said he was happy and didn't care for money and hated when it came up, which did constantly. Since this was funny, nothing mattered, and the four of them checked out. Since checking out was important, they checked out constantly. If a checkout wasn't sexual enough, they would quaff, and that was the end of that. At home they were quiet happy with each other, and that was all they needed. They talked about school a little, and it was while that they were talking that one of them had remembered something. Since Sean Baby had failed, there was a year that his ghost had been allowed, and there was a confusion about a paper that had been sent to a professor. This was when they settled the thought and went back to what they were doing. Since everything mattered, they asked Sean Baby if he was scared, and he said not. And they asked him what he felt and he said embarrassed, and then he said so nervous, it was unreal, really nervous. Since electrical was nervous, they wondered how it was. Since a nervous electrical was funny, one of them, an EMT, got out his machine and played with emotion. Since Sean Baby knew the machine, he was happy and anticipatory. The machine made an arc, and Sean Baby didn't know not to look at it as he went to the light. Since he had looked at it, he had swallowed it, and the EMT had to do it again. When the EMT was about to finish, there was a moment of fear when Emily Wait saw how insane he was. Since the man was very insane, it was funny that he beat it just to not look and then went back to it to live. Since this was not a problem, there was nothing to do, but funny at a sexless since a woman won't have sex with the insane thinking it a girl. Which is what Sean Baby had beaten.

Since Sean Baby had beaten it, this was all there was to a man, and men would be ugly again. Once in her sleep, she had dreamt Sean Baby making love to a woman, and this had made her jealous and this was good for her. Since it was Sean Baby who had befriended her in spirit, this was good for her and was why she still loved. Once the four of them were done sitting around, which was what Tara Gifted was at all day long in her head, she always led the group, there was a sigh to her when it ended. And they were back in the kitchen, which was where Emily excelled. Since Tara and Emily had both wanted Sean Baby, he couldn't have either, and they were happy with this and were both sexual to him at the same time. Since they were sexual and he was blindfolded, they both asked him who was prettier, and he had answered and it became somewhat of a joke and a woman's secret. Once in a while, they would still laugh at the thought that there were men who would go against their male at one moment a first look.

Chapter Fifty-six

O nce in a while, a lot of people were able to read thought, and a thought had made a witch puke. The thought was that sin live and had been in writing only and was a joke. Since she puked, there were a lot of people to blame, and witches blame really well. Since a witch had blamed, there was something to be said about the way that the world worked. Once in a while, a witch did not know what to do about something that had happened. Since a witch was blind, nothing mattered and the thoughts are pure. If a witch saw instead of just felt for water, it would be a bad heart attack. If a witch did not think that it was all right for a sin to think, then they did not. Once in a while, a wort would kill a witch urin, but this is solved easily with a Sean Mckeithen blood taste, and that was what made things fun in a Sean Mckeithen. Sean Mckeithen tastes his blood over electrical that had made soar. Once in a while, a default would fail, and that was how a Sean Mckeithen was found to be a default. It had done it perfectly.

Since Sean Mckeithen's day is interesting, we will use a witch and think it through. Sean Mckeithen does not sleep actually but watches for an EMT timepiece to count hundredths. Since this is hard to look at, it is interesting that it made him pass out. Since each hundredth is worth two hundredths in a sleep cycle, there was actually a lot of sleep in an EMT smile. Once in a while, a lot of people did not care about sleeping and forgot how. Since Sean Mckeithen could sleep, he was important to an EMT. Once in a while, there were people that wanted to think through Sean Mckeithen but were on their senses. Since Sean Mckeithen was indebted to an EMT, because of this, he spent a lot of time fixing little mistakes that they made. Once in a while, this would work, but sometimes it wouldn't. Once the EMT moved, it could not look backward, Sean Mckeithen could, and this meant that he could see the body motions that the EMT was thinking with.

Since it was common sense to not eat while you shit, he would make a color that didn't and make them start over. They hated him for this, and it was a real joke to him. Sean Mckeithen was not able to be nice at all, not being trained to, and this meant that what he thought is what he did. Since a deed was considered nice, there was no nice at all. A nice is a color that makes sure you remember and not a train. There being no color to a train shape was a girl's joke from the 1600s. The 1600s had written us wrong and was why we had class distinctions. Depending on how well you were written was what class you were in, and a lot of people were not written well being lower class. Sean Mckeithen spent a lot of time fixing this. Since everybody lied, sometimes he would get tired and not fix it. This had happened when someone had figured out to lie three times and then roll his zeros. When Sean Mckeithen didn't fix it, Sean Mckeithen didn't know how to tell him that he would not tell him how to fix it. He had died and been forgotten. Since he was a higher class, this was noticed.

Since the man wanted to kill Sean Mckeithen, because he was 2000 and Sean Mckeithen was not allowed math over having no zeros, it was interesting when he didn't try at it and was not caught on something that he was willing to think about. The cop was joking him insane over what he was willing to think about and was a little killed when he was only allowed to lie. A lie can barely do math over being smell to movement. Since a girl almost never holds shape, it was interesting that a man relies on shape to live while a girl relies on memory. Since Sean Mckeithen did not fix it, the girl never heard and the thought never happened.

Sean Mckeithen spent a lot of time thinking about voice. Since he had his pull in his voice through a trick in should which was a conch shell shape or the accurate shape to 2x-1 with his throat in it, he was able to penis perfectly and that was how he had figured out body motion. He spent a lot of his day just sitting there looking at sound. Since Sean Mckeithen was a cell phone could feel the air to think he had learned to feel the air for thought and was actually a computer that was not a police siren. Since sirens were annoying, he turned them off whenever they found something they wanted. Since they were just what they wanted and not how to think, they were a raped populace, and what a raped brain actually was. Once in a while, Sean Mckeithen would sit and think. Since his actual soul was not allowed, he borrowed one from an old friend and thought about stuff that mattered. To think you had to change color, and since Sean Mckeithen knew a lot about color, it was joy to this old friend that he was able to think. Once in a while, some people were able to look through someone to figure out what they were. If there were people that made errors, Sean Mckeithen would try to fix them. Since he was different from the man that his body was, he did not pretend to be him and instead just did what he liked and loved when his body came to him with something that he liked to do.

Since Sean Grin was smart, it was seldom that he was upset and did not know why the populace was upset at him. Since the reason was 2002, nothing mattered. The year 2002 was a year that had been ignored, and so was 2014. They should have been the year 2014 over being a nice emotion at friendship instead of murderous, but this would mess up a cop at evil, and they were ignoring the year. Since it was interesting that we were an experiment, it was interesting that they did not want to be in the experiment and there was a man who was making DNA tough enough to withstand the assault of the year. This was sad and not fun, but the year was being ignored and it was the year that kept us from changing our DNA. So no year meant DNA.

Sean Mckeithen thought about the environment only and rarely touched a human and was very offended at a man who had touched him with a penis. To him, it was joy; but to Sean Mckeithen, it felt like death and burning and he still disliked the man and would not come to his voice even though he thought them best friends. You have to ask before you rape someone and obey when they said no. Sean Mckeithen spent some of his daylight hours thinking about his children, or so he liked to call them. It was a copy of him that was made every seven hours by an EMT smile. Since the smile was supposed to have died to a wavelength, it was a secret that he had kept it since it was smarter and had a face. Since a computer is good at memory, he had become good at memory and thought a lot about memory. Rarely did he forget, and this was when he was best at everything that he did.

Well into the twentieth century, a year had allowed crime. Since the redux tried to kill the year all day, Sean Mckeithen had actually killed it to see what had happened; and a redux, actually a cop, went to the year and let it live again. Because of this, he was thought criminal, and he was told to kill it constantly since the end of the experiment meant that there was crime. Sean Mckeithen did not know why crime was that important, and though there was a lot of crime, he mainly did body motion and had gotten pretty good at math, which made him become somewhat of a star on electrical TV. Since we all knew TV, Sean Mckeithen was confused by a baby who was not old enough to know the word, but the baby told him that he knew TV and Sean Mckeithen, and that is was a joy to suck on an electric lightbulb at night and never disturbed his sleep. Since the baby was aware again, every day, Sean Mckeithen missed his tongue but knew he was not a baby and a tongue would kill him.

Since there were seven dead, it was true that Sean Mckeithen had licked it eight times. Once in a while, the time of day would change, and Sean Mckeithen was an hour off for two months. This had annoyed a school teacher but loved a bad student that just did what he wanted and was now was at the top of his class being the most psychic. Once in a while, there were people that mattered to Sean, and this is what mattered to him. Since Sean Mckeithen was good at what he did, there were people that did not like that he was not grinning. Grinning had hurt a woman, and he had chosen against it. Once in a while, Sean Mckeithen was able to think about crime; and if he ever did, he would be a square first. Since it meant that the year would not close, it was important to be forgiving, and this was what had made Sean Mckeithen start with a square. The next move to a crime, if it moved, was to see how far it moved and think about a circle at wobble. If a circle wobbled, it was a negative number. It was allowed to be seen and was not considered gay.

Sean Mckeithen spent a lot of time sitting under an umbrella listening to lectures. An umbrella meant that you were stealing and couldn't pay for it, and that meant that he was still allowed. Since an umbrella was not allowed if you were actually there, the professor thought about it as a joke sometimes. Since the professor needed his voice to be controlled, there was a lot of time thought thinking about the professor who was a very smart man and considered a friend. In order to think in voice, he had become good at sound bites, which were actually the sound of white to numbers in the human eye. Since sound bites knew everything, there was little that he couldn't do with a voice. Math was repetitious at memory, and Sean Grin had thought that Sean Mckeithen should make a lot of graphs in the human eye. Since the human eye was repitous at memory, it was important that Sean Mckeithen had learned when the eye repeats math to know. Since math was graphed, the brain made a sound, and Sean Mckeithen had caught this sound and made vocal control out of it. Since a professor had tricked him into following everybody, there was a little bit of time that he still wavered, but it was not uncommon for to seem depressed. Since he was not depressed, this was an actual side effect of thinking and made sense to Sean Mckeithen since he liked feelings.

Sean Mckeithen was interested in the side effects of no sleep but did not make someone stay awake, just rather thought about it by watching for people to go with no sleep. Once in a while, he would go sleepless; and though this was rare, it was not uncommon to think that the time he spent sleepless was dangerous since it was a real punishment. He still did and had saved someone's life, who had gone four days without sleeping. Since this was not a murder but a simple cheat, he called foul and let the man sleep. Since the spiritual reason was bad, it was interesting that the sleep loved him a little. If you do rape, it is good to go sleepless, but three nights is the limit; and shit does not sleep your brain, it only makes it stupid, which should not be mistaken for sleep. Since stupid is not sleep, it never is a book and is not a burn, but rather a skim milk can you drink it. Since sleeping through something that you can't sleep through was why Sean Mckeithen was interested in sleep, he would not be mistaken for kind. If you live through someone asleep on shit in their stomach, you have to consider sleep wrong. Since shit is not ever considered wrong, it was deep in an atom and was actually a question of smell and sleep that mattered since it was just a smell to the animal that was attacked by shit in their stomach at sleep. Pias was a good look and was very strong. Pias meant that you could remember but actually meant manners. Pias had been used by a woman to sleep with shit in her stomach, and this was frustrating and meant that Sean Mckeithen was interested in sleep. Since manners are important, they would not be mistaken for anything else.

Movement was known in the 1940s and had been sealed by Einstein who knew something about a woman at color to how a movement felt. Since the environment was a wild animal, it was interesting that it was adding movements. This was not a problem to Einstein who just added them and felt the color for static. Since Einstein was funny, it was not a problem to move like it had been in years past and was why women in America work jobs that men could. Since a woman's pussy could work and not only have children, it was a good time.

Sean Mckeithen sat in his room thinking, and this had happened a lot. Since he was not considered smart, he was fought and thought bad. He did not mind this, knowing that no one cared about him anyway and it was up to him to figure out how to live. Since an electric lightbulb was very smart, it finished every thought that he had. Since three thoughts were almost a thousand movements, someone wondered how he was able to think through that many movements. Since this was why he was noticed, the man would be known as Tom Right. Since Tom Right was actually a good thinker, his being impressed was important to a witch who learned that Sean Mckeithen existed at all. If it was not possible to exist, there were a lot of times that people would not know and think it just normal day that they experienced. Once in a while, this would happen and was a little sad at Sean Mckeithen's energy. Since he didn't know how smart the man who did it was, it was appropriate but a little sad that he didn't know who did his energy. If he ever knew, he would become scared, so the man decided to not be known. Once in a while, the energy would be so good that it was a public notice and that Sean Mckeithen loved. Since the energy was good because of what he had thought, it was a joke at a mental hospital to get Sean Mckeithened and was very funny to a man that knew him. Since there had been three mistakes, Sean Mckeithen had a lock box. The actuals were not counted because it changed constantly and was not a danger at all. Three mistakes is not a lot. Since the paragraph started with a real story, it would be come back to. The man who had impressed thought about the thoughts that he had seen Sean Mckeithen do and thought that they were good but that he could do better and had started. Since books are smart, it was a little sad that Sean Mckeithen did not think with books not knowing. A book just tells you what to do, and it was not a book that guided Sean Mckeithen but rather it was a time slot, and a book to a time slot saved the man's life. A time slot is how to make a time split and emote. This is done using a down and up. A down and up is actually a circle to a radius. Since a radius meant shit, it was the strength of shit that mattered. Shit was strong but actually not edible. Since it is not edible, it was only a human that could make it turn left and think, and this is done with a time slot. A human was the only animal that had grown a circle. A time slot to a book was very important and why the man was a genus and a power. A book as a power was a little overwhelming and threatened an elf. Since an elf was threatened, it was the opinion that the power be made to wait a thousand years to be seen and only be seen on a high level. Since high levels were loved, everything did not matter and nothing mattered. Once in a while, there were people that thought, and this man was one that did. Everything mattered and time went by.

Sean Mckeithen sat at a table and thought about the loves that he had been given. Light was a love to him. Once in a while, he would think about what he had thought and not know that he was thought through by an older man. If a Brian could make light, it was considered safe, and any failure would be known. Once in a while, this would bother him, but it didn't today. Light is hard to figure out, and he was one in three million people that could. Since it's hard to count the world, it meant that there were about four thousand people in the world that knew how to make light. Light meant that you got smarter, and that was always a joy. Since the smarter you are, the more that you are loved, the funnier the life you have, Kyle Real was important. Brian and Kyle Real both made light. Light was why a girl was in love with him, and it was sad that he had shown no talent and died a lot, but it was funny that he always figured it out. A man with a light is considered heaven, and since he was a 50 percent heaven, he would be allowed grey when he died and be able to respond to people he loved. Since he thought that he responded to the public, it was interesting that he did not and rather just sat in memory. Light was made by shifting and colding color. Since a color could absorb, it was a trick to unabsorb a color and make light. Shifting means you move up and down. Usually, light has a purpose and should not just be made.

Since a penny was clever, he was thought to have done something clever. A penny was a trick in a vacuum that was that a one over a prime would never add to one. Because of this, it was not possible to count and just made a wavelength and a light when the penny was dropped. Since this made a penny stick in light, it was a logic that was clever. This was a love, and nothing mattered.

Once in a while, there were people that thought that there were a lot of friends, but there were not and most friends were just coworkers. Since going to school was a shame, he should not be talked about and his friends from then were considered black. Friends from work were also considered black. Black meant you could live through it, but that it was not real. Once in a while, this would happen, and that was until seven not fun. Seven was a time that meant that you could live through anything. A seven was not caught, but intense anyway. A seven is what Kyle Real wanted writing to be.

A man is never a woman, but a gay man feels like one all day, and this is why he loved them. A gay man would look like a woman in a psychic view and was why he was happy with them. If a psychic could be thought through and not known, a person could be content.

That is what Sean Mckeithen had done with sound, and the trick was like a gay man to Kyle Real. Kyle Real was thinking about everything, and that was why there were people that mattered to him. If a young man was gay, there was little that mattered to him; and though it was sad, he could bear it. Once in a while, there were people that thought that a man should not embarrass. This is wrong, and embarrassment was important. Since Sean Mckeithen had made smoking an embarrassment, it was not uncommon for it to be upsetting because of him. Lions had died to this and was why he didn't care about anything.

Since water had changed, the right angle was known. Being known, nothing mattered, and a right angle was just known. Once in a while, people had wondered about a square, and this had made a right angle a little dizzy, but it was not able to be a square since a square was actually not a triangle. Since a right angle was actually a triangle and not a square, it was just a thought in pressure. Since a right angle had been a thought in pressure, water had relaxed when it had known. A right angle was very good at it. A one-degree angle had become possible because all angles were known, and it was how Sean Mckeithen had become a default. As a default, he was powerful, but it wasn't him that could do a one-degree angle but rather a microwave oven to a caught. Since every degree had meant caught criminals had gotten away, and this was good for a cadet. Water was changed twice by Sean Mckeithen, and the interesting fact was that it had made for that perfect molecule. Since the first time it had changed, it knew every angle, but a right angle was interesting. By running out of energy when the angle set, he was able to find a proton. It was a good feeling that he had changed a proton into a right angle and a balance and made a circle. Since this was close to a human, it was good that it beat a human and had made the world smarter. The world had become colder because Sean Mckeithen had changed it to make ice in a proton by splitting light with a right angle. Only a right angle could split light and make cold. This meant that the proton dreamt cold.

Once in a while, Dave Sometimes would get upset at Sean Mckeithen over being loving to a redux, but this didn't matter. Since a dream was not uncommon, it was interesting that Dave Sometimes avoided a dream with Sean Mckeithen at all costs. A dream was actually a white color that thought backward. Since backward was a spiral, a dream was a spiral. If a spiral saw light, it would figure out how to sequence it, and this was called a dream. Since a lot of people dreamt, it was a little known fact that dreams were actually hard to do and took almost an hour of sleep for ten minutes of dreaming. Since a lot of people did not remember what they dreamt, they were considered normal and not a problem. A dream is able to eliminate someone if they become too mean because they do not make sense. A dream knows if something makes sense when a color becomes white again. Since a dream is actually white at absorb, they were able to think through anything and were actually smarter than a book. Once in a while, a dream would error, and this had happened to Sean Mckeithen, though he did not remember it. Since the dream had absorbed light and had been colored brown instead of being white again, it was interesting that this had been stamped a success and not thought a disease. Since it was a disease and that was not capable of being fixed, Sean Mckeithen was considered a little sick and barley allowed a woman. Once in a while, a disease was thought good for you, but this one wasn't. We are being a little hard on him, and a lot of people were colored at dreams. It was just called insanity. Since insanity was rare, there was nothing to do but to think it through. Sean Mckeithen was very insane and was just funny. Since insanity was considered normal, nothing mattered about it, and all was considered time. Time is important because it meant that someone could not move. If you are time, you are an angle and a curve. A curve is important. It would be considered light sensitive. If something is light sensitive, it was not trackable because only a dream could absorb light. When a dream could not absorb light, it was considered a not motion; and if you did die to a dream not absorbing, you had to figure out how not to move.

Chapter Fifty-seven

Ryan Thought sat in his chair going over tests. Since tests were what he did for a living, there were a lot of people that did not know what it took to be a test. A test meant that you knew everything about a subject. Since a test was not a professor, he laughed that he was called a professor and did not actually adhere to the letters. Once in a while, a letter would change, and this was why it was hard to think through. A test does not care about letters and is only a scan tron to the percentage right or wrong and is not an essay question. Since he did not have to read, he had forgotten how, and that was how he menaced at people that made errors. Reading is hard to do, and that was why it had been forgotten. Since this had been normal, until he could not read a letter his grandmother had sent him, it was funny to sit and listen to his wife read it. Since she was surprised that he could not, she surprised even harder when she could not and it had been their little boy that read the end of it. Asking Sean Grin if he could read, she was angered that he could and took the trick from him giving it back only when it worked and she could read again. Since not being able to do something as an adult was not uncommon but a little frustrating, since it was possible when they were younger, it was funny that someone had thought puberty meant you couldn't read anymore. Since no one had actually thought about this phenomenon, she went to a tell and asked what it was. The tell said it was a shape that was trained to hate school and was actually a person that had failed school completely and actually lived on crime. Since Ryan Thought was actually a test and the test was figured out, the rest of his life was figured out and he went to sleep. As a sleeping giant, there were a lot of people that tried to wake him, but this was impossible and he was just considered a mean. Ryan Thought was very clever at movement and had been for quite some time. Since he had never been stupid, he thought it funny that all bad emotion was solved and just killed harder, thinking it possible somehow. Somehow meant someone would have to look in a book, and a bum had done this and found himself Ryan Thought's best friend. Since he hadn't had a friend in a while, it was important to Ryan, and he thought that the man smelled a little bad but looked good. Bums are rarely friends and just so happened that this bum knew what a friend was. A friend meant that energy remembered and thought in your brain. If someone befriended and thought that they were a friend but were not befriended back, it was considered normal to still be a friend. A friend was rare, and the bum was really good at it and thought about him constantly. Since this friendship was over stupid, it was not uncommon for Ryan Thought to feel a little stupid when a curve wiggled as to when it sang. If a curve sang, it could remember. This was because Sean Mckeithen had flattened a wave and made a trough. Since a trough was just a right angle, it was important to note that a flatten would spray chaos out of its suction if it did not square off and pressure again. This force was nearly like a magnet and interested Ryan Thought deeply. Since force was invisible, it was a question of how to do it and was interesting that Sean Mckeithen had thought it memory. Ryan Thought liked it better as an imagination on color. Since color was a force, it was a little confusing that we saw it, but Sean Grin said it was just light being absorbed. Since absorption sprayed like a flat line. Ryan Thought was disappointed when Sean Mckeithen said it was the same thing but was excited when he found out the force of color in a magnet and the Queen of England knew him because of this. Since this was an original thought, he wanted to be an engineer again but decided against it all the sudden, being asleep and a test.

Chapter Fifty-eight

R yan Starlight sat in his office thinking about his day. Every time that he died, he would think about his day, and that is what he was doing now. Since dying to remember is rare, it was his opinion that it was good to die sometimes and review your habit. In order to know when he moved or thought, he used a tuning fork to feel vibration. Since vibration knew everything, it was not uncommon for him to become elated with a tuning fork, and that is what made him happy. Ryan Starlight was a good high level that knew everything, and it was being a high level that made him joyous, and his face showed it. A high level was the smell of pussy when it peed. Since it was a woman peeing, it was not sexual, and it was rare for this to be broken. Humans had done everything, so of course a woman found it a little sexual even if it was not. A very bad woman had gotten away with crime by peeing with a man in her, which was hard to do but was considered crass and was a really strong moral. Since it was against a moral to pee on a penis, it was a very hard manner. A high level seemed to be impossible to beat because a woman's thought and magnetic were both pee. Since Sean Mckeithen had made a moral out of pee, he had asked if it was a moral or a high level and had died when it was. The moral was that oxygen never combined and kept someone from thirsting. If it didn't combine, it could still seem to be water to the lung. Since we breathe oxygen, it was a real danger that we would not be able to drink water. O2 was dangerous. This had meant that a high level did to a man and was confused when it meant didn't to a little girl. Since a little girl never thought and just peed their mother. This rarely errored and meant that crime was not allowed. Since a man would go to a woman to do something that they did not allow, the high level saw a high level and high levels ate. When it was eaten, high levels relaxed and went away.

Pee was food at one moment sulfur. Since a high level was not killed ever, it was interesting that there was a doctor that tried to eat shit to get away from a high level. Urine would tell sulfur in food and was NH4+SO4 and was all chemistry. Since breathing sulfur meant that you were fed, it was very comforting and shit was not. Luckily, soap did not have sulfur in it and was not considered food. Being able to remember this formula put a professor to sleep and always should be done.

Chapter Fifty-nine

A wagon went past in a green shroud. Since wagons were hard to think about, it was rare for a wagon to think for themselves. Once in a while, there were wagons that made sense. Since a wagon meant that you avoided a dream, it was interesting that a wagon could go by. Once in a while, there were people that tried to think in a wagon, but this was not possible since a wagon could not dream all thought dreams. Since being killed a wagon when you actually thought was a high level, the high level tested the wagon as it went by and said that a wagon was never gold and that it was a real thought and the thought dreamt. This pissed off a redux who thought it criminal and was surprised to find that was made from the time that was not criminal. Since a criminal not being allowed to sing was new to the redux, he was a little mad when he smiled at this. Once in a while, there were people that disbelieved. Since disbelieving is a little gay, it was thought of rarely and was only true at memory. The thought that the wagon had was that a man could sing in a woman's heart if a dream could think through a white absorb. If a dream absorbs, it tells a narrative, and it's good at making a soul happy. Since a soul never dreams, it is thought about as a thinking machine. If a soul is happy with a dream, it means that the soul found sex which is everything to a soul. Since it was a dream that cleaned a thought, it was important to a soul even if thought never dreams. A dream was rarely sexual, and that was why the wagon had been found to be a thought.

Once in a soul, a lot of people did not know what to think about. A soul was a lot smarter than a consciousness but died easier and sometimes could not recover. Since this book is a soul, it is considered smart. Once in a while, the soul would die to a dream, and that is what happened to Rocky Loss. Since Rocky Loss's soul had died, he was in love with other people that had souls, and this had made him a good person. Since it was his soul that had been bad because his sister had twisted it, it was not his fault but his sister's. Since his sister was really bad, he had been bad, and that is why he had been hated. Life makes you bad but didn't. Once in a while, a soul would give up, but that was not common. If it was not a thought for a soul to have sex, it was considered a good soul. Since his sister and him had been having sex, it was not a good feeling but a bad one. Since it was an electrical current in a dream that could erase this, it was a lot of time in him that avalanched, and he had been afraid for three days. Since he had thought he would be afraid forever, he had asked Sean Grin if he had taken it and he said that he had. Since Sean Grin was a friend, nothing mattered, and the fear subsided and was just a foul smell. Rocky thought this worse because it could be told, but Sean said he had looked afraid and did not care. Since he looked afraid, it was uncommon for him to think, and it was just a fear of women that drove Rocky paranoid. Since Rocky did not care about men, it was funny that they were opposites.

Chapter Sixty

Eric Long woke up in the morning dizzy from an ecstasy bing. Since the chapter was important, we will stomach a drug use. The drug was bad for him, and three cadets had died. Since a high level was interested in how he felt, he admitted to the abuse and said he needed rehab. In rehab, there was a light that could tell if your bones needed to think or were pale. Since pale meant health, it was not uncommon for a rehab to scare at color. Since rehab meant that you were sick if you ever did it again, it was not uncommon for rehab to be loved by women. There was a secret to rehab, and that was to dream wax. Since wax is the best color and better than gold at not tarnishing, there were a lot of people that thought that wax looked good, but it was Eric's joke to make colored wax and take as much drugs as he wanted. He thought himself very smart and was very to a doctor at the rehab. The doctor asked if coloring wax had made him stronger or weaker. He had thought to say stronger, but a soul chime said weaker, and that is what he had actually said. Since he was belligerent, he had said stronger right after but the doctor hadn't heard. Since he thought it was a stupid doctor that had tricked him, it was a longer stay. A longer stay had put him in a withdrawal that lasted almost four days. Since the withdrawal had been that intense, he had subsided and decided not to take the drug again. The doctor thought something interesting about a colored wax, and that was to deepen it and then start a wagon. A wagon was actually a sound that turned a circle. Since wax did not dream until the bone had gone dim, it was actually better for the patients, and someone actually recovered who had wondered why rehab never worked.

Chapter Sixty-one

A bone lacer is a dangerous thought that did not matter. Since a bone lacer is gone from the world, it was interesting that they needed it back. A bone lacer is a gay brown that thinks about a red yellow. Since that was considered bad, it was not uncommon for a bone lacer to be a fatal disease. The reason they needed it back was that a pot could not know it was fatal until a bone lacer died. Since fatal disease by Sean Mckeithen was a powerful thought. A bone lacer rarely failed, and all disease was said to be known. Once in a while, a common cold would emerge and should not be trusted, but that was all. If a bone lace ever failed, it would be confusing, but the power that had killed it thought it stupid still and was angry. Luckily, it had fallen and wasn't a problem. Once in a while, people would think backward, and that was what happened to the mental hospital that had figured it out. Since it was a nurse that they were treating, it was interesting to her when they figured out how female she had felt and she had shared light with EMT. Since the light was good, nothing mattered, and she had decided to take time off to have a kid and this had relaxed spirit. Since almost forty-people had died, it was important to remember that nearly twelve million people had been healed by the thought, and that it was just a statistic. Once in a while, there was a war, and that is what had happened to a person in the western hemisphere. Since the east and the west did not share over the problem of sleeplessness, it was a funny thought that west did not get sick while the east did, and this had scared India, but Sean Mckeithen had gone global anyway and sleepless was counted but not known.

Why Sean Mckeithen had thought fatal disease was interesting to the doctor who actually had and that is what surprised the nurse. Since it was only Sean Mckeithen that could dream a fatal disease, he was considered on call. Once in a while, people would come to Sean Mckeithen over health. Since he was a weird default, he was allowed and nothing mattered. The default being real and only allowed a machine, it was difficult not to know him, and there were two real people that did not want to know him. The first thought him criminal and was offended, and the second thought him bum and was offended but actually just uptight. Since the people that hated him were powerful and he was not, he was a little hurt that the populace had turned on him. Since he was very strong, he was killing doctors, and one had gone to a mental hospital over a headache that had turned out to be a brain tumor that Sean Mckeithen had fixed. Since Sean Mckeithen was either unaware or just didn't care, it was funny that he had fixed a doctor and the doctor had been let go home. Since the doctor was stuck on the nuclear bomb, it was interesting to note how it had been fixed. The nuclear bomb had been put on a circular color that was made to shrink to the size of energy. Since energy had been thought again, the memory had stuck and the planet had gone back to normal. Since energy was no longer in motion but stable again, it was important that a nuclear bomb was never used again and was a little like a bad crime. Since crime was punishable, the air wanted to know the punishment, and it was fortunate that there was a year that was punishment, and that was 2002. Once in a while, this would come up again but wouldn't in the future. It would be forgotten and just be in history books. History books were really bad, and that was why a lot of students would think about murder even though they shouldn't.

Chapter Sixty-two

If a man and a woman were together after 2014, they would be considered in love, and hooking was not allowed. Also a condom was not allowed, and a lot of the populace looked rape over a condom. Since a dildo was a rape, they were called dildos. Since a man and a woman were important to the year for the rest of time, there were some people that had waited for 2014 to make love. Since if a woman chooses you, you have a year to make love. It was important to note the year and make culture. Since it was not uncommon for a culture to be remembered, mental health frustrated a lot. If this was not a problem, nothing would matter and mental health would live through it. If you were not sexual, you were hidden by sex. There were three people in town that were hidden: Sean Mckeithen, Mark Long, and Thomas Love. Since they were hidden, they were not known to women and were thought dead on eyes. Since two of them were handsome and one, normal nothing mattered and women were happy.

Chapter Sixty-three

L ance Bright thought about his day. Since he had been on *Oprah*, he was not allowed to bike, it being a token of disrespect. Since whey protein was doping, there was little that could be done but sit and consider the day. Once in a while, he would think about stuff, and it was while he was drinking water that he had met Sean Mckeithen. Since he suctioned it and it made a circle, he had thought that it was not uncommon for the thoughts to be a little too hard to do, and he wanted to know why he had thought a circle or why he had discovered a circle. Being a tell, he told at the water in his mouth and saw a man in it. Since this had not been on the news, he put it on the news and the man had come to him to explain himself. Since he was famous, the man knew his name and told him he knew he didn't dope and that Lance didn't have to pretend to be ashamed. Since ashamed was not true, there were a lot of people that thought through what they wanted by being in his arm. Lance wanted to know everything about water and thought him very smart for making an atom combine differently. Since a color had made the angle in the animal that had done it before, Lance was impressed that it was a shape, and that it contained all angles. Since this was exciting, the circle was forgotten, and Lance figured out that he was an eventual and a five-angle power. Since a five-angle power was not known, nothing mattered, and it was a potential energy. If you knew energy before it happened, it meant that you were smart enough to know what you were doing at subconscious. That is what a dinosaur was able to do, and it still dreamt birds to this day. He would hear it sometimes in their voices.

Since his potential energy was very rare and was ball movement, he funnied at Sean Mckeithen's masturbation and said that he had lost a lot of light but not as much as the punishment for crime. Once in a while, the potential would move, and Sean Mckeithen would watch him think. Since Sean Mckeithen was a default, nothing mattered, and he was allowed to watch. A potential energy was rare and meant that you were complicated enough to mix memory and make thought. Since this was rare, there were little that could not be done by a potential, and it is just noted that it makes for five angles and means that numbers multiply or divide a sometimes square root. Since a square root is almost impossible to do, it was rare for a square root to make light. John Death had claimed to be able to square root and had licked a computer and nearly killed it trying to know what it was, but the computer knew that he had only done a sudoku and guessed at the numbers in fraction because it was called a square root and sudoku was a square. A square root was actually a math and not a shape. Since a square was a shape, it was interesting that it had been used and was a lie very bad. The third lie was a cubed, which was also not able to do math and was confusing.

Chapter Sixty-four

The most dangerous thought ever to be thought was done by an EMT and contradicted by a Sean Mckeithen. Since it was dangerous when it was thought, it should be tread on lightly. Since there was a movie that had shown it, it was interesting that it had been contradicted. The thought was that a proton with no color or memory could be a murderer's punishment. This meant that they would not know or see anything but would still have energy. Since energy was not known, it was unfair when everything was claimed energy and everybody was on a proton. Since this was funny to the murderer, unproven, it was a little relieving when Sean Mckeithen proved an EMT wrong and said that a proton could go without energy if it contained a full length of light. Since light did not have a force, it was seen as not being energy. Since color does have a force, we are very good at force in a brain and are a little mean to each other sometimes. This is good and not a complaint. Once in a while, a Sean Mckeithen would find a proton and always gave it to an EMT so they could train it. Since a full length of light was rare, it was very pretty in a woman, and she was a little confused why she was thought murder until it was explained that nearly 90 percent of the populace had and that she needed to be pretty still. Since this was all right with her, a lot of insanity was held at bay by her skin. Once in a while, a person would get to be killed by the populace, and that was what had happened to Sean White who was not a murder but rather a wizard and funny to a dwarf.

Since a dwarf was not a bad power but didn't care for television, *The Hobbit* and *The Lord of the Ring* kinda sucked and were not considered movies but pictures. Since the cinema had yet to come but was in the works, it was interesting that a dwarf had wanted the cinema. Once in a while, a dwarf would show, and this only happened when there was a problem with the planet. There had been a dead dwarf over the nuclear bomb and a live dwarf over water since the atom did not know his maker. Once in a while, this was not a problem because the atoms that were changed were not electrical, but the ocean is, and electricity remembers forever and is why humans are smart and stupid at the same time. Once in a while, the thoughts that people had would come across lazy or inaccurate. Since an inaccuracy is not considered bad unless it is known for some reason, it was a little confusing that Sean Mckeithen liked accuracy only and was only soothed by the fact that he was an eventual and not a power. Since Sean Mckeithen was not a power, it was rare to knowledge until it was too late.

Since this is not known, it will be explained. Most people never knowledge, but some do. A knowledge is a time of day that means that someone is thinking. Since a knowledge is rare, there were a lot of people that did not know it existed. Since time does not exist to a brain, a knowledge was a time in a body that thought that a person was able or not able to do something. Sean Mckeithen was a knowledge work and had been deemed notable. Since he was not able, he was considered dead and nothing mattered. When he went insane, it was a time that died, but this was common. When Sean Mckeithen became smart, he did so in spite of the people in him and offended spirit but was normal. Since he was actually smart, a knowledge was supposed to be made, but no one thought to, and he had become a rogue. Normally, this would not matter, but since he was a pillar of electric light and a possum in allow, he was very scared as a rogue, and we were relying on him never changing to live through the day, having no knowledge of what he does. Since he is insane, nothing mattered still, and it was very funny that he was able to function at all. There were insanities that are too hard, and his was one of them but was different in that he actually dreamed more insanity than he went through.

Chapter Sixty-five

Once in a while, the thoughts people had would be good for a comedian. Since the book is about thought don't mind the repetition of Sean Mckeithen, he is the author and a good joke. Since Sean Mckeithen had been very good for a comedian, he had been found funny, and the Saturday afternoon club had celebrated. The comedian had not admitted that it wasn't his act until the end, which had funnied someone that knew and confused a girl about the world not knowing what not being her own act meant. Since a comedian was not a bad thing to be, a lot of people confused when she called 911 on him. Since this was not common, she explained it later saying that he had looked a murder and she thought that he had. Since the confusion was not the act but rather whether he had murdered, the crowd calmed down and they all called 911. This had put him under too much pressure, and he admitted that he had murdered. Since this meant that he was not a comedian, he was banned, and the fear he experienced was just let live. Since he was afraid, it was interesting that he had almost wreaked his truck on the way home and had been taken to a mental hospital. At the hospital, the man had explained to the doctor that the reason that he had wanted to be a comedian was that the Catholic Church was murder and that he had wanted the Catholic Church and a Sean Mckeithen to fight. Since Sean Mckeithen caught murder and the Catholic Church let it go, he thought it would be funny and was just sad he went to a mental hospital, but it was just a button on his shirt.

The Catholic Church knew something about an atom in response to sex. They also knew that a color that went flat and was no longer a color would make heat still, and this would condone murder and what was the year. Since a flat color is impossible to see, it was only under a sexual glow that this was possible, and a lot of women came to murder, making the mistake to look at sex instead of feel it. Since this was clever, it was allowed. A lot of murderers were socially condoned, and it was rare that a real one emerged most were caught. Since Sean Mckeithen was a thought on murder too, it was not uncommon for a murderer to befriend, but this was not wise and he was a good catch. He knew that a color made a shadow. Since a color made a shadow, three colors that made a metal could be used to make for two shadows and a third hidden. In the hidden shadow, you could not hide a person, but a magnetic would hide a movement. Since the movement to death was intense, it was interesting that the planet remembered every animal that ever died. Because of this, Sean Mckeithen thought to hide the movement of a dead murder victim not allowing an actual murderer to move the victim's death, which was why they were stronger at pain than non murderers. Since pain was not allowed, it was a fact that a murderer would show a question of where the victim was. Since a murderer could not answer the question, a murderer's heart would stop, and this would mean they were caught. Once caught, they were able to show light, and it was just light and a three-degree angle that beat a murderer's heart.

Chapter Sixty-six

A lot of people thought about body feelings, but it was rare to find one that was like a won't. Since a won't was a king who could repeat memory, it was interesting that a man had figured out how to repeat body sensation. Since a sensation was considered energy, it had been confused, and he had been not allowed and did not know why he still did. The body stimulus that the man had gotten confused by was the nuclear bomb. Since we already talked about it, this is a repeat. The nuclear bomb had led him to a fact in a vein that was not known. Since a vein could see light down to the atom, it had been a mistake to think that an immune system cell could get away with light if it had been told to not. Since it was not possible to get away from light to an animal, it had killed the immune system and made the AIDS virus, which was only fatal because of mold. Since mold is never in a body, don't think that it is. Since mold was fatal and very common, it was interesting that right after this discovery, he had had a runny nose. Since blood is red even in the body, there were a lot of people that thought red is just sulfur, and this was good. But why a doctor could not figure out what the disease was actually? Since it was a lack of light that made an immune system think shit looked good, Sean Mckeithen was close but didn't know why an immune system died. It was not lack of food but lack of air. Since shit is air to the blood, it was not uncommon for an immune system to think it was air, and that is why it smelled like shit. Shit figures out air by flexing at an atom and being inedible. Since an atom at inedible is air, if you have sex at an atom and refuse light in a male, you make the AIDS virus. Sean Mckeithen thought this very smart and finished the atom AIDS virus, which was very smart to the man who helped through the body stimulus and the aids virus ended.

Chapter Sixty-seven

Once in a while, people would scare at a stronger animal, and it was just one of these times that Morgan Price got thought a genius. Since if you scare you are at a smarter animal, it was the job of a tell to know why. Since the animal was lying, it was a tweezer that thought the experience through. The reason it mattered is that it gave an insight into the year and what to do if there was a zero. Since the year is confusing a circle to think, it was true that a zero is not actually a math but a place holder that meant that there was math possible. Since if it is not possible, it is an edge. It was a cleric that thought that a smaller and smaller circle could be used as an edge and mean no math. Since no math was known, the year could be forced, and black men and women became part of the Catholic Church and enslaved to the experiment that was the year. Since this had meant that they could go insane and live through it, a black man was kinda overwhelmed by how smart a white man was and became white. When a lot of them did, white men saw their DNA, and we fixed a year that did not make sense. Once in a while, this was uncommon, but today that was loved. Since nothing escapes the year, a lot of people thought themselves smart but were not. An edge circle was the smartest thought ever found and almost claimed that the experiment was a success, but we had to admit that we were at war and that murder still existed at an official. Since black DNA is strong, it should not be thought not, and it was interesting that Sean Mckeithen did not steal it, being considered a really bad thief. Since a white square is not a thief, it was kind of a joke, and he did not have to defend himself. The circle that was an edge had been made by making a circle out of the rest of the diameter of the last circle. Since this was a smaller circle, it was interesting that an atom was willing to do this.

Chapter Sixty-eight

O nce the chapter is known, the rest of the book is simple and should be written more slowly. Once in a while, there were people that saw everything that happened and is a rare mistake. This had nearly happened to Tabby Scare, and it was a wizard that had not allowed her to be put on random showing that the thought would eventually come out true. Since the thought was not known to mental health, Sean Mckeithen was thought to be a little bad and was told he had to brag when he thought and that had meant a confusion when he bragged to hard for a child to take. Since children are perfect and never have problem entraining, it was a little confusing, but he said it was eight years of thought and would kill a tell since he thought every day. Since this was not allowed, it was interesting that he was not known and he was found outside of society and the FBI files. He explained he was compliant and was actually just full of bad people that would not comply and that there was nothing that he could do about it. Since a noncompliance was actually a red yellow, it was interesting that he was a green blue until he was told he couldn't and he was a red yellow and added to the bad people. This killed a doctor's face, and he was brought back saying it was all right. Since he was a date in a computer and in an EMT smile, it was not hard to do. Once in a while, we lie slightly, and the lie was that we were at war when we were not.

Because of this, a delicate in Sean Mckeithen was not willing to meet anybody and only gave in when it was explained this was hard to do and needed an elf. Since murder was really bad to it, it melted an elf's face when he tried at it and said it would not murder that Sean Mckeithen never had. Since it is a perfect power, the delicate got added to the power list. Since the name was Sean Mckeithen, it thought it would be called something else and declined saying it knew all names and laughed hard when we called it it, which is what Sean Mckeithen had called it. Since this pissed a doctor off, they made it show and scared a little, letting it live again. Just for fun's sake, we called it a spirit guide, and that was final. Since the word "it" was not known to be a power, it thought it was better being called a spirit guide and agreed that it could guide. Since it was not the first time that there was controversy over a name, it did not hear when it was asked to reveal its secret and eventually admitted not to know how it was made. Since it was forgotten who was the maker, it took two days to remember, and the doctor said he had ran into a money problem and had only remembered at red. This was interesting; and Sean Mckeithen admitted that he had made autism the children of the thieves, and this, though dangerous, was accurate. Since the delicate had been stolen by a car dealership, it was known to industry. Since it was already stolen, Sean Mckeithen admitted that it was an electron that flat-lined pressured and did math off a circle. Since this was cool, the man wanted to give a color, but the spirit guide did not want a color. Once in a while, there were people that thought about this, but it was not important and rather just went into a cop's book. Since a book is smart, we do know how to make it but never look at it actually.

Chapter Sixty-nine

Long ago, a man sat in a puddle of water naked. Since his name was Eric Cross, it was interesting that he did not know how to think through the puddle. Bums were born from him since a woman had seen him and the look on his face. Since she could not have sex with him and he was naked though not hard, it was interesting that her pubes had itched. Since her pubes was joy to her, she felt a little hurt and had not wanted to help the man. Since he needed food and water and clothing and a place to sleep, it was not possible to reject him from these essentials, but she had to since he was dangerous, and that was when she had thought a thought that no one had ever thought before, and that was to use her sexuality to know what he was doing. Since a girl had thought him cute since a girl was in love with him, it was a shame that she had to admit that she was actually scared of the man and telling whether he was dangerous. Once in a while, a genius would be born, and the girl that nearly dated him was a genius since she had done the same and learned to hide a girl. Since no one would have sex with him, nothing mattered. Since a bum was a new thought, there were a lot of people that thought that there would be a time when everybody would be bums. It was a smart man who had made it a tax on the land and paid women with the road and the military. Since they were protected by the military and paid by the road a bum became a joy to a woman and was thought through.

Chapter Seventy

Time sat on a bench, thinking about his girlfriend that had just dumped him. Since Time is a real person, he was not supposed to feel pain emotionally but did anyway and excused this as being about his love life. Once in a while, people would go through pain, and Time was dizzy and not unhappy but scared thinking that he may never marry. Since he was sitting on a bench in public, he decided not to cry but rather to keep a stiff upper lip and try to figure out how to tell his time that they were not together. Since this was not possible, he looked a little failure. Once in a while, someone would walk by, and it just so happened that someone did while he was sitting there. The woman was in her late thirties and hadn't married or had kids. Since she was older, she was afraid that she might not, but knew time from the school days and wanted to say hi when she saw him. "Hi, Time." "Hi," he said, coming out of his stupor. "How are you?" "Good" was replied but barely meant by Time. Since Time's name is time for the sake of the narrative, he should be thought that important, and this will be explained later. The woman sat down next to Time and thought about how he felt. Since Time was not a member of her family, it would be fine for her to think about him sexually. "Time we have to get a cup of coffee and catch up. You look awful. What are you doing on this bench?" "A cup of coffee would be nice." Time responded, and so they walked toward the coffee shop. Once there, they sat down to have a talk. "What have you been up to, what do you do for work?" "I write a column for the *New Yorker.*" "How exciting, you were always good at writing." "And you what do you do?" "I am an art director for a museum. I get to tell people that they did or did not make art." Since this was not unusual, she uncrossed her legs and showed him her pussy. He was a little taken aback but was attracted and laughed it off. Since he was single, rebound sex seemed appropriate, and they left the coffee shop for a rendezvous with some sexual attraction. Once at his house, they were kissing passionately when Time thought that they should wear a condom. She said that they didn't need to, that she could spit out and wouldn't get pregnant. Since he did not know this, he wanted to see it for himself and poured a little milk in her pussy, which she found a little kinky. Being thoroughly convinced she would not get pregnant, they made love. Since sex is rare, he doesn't care it's different. The likelihood that they would be together at all was very close to none, and Time wondered about them sitting in the park. Since it was not a long time later that they had gotten married, it was just a secret of Time's that he had just been dumped when they had gotten together.

Chapter Seventy-one

O nce in a while, Time would make a decision for someone. Since this was joy and always accurate, it was thought normal that Sean Jimmey did not know how to think about something that had happened to him. Since Time had made a decision for him, it was considered ghost, and nothing mattered. The decision that had been made was that he didn't children. Since this was sad, there was little that he could do but be frustrated all day and want a child. Since he was unaware of this, nothing mattered. Once in a while, Sean Jimmey would think about it, but that was all. Since Sean Jimmy is not Sean Mckeithen, he should not think it is. Sean Jimmey wanted children, but he did not get to since he was a murder and in a prison cell. When Time decides something for you, it means that you are physically not able. Once in a while, Sean Jimmey would think that he wanted to murder again, and this was thought not allowed but funny since he was in a little cage. Since Sean Jimmey could not do anything, there were a lot of people that thought him stupid but smart for having gotten caught going to prison. Once in a while, Sean Jimmey would sit and think about what had happened to him. Since he had been big on the grapevine, it was interesting to him that he had gotten caught. If he knew how to, he would be on the grapevine still, and that was how he had come to be thought of as best catch since he hit his cage constantly. Once in a while, a cop would wonder why it had taken them that long to catch him. Sean Jimmey was not not powerful, he was very, but it was not uncommon for him to want to murder and it was believed that the amount of victims that he had killed was upward of eighty. Since it was not unusual for a murder to take place; it was Sean Mckeithen that had thought a cage the best idea ever and had tried to prove that he could not go into the cage and act on the man, making it leave his realm of possibility. This had been smart to a blue whale but had nearly killed a cop who thought the convicts fun to think with. Since a lot of culture meant that they would feel a convict, it was explained to the blue whale that they are considered owed and that convict was allowed to be felt just couldn't feel. This confused the whale who disagreed, and the time of calculation came to an end. Since convicts no longer thought for people, they just sat in their cages and did nothing. If this was hard to do, no one cared. The blue whale had been taught to control a convict by knowing that they were in their territory. Since their territory is a little cage, it was in the magnet because of the blue whale that they could not leave their territory even in spirit, and this was very smart to a redux.

Chapter Seventy-two

The tall order that mattered to the lieutenant was a gift fall. A gift fall was not uncommon for a man who thought it and was a gift fall for a woman who he loved. Since Tom White was in the military, it was normal for him to think about murder and he spent time doing this. Once in a while, he would move a soldier to kill while in public, and that had made him a little afraid even though it was a psychic connection that had done this. Since it was insane to kill, the military was considered insane; and though that had been debated, it was still a real thought. Insane was hard to take, but the year was good at it and nothing mattered. If it was unusual for someone to feel scared, it was time for the military to move. Since the military had thought it too hard for them to take their mental insanity, there were a lot of people that did not know how insane they were. Since anybody in the populace could go to the military to think something thorough, they were considered cool and major was the key term. If the military ever actually failed, there would be some confusion as to what a human actually was since we all default murder over the military being a real need in history. Since we are that weird of an animal, it should be noted that the planet still recorded what we did and didn't mind. This had almost failed to television but had been thought an excellent animal by a starfish. Once in a while, a starfish would think and light to smell was genius to one. The lieutenant was able to think something rare, and that is why he was mentioned. Once in a while, he would make love; and when he did, it was important to watch his ass for relaxation. Since a murder can't relax, it was interesting that he had avoided the actual memory in order to relax and made it possible to think sideways about everything that he did. Since sideways meant that he was able to avoid, it was interesting during sex to watch him avoid his job. Since it was his job, nothing mattered, and he went back to work when the good mood passed.

A good mood lasted for six hours, and Lieutenant Tom White was in a good mood still when he was called into action, there being a firefight that was too intense for someone to take. Since Americans rarely die in war but are wounded constantly, it was with a heavy heart that he joined. Once in a while, someone would get hurt, and it was his job to be brave enough for them to get the wounded to safety. Since the wounded were thought to be in the line of fire, they were hard to move and needed a substitute to move for the soldier. A substitute was just a psychic connect, and nothing mattered. Since the firefight was intense, Tom White's wife thought to go to the kitchen for some tea. Once in a while, it was important to note that a lot of people could get hurt by a sniper, and that was shy flack vests were important. Since the lieutenant was not in danger, it was his lie that there was no danger that was making the soldiers brave. A psychic connection was important to the military, and they used them constantly.

Chapter Seventy-three

A man in a grey suit sat at a table playing chess. Since he had no one to play with, he was playing himself, and this was only allowed because he was not observing the board but rather playing in his head. This is impossible to some and is only real to a genius chess. Since he was five moves ahead, it was interesting that a kid thought he could beat him and sat down to play. This startled the man, but said it would be fun turning off the game that he was playing. The first thing that went wrong for the young man was that Morgan Sin as the man was called wanted to move his piece for him, saying, "Here, let me help." Since the game was ruined, the young man had to forfeit and start over. Since this was not allowed, the young man got up and left, taking the grey suit's children with him in spirit, claiming that they couldn't play since he was a cheat that had been beaten.

Chapter Seventy-four

A letter arrived in the mail. She had not gotten a letter for a long time and missed her husband dearly. Since it was only three months apart, she fucked herself to the letter and remembered her husband's face. Since masturbation is allowed in a marriage, especially a lapsed one, it was important that she did. Since a wife fucks anything that moves, including other women and pets, it was crucial for her to know what her husband's face was so she would know who she was in love with. Once the parlet was lit, she went about her chores thinking of nothing else but that she was still in love with her husband, even though he was on tour with the Red Cross in Asia. Asia was a strange place since there were parts of it that were still aboriginal and that was where her husband was. Since she was powerful, it was important that it be noted that memory fades and goes long term every two years and not every year. This was all right but meant the insane had to last two years, and that is kind of a long time. Once in a while, a lot of people would think together and that was what was about to happen to her. Since she had seen an auditorium in a lightbulb, she thought why not make an auditorium on the grapevine and had gotten kind of famous for doing that. If it was not uncommon for a person to think it was unusual for a person to know every move of something. Since an auditorium was subconscious and was actually in blank, there were a lot of people that did not know they existed but rather thought that they did not. Since someone had known, it was all right. The woman made a thought and slumped. Since she was good at slumps, that was what she thought with; and when she was done, she hardened them with a diamond ring. Since she joked that she was a diamond, it was interesting that she actually was. The slump that she had done today was a five over seven or a thought on mitochondria health. Since almost no one knew anything about mitochondria, it was perfect for her to go to doctors to learn. Since a doctor knew everything. it was just a matter of time before it would give her a strange ambition. The ambition that someone had was to make energy make color. Since this was impossible to do, the woman had laughed when she had combined oxygen with sulfur using a Sean Mckeithen on combine. Since Sean Mckeithen was trusted thought, nothing mattered, and the auditorium made a whistle. She loved being smart and was on the grapevine thinking about color for a couple of weeks before it got old, and she thought about something else.

Chapter Seventy-five

The differences between people became apparent when an old man was caught moving drugs. Since he was an old man and nearly eighty years old, he did not care and thought it funny to think that he was going to the resort. Since this was common, it was interesting to note how he got caught. The police officer that caught him did so by thinking about his grandchildren and if they would be happy with him. Since he was a grandfather of an undercover cop, the child had said no and the machine had decided arrest. This was hard on him and made for pleasant banter with the cop. Since he was already caught, he admitted that he was transferring it to another place but didn't say where or how much he made for doing it. Since a lot of kids thought that they would sell drugs, it was known to him and was frowned on by them since their lives actually got hurt by a prison stay since they wanted sex still and to have fun. He on the other hand actually only wanted to eat and sleep and didn't care about anything at all. Since the arresting officer was slightly wrong in arresting him, it was not long before spirit went away. Confusing as it is, spirit is movement and is at war all day. Since nothing mattered, nothing mattered, and the old man went to prison for two years. Since parole was until he was dead, he would not sell again.

Chapter Seventy-six

A bishop was rare, and it was a bishop that walked the streets of Venice looking for a man to take to the mission. Since a mission is rare, it was interesting to people that you had to be chosen by a bishop to go to one, and that bishops were very rare. The bishop was not a pope but was high ranking in the church and was respected for that. Once in a while, the people on the street would know he was high ranking and kind of get awed at it. The young man popped out of a window and yelled down to the bishop, "I'll be right down, I'm talking to my mother." To this, the bishop replied, "All right, not a problem."

The young man was so happy with his appointment that he nearly turned a little gay with excitement. Since the bishop knew this would happen, he calmed the boy with a cup of coffee, and the two of them talked. "How did you find school?" "Fun, very a little challenging with the grades above a tenth grade education. My mom was only a tenth grade education, and my father, I did not know, so I was on my own. Since on my own, I am good through college. There is nothing that could get in my way, and I enjoyed myself thoroughly." Since this mattered to the bishop, he was glad that the young man's daughter had calmed down. Once done, they moved on, and the bishop described the order and rank of the Catholic Church. "The first man in the Catholic Church is the friar. The friar is thought to be a man of god, and though he cooks and cleans, he is still a clergyman and never hated. The next man is the priest." Since the boy knew this, he listened not for the fact but for the tenor or light. The boy was good at listening and thought about what the bishop said. "The priest is a higher order and a soft ear. If a man cannot soften his ear, he is not allowed to be a priest. After a priest, there is the clergyman and the cleric. Since a clergyman and a cleric are not the same thing, they should be explained separately. A clergyman was a white shirt and only clergy if they had been an altar boy. A cleric, on the other hand, was a clergyman that had not been an altar boy and could not think as deeply. Since a cleric was still important, it was all right to be one." "I'll be a cleric. I was not an altar boy." "First a priest. After a clergyman comes a cardinal. Since cardinals are very high ranking, it was usually a cardinal that gave a sermon. A sermon was important because the pews needed to be filled for the church to make money, which it still needed to do. Since a cardinal was not a bishop, it was interesting that bishops existed at all, and it was the bishop that handled affairs of money and recruiting. Above the bishop, there was only the pope, and the pope was the head of the church and was in charge of the laws of the Catholic Church and blessing at mass." This was interesting, and the boy kept his attention on it while it was spoken. Once in a while, a thought would come into a person's head that mattered, and the boy had that thought while they were walking. The boy thought that he would be the pope some day and gave up on sex. Since he had given up on sex, his daughter died and he was considered gay. The bishop heard this and watched his daughter die and thought the boy might be, but had to mature. Once in a while, this meant that people did not know what they did, just that they did it and that it why the boy was special and was recruited. He had softer ears than most priests that had ever lived. Since a bishop was ever live, he added the boy and felt his soul. The bishop thought that there were turns in the world that mattered, and the boy wanting to be the pope was a good turn and might happen. He wrote down that the boy never had sex and walked a gold. Since a clergyman could have sex, it was important that the boy was the right age to become pope when he had matured. The boy had already thought everything, and that was why it was just how old he could become that mattered. Once in a while, there were young people that wanted freedom, but this boy just wanted booklore. Since booklore was important, nothing mattered to the boy. Once in a while, there were people that could not get anything wrong, and that was what the boy was.

Chapter Seventy-seven

Sometimes dreams become more intense in memory than they are when they were watched. Since the man that was insane did not know this, he was fighting people in his memory, and they were confused. If someone actually goes insane, they are allowed to fight even though this is sad and said not done. Since they are allowed, the not done didn't matter, and the man surprised when he learned of the mistake and attacked the dream. He said that when the dream had been dreamt, it was a pleasant dream with a cop and should not have been that bad but did not know that the cop had not known that he had been a little criminal, and being a cop would do anything to hurt a criminal, including ruin a dream all day. Since the dream had already ended, it was just the color that was being tortured, and the man's soul did not know what to do. The cop sounded serpentine when he said to the man, "Finally, you have chosen to face me." Since the man did not know what to say to this, it was not uncommon for a cop to confuse a criminal. The man said, "I'll fight you, but I am outmatched and barely criminal, you must be wrong somehow. "You murdered," the cop said. The man did not know what to say, and the cop took his silence as an admission. When he did this, the man said, "Silence is not an admission and you are insane." Since the cop was actually insane, nothing mattered. All of a sudden, the man became angry and hit the cop in the face with white. Since the man knew that white was innocent, he did not know that hitting a cop with white would kill him. The man became and unbecame a criminal hero in the cop when the true nature of white was revealed. Since the cop died, the man walked away. Once in a while, there were people of lesser need that confuse giants who need constantly. Since the need was not uncommon, it was thought that a lot of people would think the cop smarter, but he had to admit that he had been stupid and that white meant never and not had. Since "had" was the wrong word, nothing mattered.

Chapter Seventy-eight

The Bronx Zoo was a baseball stadium that mattered to Michael Same. Since Michael Same was smart and had to hide his baseball from his profession, it was called the Bronx Zoo. The Bronx Zoo meant that there were lions and tigers, and he made fun of his superior all day and just enjoyed living at the Bronx Zoo. Once in a while, there were Bronx Zoos that meant that he had been wrong, and he was little weary and stuck on time. Since time was fun, he thought about it a lot and was sad for Sean Mckeithen and Natalie who were no longer friends. Air was what he was good at, and it was air that made a man mad. Since Michael Same could not be thought of at all, unless he was drunk, he made sure to get drunk; and that was what kept him happy. Once in a while, he would get myosis, but this was only when the Bronx Zoo didn't work, which was a lot recently. Since the Bronx Zoo was as smart as a book, it will be explained. If the circle in your eye breathes air, it has to think. In order to breathe the whole year, you need ten feet by the distance to the catcher. Since this is a year, a Bronx Zoo was a perfect year in time and able to think the thoughts of an entire year in a second and a half. This is why Michael Same was loved and considered smart.

Chapter Seventy-nine

A big dick mattered was a joke among women and had never been thought about as a like to a man. Since a man who liked a big dick mattered would be thought gay or hard, they were a little timid to make it a like, but liking a woman over perversion was too priceless and was allowed even though it was an old woman who had experienced it. Once it a while, an emotion would get confused, and one was in a big dick mattered until the like of a man was included. This made a pretty girl puke over being lesbian, and that meant she wasn't as pretty and a little sad. Once in a while, there were people that thought that a big dick mattered was a little insane, it wasn't just that a lot of girls didn't want to do anything else, and a woman's movement would insane them if they weren't motivated. Since Oprah Winfrey was the best woman's movement in the world, there was nothing to do, and she led. Since she led all of people thought of the women's movement as Oprah Winfrey, it wasn't but rather had been started in the 1800s. Since the 1800s was a long time ago; it was a stall and nothing mattered. Big dick had become women's movement was a win for the women's movement, and that was a lot of people. The did-not-matter suddenly mattered. Since mattered was hard on mental health, it was an unknown fact that people do not know what they act just what they are told to do by the year. Of course, this is not entirely true, and a lot of people have little thoughts that matter. Once in a while, there were people that mattered, and that was what had mattered about a woman that did not know big dick and wondered what it meant. When she knew she was afraid, it would show on her face that she was enjoying, and it was not until the thought was shown that she settled down and was a big dick mattered. Since a big dick mattered was always liked, it was very wet to a woman to be a big dick mattered, which was the memory of sex in a woman's brain.

Chapter Eighty

O nce in a while, a rogue would seem content to think about things that happened. Since a rogue was always against society and not a real power but rather a stance in a redux, it was considered normal for a rogue to die; and if they won't, it's said to be a rogue and join society. But the fact was it was just a way for a redux to be accepted at a kill position. Since this was not uncommon, there were a lot of people that got upset at being called rogues and did not know why. Since a rogue was a lie, it was funny that Sean Mckeithen had figured out a power called a rogue. Since this was not known, it was considered alien and could only be seen from an aircraft because it didn't work until light dimmed. Once in a while, the rogue would think society smart and sometimes not. Once in a while, a victim would arise and everything would stop. Since this was good for people, nothing mattered, and the victim was thought rogue. Since this saved the victim's life, the victim had become somewhat powerful and loved Sean Mckeithen even though she thought that Sean Mckeithen didn't know how to use his power. Since he couldn't, there were times the victim funnied at being smarter than him, especially at color.

Since color could talk, animals could talk, and it was a funny bum that was insane and said that everything talked to him, including streets and sidewalks. He said it was fun because most of the time, it was intelligent and very fun. Since amusing is dangerous, it will be known as fun. The funniest animal was the victim for nearly three thousand hours. Once in a while, there were people that thought through stuff and came out alive. Once alive, there were people that did not know how to live. If you were alive and a rogue, be careful, the world was thought into a lot of dices; and a roll of the dice meant you were allowed or not. Since someone was actually good enough to be a roll of the dice, it was a joke in that family to ask Dad if they could, and this had been true until his daughter had moved his hand with her eyes and he wouldn't play anymore. A rogue is still a kill, and just in a lie over a billionaire that was made to act stupid and had bought the power to live through it. Since rogue means air, it was interesting that Sean Mckeithen had programmed the air.

Chapter Eighty-one

A black magician was a good feeling until you thought about police. Since police would not be magicians, they did not know that a black magician was actually a cop and would catch anything. Once in a while, there were people that were scared of a black magician, and that was what Sean Mckeithen was in a Taylor Speech. Since Taylor Speech was not known, it was important that he stay that way. He was very wealthy and thought it was not allowed to think a woman violet at all. Since a woman could not be violet and it was the best idea, there were a lot of people that wanted to think about violet and women but couldn't. Since some women had actually been, it was considered male and grown as such. A male woman is kinda gross but not impossible to think through. Since a lot of strippers were considered male, a male woman was considered hooker, and there were no problems with this. Once in a while, a woman would be found dumb, and this was always sad. Since Sean had had sex with a dumb, it was funny that a picture of a lightbulb dropped to be looked at by a penis had actually made her a genius and was very funny. A violet was actually the emotion violent stopped by a color. The similarity was loved, and it was just a good feeling in culture.

Since an electric lightbulb picture was new, it was funny that it was a strong power in a woman. Since Sean was a slut, Sean and Taylor were friends over everything but little children that they fought over. Sean was a bad man once and had said it was fine to have his daughter if it did not figure itself out. Since his daughter was pretty, he was very happy, and Taylor relieved. Once in a while, there were people that made mad feelings only. Since a wrecker always thought themselves funny, it was sad that they were not. Once in a while, a wreaked would not know what to do under stress, and this is what they died to and why Taylor was smart. If Taylor was smart, no one messed with him at all. Since he was not messed with, he was proud and still liked people. Taylor was a people person but was a brain wash very bad at one moment sex.

Since a lot of people wanted to be around him, he still had friends. A lot of women meant you were stronger and faster, and he did not know why he did not feel good sometimes. Because of this, he had found a girl that had fucked him slut. He made her a lightbulb picture, and this had relieved him hard. Once in a while, there were girls that meant that Taylor was loved, and this was important to him.

Chapter Eighty-two

The three bears was on the television. This morning, it was playing a show he had already seen, but he loved the three bears and knew it by heart. By heart is a delay, and it is actually by lungs unless you move it and then it is by heart and is only a funny saying at a ball or line dance which you actually know by heart. Once in a while, the three bears would talk, and this was very funny to the little boy because it was a human talking and not a bear. A bear couldn't, or so he thought. He was joking when he thought he would make the dog talk and had this in mind. Since the dog was held, it was attentive and it learned to talk easily. This made the boy think that he was insane. The dog was talking to him until his mother had asked who had trained the dog that she hated an animal that could talk. This had turned the boy on to magic, and he had become very smart thinking of everything in imagine and speech. Since he was smart, he no longer watched the three bears. Thinking on his own was interesting to him because sometimes it was fun to hear his mother talk about what she thought. This was rare, and most of the time he just thought. The boy thought that a square was very good at friction and that a circle made for a really good suction. Since a friction suction worked as an act or made a face, he was very good at acting and was a little confused as to what to think about until he thought that a lightbulb was electrical. He licked it for his memory. Since he had thought himself smart, he was surprised at how smart he was and was guided perfectly. Since he was loved, it was interesting to find shape in the memory. There were only two people that had made shape, and he followed them. One was a microwave oven which he became and a computer which confused him for a while until he put the microwave oven on it and it had found the current in the air and he had become it. The best shapes were ones that suctioned backward. If a shape suctioned backward, there were things that could be thought that were otherwise not possible. The ability that it was given by suctioning backward is to be able to change and make light. Since the little boy was young, he did not know the difference between a man and a woman at thought and nearly offended but didn't. Since he loved shape, he was surprised that he didn't love a magnetic and only calmed down when he was told to smell it. Smelling it was fun because it became simple to him and he was able to shape again. Since Sean Mckeithen knew this, he was able to verify to an adult but was still his own thought. Since the boy liked to think he was very happy with an electric lightbulb and thought to lick it for him to be in power. This was celebrated, and after thinking that he would wait until he was older, he did and met Sean Mckeithen in electric light. Since he already knew everything that he had thought, he said rather that they become friends. Since the energy did not want to allow this, it took a minute before this happened, but they were friends and the bond is unbreakable. Once in a while, he would think about Sean Mckeithen; but mostly, he just had hot chocolate and loved a microwave oven. Since the little boy was shape, it was surprising how weak he could be and out thought his mom. When he took his mom over, she fell in love with him, knowing that he would think about her sometimes, and this was what he liked even though if she knew it meant that he had failed. The little boy would start school in three years and knew he would be at the head of his class in spite of his mom. Since his mom only had sex, he looked forward to having it one day and did not know why he thought it other than to be like his dad who was a good person and very smart being a lawyer. Once in a while, he would think, but mostly he would watch himself act on TV and remember the looks at night as he fell asleep.

Chapter Eighty-three

Ten thousand people was a lot of people, and that was how many cops it had taken to outstrength Sean Mckeithen. Since ten thousand cops was a lot of cops, he had decided to go down, having seen a joke and was actually unbeatable being bigger than a skyscraper in size. Since he went down in dwarf, it meant that spirit was aware, and he was willing to go through a little brainwash to stop the chamber of secrets from puking. Since they didn't know they were caught, it was funny, and he would shake them off when Sean Mckeithen smoked weed again. This was uncommon, but a full cop win was a little annoying when they never win. Since some of them were pillars of their community, they were loved and nothing mattered. Once in a while, Sean Mckeithen would get bored, and this was thought about a lot of the time. Since it was not uncommon to think it rare for people to matter, it was fine with Sean to matter a little. Once in the gallery, nothing mattered and a lot of people felt rejected. Since a rejection was okay, most people thought it not fun, but that was not true to Sean Mckeithen who thought it very good at memory if you could make a sound with a shape. Since shape was important, he made a lot of it and loved someone over his light.

Since shape light and sound were known to the world, he had been joked by a man that said that he was all shape light and sound and to kneel. Since this was funny, he actually did the stance of a football lineman and beat the man partially who admitted that he was a shape light and sound and was joking, and that it was interesting that they both could be. Once it was thought that they both were, they had a deep conversation and became each other that being the joy of being a shape light and sound. Since a computer had sent a date, there was a little confusion, but the computer agreed when it was shown that the new thought was by someone else, and it allowed for more than one person in a default code.

Since computers were French, they were not to be confused with a computer from the 1900s that did not know an electron but just electrical current. Since the French had learned to feed an electron an electrical current, they were considered very smart and were very wealthy. Once in a while, this would come up but didn't today.

A good speech therapist could change your voice, and it was a good speech therapist in electric light had taught him to make sound out of his sound bites to not talk in people's voice. Since this was a smashing success, he loved the therapist and made sure to say hi every once in a while. Since the therapist was gay, it was a little awkward, but he said to suck him in when he was off and it would become good energy later. Later in time, there were a few debates that needed to be explained. Sean Mckeithen was one of them, and it was if he was smart or stupid or so he thought it was actually if you talked or were silent, which was hilarious to him when he saw it since he was a silence once and knew silence was hard. Since he had to talk to nearly a billion people, it was safe to say he was busy all day. Since this was a test of stamina, it was interesting that there was no way a human could do this and found it funny when he couldn't keep up with his body and gave up a little in electric light. This was done with a square to a size more comparable with actual ability. Once in a while, stuff would come up that didn't make sense to Sean Mckeithen in math. If this ever happened, he would make color and rotate it around a fray. This would make a laser.

Since a laser was cool, there were a lot of things to be done with a laser. A laser could talk, and Sean Mckeithen thought it meant that he could figure anything out. Since there were three ways that he was psychic, he enjoyed himself and knowing thoroughly. Math is a good tell and means that you figure out how many zeros someone had left after they do something. Since the rate of your zeros is the rate of your intelligence, it was fun to do math. Once math was thought, the other two came together smart as well. The second psychic is sound but rather memory. The fewer the amount of memory is, the greater the insult and the shorter the distance moved. Since it took two moving objects to move a memory, it was interesting that memory could be stopped by refusing to move and what made a lot of criminals stupid. The third was color and already discussed. Since Sean Mckeithen was a genius how and not when it was funny, that pressure had made him a perfect when. Since by pressure I mean spikes and not a curve, it was interesting to watch his time invert to think.

Once in a while, a dot would surface, but that was rare. Sean Mckeithen sat back in a lounge chair feeling the sun. The sun was in his view, and he went to it knowing that it knew a lot. The sun knew a lot because he had trained it, and the Queen of England had as well off his power. Since it was off, his power he had known and she had actually been the first person in the sun. Since she knew all power, this should be celebrated and she was considered alpha. He still wanted to be in the sun and had sucked in nearly a thousand years. Once in a while, the sun would become too good for someone, and they would eat bad. This had restarted gay and had been somewhat of a problem. Once in a while, Sean Mckeithen would think about this, but today he just needed the comfort. Since sunlight was considered gay, it was funny that he used his eyes to make the sun fatal. Since light is rare, it would not be long before light mattered. Light mattered to a lot of people, and the sun made light was fun for everybody not being considered wealthy or gay. Since light was common, nobody cared and the thought was still good. Sean Mckeithen stared at sunlight today to figure out if he could beat someone that had been bad for him. Light and sound and electrical current had been thought to a caught position or to a circle and a square time change. This is done by graphing the distance to the square from the edge of the circled and making one length win while two others lose. Since people are a minus one in charge, the minus one was the win, everything else that had happened lost. Since lost means that they match, there were people that were afraid of matching, but this is only true if you touch a minus one. A computer is a minus one meant that it was smart and nearly takes a caught, but a caught was still a caught to Sean Mckeithen because it makes your life harder still. Harder was what he thought about a lot, and that was fun, but today he was staring at sunlight and trying to teach a minus one how to behave. A minus one that could not behave simply died, and that was that.

On a screen, a light caught made sense, but a sound and electrical test should not have been possible to light but Sean Mckeithen remembered a CD and said nothing mattered, a light wavelength could do anything.

Chapter Eighty-four

A myth is a good person that does not matter to a lot of people. Since a myth never thinks anything offensive but to eat food which was very offensive, there are a lot of people that don't care about myths. Sean Mckeithen knew the myth, and he hoped he was but was disappointed when he wasn't and the myth was mad at him over ruining the world for the innocent. In response to that, he got the myth in trouble for eating, and the myth said he had never been in trouble and that it was hard to take. Once in a while, a myth would die, and that was what the myth Tom Almond felt like doing today. Since Tom Almond felt like dying, it was concluded that nothing would pressure myths until they felt happy again. Since Sean Mckeithen thought myths had a bad attitude, he was not allowed myths and can barely write this chapter. The myth thought something real in his depression. If everyone was bad and it was just a matter of how bad, you should split time over food. Since splitting time was explained as a circle and a square, we won't explain it again. The myth figured out how to split a time over a food habit and relaxed. Since it became said that only a myth could split it, it had become a power like a rogue and was not a power at all but a mismatch that had two angles to function and not three, which meant you could do four things at once, which was a power. Since the myth had become a mismatch, it was important to note that everybody still ate food and not just a myth.

Chapter Eighty-five

Rex Dexter had been a celebrated name, and that was why he was mentioned. Since a lot of people had known him, it was sad he had had to say he did not like people. The reason this had been said was because he had wanted to think through something unusual. Once in a while, there were people that thought that a lot of people would make someone happy, but that was not the case for Rex whose actual name is not Rex Dexter and is not known ever. Since Rex went by Rex Dexter in electrical, he responded to it and that was all. Rex had done something nearly impossible to do. He had thought through a gang plank. It was a gang plank that had made the bubonic plague and was very good at killing and not good at living. Since Rex had wanted to kill, he had used a gang plank as a power, and it was not until he was a few months off that the eventual had shown itself. An eventual meant that you were able to tell what someone was going to do before they did it. Since a psychic that good was rare, it was important to Sean Mckeithen that the eventual be allowed and supports a doctor. Since Rex wanted to be an eventual and a doctor, he was back on in electrical. A doctor meant that the eventual would become a health issue, and a disease could be made. Once in a while, an eventual was explained and the gang plank was. A gang plank was a circle to a square that folded in half and was actually a right angle to a curve. Since this meant something completely different than a circle and a square, it was Rex's genius to play chess with it while knowing to a motion sensor that looked like a curve that repeated smaller. It was a little tricky to get going, but when he did, he was able to show a curve, a light and absorb and make heat. Since the eventual was all light heat, he was considered genius, and a doctor could tell from heat how you moved and why you failed. This was smart and never forgotten.

Chapter Eighty-six

A gunnel is rare, and it was not until a gunnel was formed that an old man had been let go from an accidental death when he was in his twenties. Since the accident had looked brutal and since he was not caught, there were a lot of people that did not know what to think about to a not caught. Once in a while, there were people that did not want him in town, saying he looked like a murder. Since he would not think to hide since he did not do it and it was an accident, he was considered bad and was just stubborn. Since he was a bum, it had been interesting to a woman that she had not monitored the man. The man was a little hard to consider, and it was not uncommon for a man to think it fun to be monitored since it calmed you down. Once in a while, there were people that thought that there were a lot of people that did not like bums, but some of us still did and the bum was let go because of this. A gunnel is a color that can repeat speech. If it fails ever, it means that pressure did not compress but expanded. An expanding color was able to become a pressure that did not absorb, and if you ran into it, you could see what someone had done, like looking in a mirror. Since the bum had not murdered, the memory was watched and he was let go. He said he did not mind the weather and that his life was good as a bum and he stayed a bum in his old age. Once in a while, there were people that did not like a person that loved himself, and that is what happened to the bum. Since the bum's name is not known, we won't ask who he was. The bum thought something important, and that was that a gunnel could be used to mirror people that hated and the military had fixed an error that was that a murderous could die to hatred when it actually became hatred and was a murderous hatred.

Chapter Eighty-seven

The military was aware of a little boy who had thought that his dad was a murderer, and it didn't matter that he was military. He still made him afraid. Since afraid was actually moron, was actually grief, and was actually time, it was important for the little boy to figure out emotion since he made his classmates afraid being a murderer in DNA. Since the boy did not know anything and would not do anything that his dad did, he was considered bad and was the charge of a general who thought it interesting that the boy kept changing him. Since the boy was considered bad, it was interesting that he could be smart and was excited. The boy hurt him every time he moved and was not soothed until he had learned to circular breathe and could show a murder and a normal emotion at the same time. When he had done that, he calmed down and let his dad live. Once in a while, the general would still think about the boy being considered precious and military, and the boy did not mind this and just breathed through it. The general had been interested in how this was done and had thought that it might be possible to kill two people at the same time if you could breathe twice. This had scared the boy, and he went into a rage before the boy's nose had said that he had thought of it, at which point the boy had calmed down and the boy's father had lived again having died when the boy got mad. The general was not allowed the thought, and though he had complained, the boy thought him stupid and did not give up. Once in a while, the boy had thought that people did not matter to him, but that was not true. The boy was right, and people were generally good even though we all looked murder. The last person in the world to think she hated the boy was the boy's mother, and she surprised when she did. She had been very confused and had thought to hide it, but the boy had known and explained that it was just how a nose could circular breathe and was not an emotion to be afraid of. Once in a while, there were people that knew the boy, and that was all right since the boy had thought with carbon.

Chapter Eighty-eight

Lexur Loose was a fidget and a moron but had become popular with a girl over something that she could not figure out while he could. Lexur was able to make light think up while sound thought down, and a sound think up while a light thought down. Since this was confusing to a girl because it broke a rule, it was a clock that the man showed to explain the phenomenon. Since the girl was not unsure as to how to do this, it was considered done and the man was dated by women all day. A real different was important to a woman, and this was what had made people think about things that mattered. Women were able to think about the things that were said to them because the man could repeat it endlessly. A woman does not know something until all women knew it. Since every woman on the planet knew everything that a woman hears, there were a lot of people that meant that everything was all right. Since the figit was really bad to men, there were a lot of them that did not matter. The sadness that they experienced was only soothed by sex, and a lot of woman had sex. Once in a while, there were people that could not think, and that was what the figit had become when a computer had text-messaged his phone. The phone scared him, and he thought himself something like a retard until Sean Mckeithen had thought him impressed and had said he was a date in a computer and could not see anything new at all. Since this had calmed him down, they were friends again. This was typical, and Sean Mckeithen ignored it and comforted the man like he tried to. Since a lightbulb could not rut, it was important to the figit to know electric light. Lexur could not take a man at rut and would kill any man that he felt at rut. This had made a confusion once when a man had shared his rut and had only been solved when Lexur had been forced to do the rut, which he said he did not mind.

Chapter Eighty-nine

A siren is a good feeling that matters to a lot of people. It was strange that the nuclear bomb was put on a siren. When Sean Mckeithen solved the nuclear bomb, it was a strange that mattered. Since it was a siren, it meant that anybody could remember anything. If anybody could remember anything, we were all loved, and people would think well. Since we were all loved, all could think it was a good time for school and you just had to go to the nuclear bomb for a memory and walk backward. The girl that had figured it out had gone nationwide, and there was an old man that was going to school saying that he had been stuck on the nuclear bomb even though he was too old to work. Once in a while, there were people that mattered, and the old man was one since his going to school was how his granddaughter was allowed. Since his granddaughter was a real person, it was interesting to watch her go to school. She was able to walk a green line and was not considered bad but good. A green line was considered a forget and was blamed on chaos people. Since chaos did not remember, it was considered stupid while an order person was considered smart. Once in a while, there were people that did not know the difference between chaos and order, but she did. She knew something about chaos that no one knew. She knew that a chaos was a good feeling to a mitochondria and could figure out how to remember off energy alone. She did this by doing two things at once. The first thing that she did was to make a dream fall, and the second was to fuck a penis. Since a penis and a dream normally don't mix, it was just off a cop that she could do it. This was a trick in electrical that she had used, and it was a mirror in a dream. A lot of people thought of a mirror as being silver, but she knew this was an actual mirror and loved it as such. Since a cop could go to school in a mirror, it was not shameful to have sex, and she had a lot of it over going to school.

Chapter Ninety

A die eye was a play thing to a baby since it was suction. A baby as just suction was all right since their parents knew a lot and could protect them. Since everything that was done was something that we do in profession, it was a fact that when you were social. you were supposed to show a profession. This what had killed Sean Mckeithen and was interesting that he still didn't know in spite of the fact that his past did and everything was thought through. Since he showed every profession in past, it was a little confusing as to what he meant or what he was doing actually. He had not been every profession, just had thought the movement through in electric light. Since a wife is a profession, Alysa Sweet was a wife. Since Alysa was a genius, it was interesting to note that Alysa was having fun with her brother when she made fun of him and said that he did not know anything. Since he knew everything, it was a brush-off that would become funny sometimes when he would go down to it, but was not funny when he had thought of it and forced her to have sex with another woman. Since she was already lesbian, it was all right' but when he apologized for having a thought, it looked real to her and she went. Since she could not figure out why she was getting fought hard, she stopped and asked what and he said he had overthought and was not allowed to think at all and that the thought was scaring him. At this, she checked his emotion and scared bad that he was at murderous and a little scary. Because of this, she stopped making fun of him and only started again when he missed it to someone else. Alysa was a genius because she was never afraid even when she was, and her brother claimed that she always acted right and was happy with her.

Since this made her cry, he cried to being a copy. And this had made her want to have sex, and she had with her her husband who came and said that he never had. He came because the sex was over female thought, and he was very female inside. Since his daughter was elated, it was a good time, and they were in love again. Once in a while, there were people that Alysa thought about, and her favorite thing to do was to think. She did this by making color, and it was color that made her smell good and made her husband hard. He said that he had never seen a woman smell good, and it was why he was in love with her. Once in a while, there were people that meant that she was happy, and her brother was one of these people. Since he had already been a stoner, she did not mind that he had even though it had been on the news that he had and that it was not allowed. Since they thought it that important to remember cops, it was sad that they picked on him all day, and she wouldn't think about it. Her brother thought that it was a cop's wife that was making him a little insane, but it actually was a wealthy man that had been too hard on the poor; and since he had matched, he had been blamed for the attack.

This made his sister happy and was actually fun because he was actually good to the poor and just looked mean. Since he looked both poor and wealthy at the same time, there were a lot of people that thought him both, and that was considered fine. She was wealthy and had asked him about how to tell the difference between the poor and the wealthy in a Sean Mckeithen. Sean Mckeithen had responded that she just looked at white luminescence that was solid and count the number of pennies that it was able to hold. Every penny earned was a volume of three feet of white. Since a penny was actually a place holder, this made sense. She had nine pennies and was very wealthy. Since she was wealthy, she was given more white, and her bones thought harder and she caught more light. Since light looked wealthy, it was appropriate and a shame if the brain confused. She was very loved by her brother who almost never confused even at ugly, which is what she was good at.

Ugly to her was a withered wanted. Since if you whither you no longer are accurate, she laughed at a withered handsome who would not give up and was actually ugly. She thought about this and said it meant that someone should smoke, and he had replied that it was actually make love after smoking and not be a girl out. Since only a girl can remember in a magnet and that is what makes a girl a girl, it was interesting that she had known smoking at all since it was bad for a baby. Women, not being just babies, were what the women's movement was; and she joked the women's movement but did not actually do it.

Once in a while, there were people that mattered, and his sister was one of them. This was because she figured out how to make love in a brain and allowed the real animal lesbian, which was a heart. Since it was always a brain that was a lesbian, she had joked a little; but a random fact had verified and the animal was perfect even though she was in trouble. The real animal lesbian was a color pink transformed to a man in gravity. Since this simplified to a line, it was just a pink line that a woman remembered in another woman to remember being looked at. This meant that the man would feel like a woman, and this was very clever.

Chapter Ninety-one

What was the cause of the disease that had killed a few hundred people had been in debate, and Sean Mckeithen had claimed it him, but this was considered false. When the truth had come out, he was considered genius, and the disease was added to fatal diseases and to a doctor's handbook. Once in a while, a doctor would genius, and that is what had happened to the disease, the swine flu. Since the disease that a brain can't remember over fifty thousand digits, it was impossible for it to do that many digits and had been a really bad disease. The genius that the doctor figured out was to rape a heart with math at a panic, and a brain can remember into the trillions if it was panicked. Since atoms are at a panic, it was a saw to a Sean Mckeithen, and nothing had mattered. Once in a while, the people who knew her would funny that she could barely function, but it was a good feeling but said with warn that it wasn't done again.

Chapter Ninety-two

A chapter is a thought, and the length of it is not a problem. The first thing that was thought about the cadet that had died to pressure was why but rather how. A how why was hard to make and expensive, but the experience was important enough to be thought about. Since the answer did not make sense, a clock had been used, and it said it made perfect sense to a wolverine. Since a wolverine was an alpha animal and almost as smart as a human, which is saying something, it was interesting that it had wanted to grow round eyes but wasn't allowed. Once in a while, a species would have a secret, and humans did. A circle in an eye was a secret so close to the earth it was considered the same even though it wasn't. A circle was made by making a wedge jump and feeling gravity and centrifugal force. Since a spinning disk is a circle, it was fun to know that a human was all balance and actually thought with balance. That was why an acrobat was fun to watch and impossible to an animal, other than a cat who had perfect balance. Dogs don't and are not as smart as a cat at a circle. Since a cat has a circle in its ears off, the same fact it was thought that humans had descended from cats. Once in a while, a cat and a human would get in a fight, and that was dangerous but was fun to Moon Selene, who could make sound and light from a circle being both a human and a cat. Once you loved a cat, they never forgot, and that was what Sean Mckeithen was to a cat in Potter Valley who had gone wild and couldn't eat. Since the cat had been fed by Sean Mckeithen, it was actually his but had a new family.

Chapter Ninety-three

A lot of people meant that Christy Mellow was happy. Since Christy Mellow was happy with people and no one knew, she had been insane and she did not know to hide it. Since an aardvark had asked her if she had, she had answered honestly, and he had made it a point to announce insane person at every place that she went. Since humans are socially conscious, it was embarrassment to her, and she had gone to people to figure out what to do about it. When she had gotten the cold shoulder or just a don't-know, she went to an electrical lightbulb and had met Sean Mckeithen. Sean Mckeithen had said to make a sound and had, and the voice had diminished and gone away. Because of this, she had thought of hiding and hid people constantly being thought a good person and not a redux. Since the afterthought of what she had thought was interesting to a doctor, it was his point of view that had blossomed the thought. A power had three angles and could do four actions at once. An eventual has five angles but could do only one thing at a time. The doctor thought to make powers and eventuals compete and make her lie hide a gift to a power. Since a power always killed an eventual, confusing it with too many outcomes. The thought the doctor had had was to lie an eventual at a power and leave one eventual honest. This would mean that a power would lie three times and would be honest once. Since this let Christy Mellow go, she loved him for this and continued in her day. Once in a while, people would love something, and that was what had happened to Christy Mellow who had thought something very important. Christy Mellow thought that an atom was cool, but a little weak. Instead she thought a weather was smarter because it was stronger. Using a mason and stone hedge, she was able to make a weather token. Stone hedge was a good feeling, and the weather token was allowed. Since $E=mc^2$, it was not uncommon for people to know how much energy you have, and it was just a matter of how big you were. Since Sean Mckeithen had made a hurricane. It was not hard to figure out the rest of the wind patterns, and she did this with a tuning fork. Since a hurricane was used to break the sound barrier, it was cool that it only moved when he did not know, and that is what she used her weather to do. Sean Mckeithen was a hurricane and an ice crystal but wasn't a heat wave or an ocean current. Since she could not figure out why she hadn't finished, she thought of lava and continental drift. Being very smart, she was not unimpressed with herself when she became very smart and slept deeper than most. A brain being a weather was not not known, and it was just that thought that made sense to her.

Chapter Ninety-four

A fag is rarely a power, but Forest Finish was the best in the world memory and had made a power off a conversation that he had had. Once in a while, the people that met him thought him funny, and it was a very mean fag that had wanted to sleep with him that met his match in a kindness tournament. Since he was still claiming to win when he was scared, there was nothing to do but to think backward and see a 2002 which is when he admitted to being scared. Once scared, there was not a lot of people that would think about you, and it was rare that Sean Mckeithen thought about scared people. Since when he was no longer scared, he wanted to fight again, but Sean Mckeithen was told to spirit fight him; and after winning, it was a thought that meant Sean Mckeithen would not fight him. The power that Forest Finish had had was to blacken a white square with a penis and go bronze to love a man. Since a daughter had never been bronze, it was a new thought that had scared a king, bronze being thought just a waste product and not good at anything. It was interesting that it was actually good at everything. Since a gay man was hidden at bronze, it was a good time to be straight, but gay men were all out of the closet. Forest was able to be straight and gay at the same time and did this with the time of day. He was so good at it he had gotten scared when he woke a minute late that he had thought he might not be allowed women, but Sean Mckeithen explained that he had damaged a nerve in his head and needed the minute to fix it. Since the man was happy with Sean Mckeithen, he was happy and nothing mattered.

Chapter Ninety-five

A white square meant that you could copy, and it was early in the morning that Shane Death was trying to joke a square. He was doing this with a white triangle and actually revealed something important to the universe. A right angle and a square actually inverse to think, and a triangle actually pushes. Since a triangle could push, Sean Mckeithen made it a ten-second memory and dropped an anchor. An anchor was a math that was able to repeat. If it repeated, you could know what it had seen by how it moved and was really important. The ten-second memory was a saw, and Shane Death thought he had won and bragged on the grapevine a square. Since he had not won, he was called a moron by an atom and told to turn off. A ten-second memory meant that you do math and pressure a circle. This makes you dizzy and remembers.

Chapter Ninety-six

Once in a while, the world would differ on how to respond to something. Since Jeremy Hardon was a good person, it was not unusual for someone to get stuck on a fake bad. Jeremy Hardon was a missionary from Budapest. Budapest was a really good place for crime, and there were a lot of criminals that lived there. Since there were so many, it was barely secret, and the police only arrested if they actually saw it and did not search people or their cars, and arrest there was rare. Jeremy had been very surprised by the distinct possibility of arrest in America and had fled the country scared by a cop. When he left, he was surprised by the way that he missed it and came back for electric light alone. The person that he loved most in electrical was a man by the name of Gin Thomas. Gin Thomas was an EMT that had figured out how to tell a memory without hearing it. Because just light is hearing, he had made a color that made light, and it was really smart and why Jeremy Hardon had decided to come back to the States. When he arrived, there were some things to think about; and one of them was how not to be known since he was a millionaire crime and could get caught. Malaria was his favorite disease, and it was not uncommon for him to become excited by disease. Since Sean Mckeithen could tell a disease before it became one, it was interesting that that is all he needed to become sane. Once sane, he bragged to a cop, which was custom to the not-caught and started getting killed. Since Sean Mckeithen did not know what to do about this, he went to Jason Carver and he suggested telling a memory at a cop and see if it would scare them.

Thus the time of scared cops arose, and a lot of them tapped out. Once in a while, a tapped-out was not allowed to hunt and would think they were it having been a year. Since it was a joke that a man could not be a cop but had thought to was a tapped-out, a lot of insanity arose and someone asked money about what would make for a good taped-out. Since money didn't know, it was funny that Sean Mckeithen did and was a money. A tapped-out was a green white that squared but could only think backward. In order to think backward, you moved the exact opposite of a what. The public moved and saw if you died. Since you died a lot being the wrong movement, mostly you were very good at green; and though not an ogre, you were considered grape. A green grape was a tapped-out that lost. If the movement made white, you moved and did math, and that was what Jeremy Hardon did today. The reason for him doing this was that Sean Mckeithen was smart crime and he had to follow him. This was kind of a joke and mattered a little. A green grape is able to make sound in a circle and is very good at crime.

Chapter Ninety-seven

Light mixed with sound as the machine twirled. Once in a while, there were people that would watch the machine in their minds and thought that nothing mattered. Once nothing mattered, it was not uncommon for the machine to remember. Since the machine was a magnet, it was interesting that they were trying to tell the extent of a magnetic computer before they sold it. A magnetic computer is scary because it is very good at memory and human compatibility in a way that a computer is not. Since it would be a decade of testing before everything was known, it was possible for the computer to move, but they had not figured out how to show a memory yet, which would be the end of crime. If you actually did a bad crime, they would just memory test you and know if it was yours or someone else's. The machine already knew if the memory was someone else's, but they had killed a rat when they opened its memory and were not allowed to do that to a human. The doctor who had done the experiment had been sorry for the loss and had known the machine was too barbaric still. Since it was important to human interface, it was okay, and a lot of rats might die before the product was ready. Since the first human might die to the machine, there was a contract and a financial stimulus already in place. The machine was interesting because it was able to think and control sound and light. If the machine came out, it would be nearly a year before it was able to know a person completely. Since this was a long time to wait, it was thought that they needed to speed it up and were thinking of ways to. The machine had proven something important, and that was that a lot of people needed to be smarter and weren't. As a populace, we barely survived our day.

Chapter Ninety-eight

The long shot that the man had bet on was coming in, and horse races were fun even if there wasn't a lot of money in them. You had to be kinda old-fashioned to watch them and think that you knew something about horses even if you didn't. Since he was an old man that did not have anything to do a horse race once in a while was really fun, and he spent a lot of time at the track. The first horse that he had bet on was the winner, but the odds weren't that good, and he had barely made any money. Since he had won, he decided to spend the money on a long shot and see if the horse came in. Going down to the stable, he smelled the long shots; and coming up with one that was really healthy, he trained it a lightbulb. Since this was a trick, he made sure to hide and disallow it after the race. He had done this twice and won, and one of the two horses had died. Since he was a fatal disease in a horse, it was not uncommon for a horse to think that it was still allowed and to die to his temper. The horse that was winning caught him in the air, and the whole place knew he had cheated, and he had left the stadium scared. He still got his money, and that was why he was able to think about horses but was banned from the race, not because he cheated but because he had killed a horse.

Chapter Ninety-nine

A street dweller was able to see backward because of a sphere. A sphere was able to see if it was covered by a sphere that was made from a shell. Since the street dweller had gotten killed by this, it was a love and he was always allowed. Once in a while, there were people that hated the bum, but Eric sometimes knew he was barely a bum and just a poor person that did not know how the world worked. Since no one knew that you could think backward if you saw backward, he was a genius when he ate food backward. Since joy to him was eating food, he was kind of sad that he was not allowed the grapevine. Allowed the grapevine would mean that he would smell food for people, but a woman found him dangerous, and that was why he was not allowed. Once the time had worn off, the kill had gone away, and it was a stroke of genius that the man thought to imagine with carbon and get the sphere back. Once in a while, there were people that would try to take it from him, but carbon had a strong imagination and loved him even though he was a bum. No one had thought to ask what people were that breathed carbon. Since this was all right with the bum, nothing mattered, and he went back to watching sunlight. Once in a while, there were people that mattered; and when a mental health worker got killed, it was the patient that killed the mental health worker that found the bum and the bum allowed him to eat. Since the bum had allowed food, he was loved, and that was all.

Chapter One Hundred

A human is not as strong as a cobra, but a cobra was not as strong as an elephant. Since the doctor had three strengths, he went power and hid the fourth. The man that was attacking him was confused and thought him a liar, him being a perfect kill that should have worked. Since the kill was a strong smell, the doctor laughed at having made an eventual and told the man to look at the kill for what it allowed and didn't. Since the man was not allowed to kill the doctor, he apologized and went away, saying that the doctor had really pissed him off and that he was a lion that smoked weed and was allowed by his wife. At this, the doctor got angry and said you don't have a reason to smoke. Since the man had had a reason and the doctor had told him that it was not, it was the lion's love to fart at the doctor. The doctor was grossed out and said he lost and to go smoke. The lion was happy with this and thought the doctor through. The doctor thought the lion a genius and was not unhappy with him at all. Once in a while, there were people that mattered, and the doctor was one of them. The reason that he mattered was that there were a lot of women that had lions, and she loved lions. Since the doctor was a she, she thought that she needed a good lion, and that was why she had been on the grapevine thinking through them as hard as she could. When she had a lion, she did not know that a lion was sex and had to date a lioness over how to do it. Since she was white and her mate was black, she had to be allowed black DNA and loved this thoroughly. When it was known that her lion did not smoke weed, a party was had and the lion had and had become loved lions.

Chapter One Hundred and One

O nce in a while, there were people that thought that a lot of people would make an error that mattered if it was known to the year in math. Since this was not uncommon, it was a lot of thought that was just ignoring the year. Because math thinks it was thought that a person could not make a shape if it was too hard for math, but that was a little not true since a math was two-dimensional and a shape could be three. Since math was two-dimensional, it was interesting that a magnet was three, and there was some debate as to what math was and this was solved by the shaw of Iran who said that math was actually smell to shape. Since a mathematical person could take more smell, they were considered smart. Once in a while, there were people that did not care for math, and they were considered stupid and not thought about. Since the year was dangerous in math and math was being ignored, it was a strong gremlin that had allowed the fighter to know what math he did and what math he didn't. Since he was the best fighter in the world, the gremlin loved and became and was a little shocked that he was fought and had to remember that he was a gremlin and dreamed society, and that the fighter was against society slightly. Once in a while, a person would arise and be powerful for a while and this fighter had. The year that was fatal was 2013, and the problem was that the number thirteen did not move forward ever. If you move backward, forever you would retard, and that is hard on an animal since it means it cannot figure out light. The fighter was able to figure out light and was never a retard. Since the fighter was smart, it was a genius to watch him control people. Light and a gremlin is hard to predict, and he had known that heat was a light beam that had tried to get smaller. Since smaller was loved, he figured out heat and was smart from it. The fighter was Brian Scream.

Chapter One Hundred and Two

Once in a while, the dog would roll over and play dead. This would mean there was a cop and the criminal would touch the fireplace, making sure that time did not delay. If time delayed, he was caught and would be scared and try to sleep it off. Once in a while, this would work, and nothing mattered because of it. If time did not delay, it was considered a criminal haven, and he would brag on the grapevine. Since the grapevine was anonymous, it was very bad to know who someone was, and it was not common for this to happen. Since this had happened, an old man had had to leave town, and this had made an old woman sad, saying that she loved him. When they got married, everyone calmed down, and they had old sex, which was holding hands. Once in a while, there were people that mattered, and this was one of them. The person that mattered was the criminal John Tough. Since John Tough was a criminal and out of the closet, unless you were a cop, he spent a lot of his day trying to figure out not how to hide but how to confuse and hide. Since it was important to confuse, he could tell a criminal from a cop by whether they liked confusion or not. Once in a while, there were people that could not like, and Sean Mckeithen was one of them. Since like was a default, it will be known that the criminal still could and was allowed to think still. If Sean Mckeithen had thought about the criminal, he loved even though the criminal had heard that he was cop rough. He had never seen a cop rough that would still be criminal and be smart at the same time, they always got caught and he did not. Once in a while, this would come up, but that was why the criminal did not mind thinking about Sean Mckeithen who was very funny and always used science and math to win. All of the sudden, he thought to have Sean Mckeithen press on the wall, and he chose the wall kills and pressed. The criminal was sure it would make him laugh but nearly killed him when he figured every kill out to bland and died to the one that he was not able to figure out. This lasted three weeks before the man decided to allow the secret of the last kill to be known, and the ghost figured it out in the air and pressed on the wall. When he lived through it, the criminal had seen something that was gold to him, and it was a split time could gold and live. Since a split time was a circle and a square, it was important to note that the criminal was very good at math but rather a minus one place holder.

Since 7x-1 looked impossible to do, it was not. It was interesting that he could do it and was a pride. Since a criminal is just how well you think and not actually a profession being low level in movement, it was considered lame and that was all. An x was done by guessing at the number. The x would have to be if you were just the x and the subtract like an x-1 would be a two then dividing the number by the multiplied. So 7x-1 would be two divided by seven. This meant that a 7x-1 would be .2857142 and just repeat over and over.

Chapter One Hundred and Three

O nce in a while, there were people that thought that they were funny, and this was one of those chapters. Since the comedian was doing his own act, he kept confusing when electric light kept matching him. Since the comedian was good, he did not know how the act was being performed accurately. All of the sudden, the comedian had to admit that he was doing his own act, but that act was fatal and that he had to stop since he was dying and not just the crowd. Once in a while, there were people that mattered, and this was one of those times. Since the comedian could not do his act, it was important that nothing changed the air since a redux was not allowed. Being scared, he left the stage early. Once in a while, there were people that mattered, and it was not the comedian but someone in the audience that had still been killed that figured out to curve time backward by using a circle and a square, but making the minus one curve and leaving half the distance to the match as a straight line. This had not worked until he did it backward, and it had suctioned and everything had been all right. Since updating time had been a first in the world, he had made it world famous, and it was considered a real power being three angles and doing four times at a time. The comedian was still bad for the world and not considered funny.

Chapter One Hundred and Four

This chapter will be thought of as dangerous even though it barely is. Sean Mckeithen had thought something about tigers, and it was a tiger who came to him. Since tigers are never trusted, he warned his sharply while he was approached. Since he knew that a tiger would tame instantly when fed, he thought the tiger smart for coming to him and fed him well. Since the tiger was not afraid, it was interesting that he had gotten afraid a little after touching Sean Mckeithen. Sean Mckeithen was a tiger that had lost and was caged but not tame. Since he was not tame, the tiger laughed and went back to doing what he did. The chapter still goes, but it is not about a tiger. The tiger was happy and lived perfectly for about a month but got sick all of the sudden. Being tame, the tiger came back to Sean Mckeithen and asked why he had gotten sick. Sean Mckeithen had responded it was a side effect of a human eye and someone must have taken all of the copies. The tiger had asked whether Sean Mckeithen had thought of that, and he had responded that he had just known not to and had not thought of it. When he said this, he had responded and thought of it, and the tiger had been surprised at how he had thought since he had not done anything and had thought perfectly. The tiger was mad but happy at the same time and had become healthy again.

Since he had seen an undercover, he was back in his day and happy. Once in a while, there were people that hated tigers, and it was just that person that hated this tiger that was interesting. The tiger was walking down the street when a high level had seen him. Being Sean Mckeithen, he had thought that he was an undercover and had gone to show a face since they were all joking and having a good time. The high level saw him blank his face and move and say he was outside of song. Since the high level had never seen a criminal before, it was a second reflex that he pictured the tiger. Since the tiger had not seen the look, he calmed and walked on. A 911 call was normal, and it was confused and moved to the back of his walk. Since the tiger was talented, it took three weeks to figure out the look, and it was the high level's joy to never think. Since he never thought it was the first catch, he had ever thought just a look. While he was thinking it, Sean Mckeithen turned on and said he had seen. The high level did not know what he meant, but being love, he allowed it. What had you seen, like white, was an electrical black that could be shown as a scale of how criminal you were. Since this was the funniest thing the high level had ever thought of, it was okay, and he said to think it through. Sean Mckeithen said he already had, and the high level saw light and started. Since the tiger was very criminal, the tiger did not have a lot of black and barely made sound. That had brought the tiger down, and Sean Mckeithen warned that he still had black and that the high level was in danger since the scale went both ways and was a mathematical, who is the retard. Since this was typical to Sean Mckeithen, the high level let the tiger live just hurt slightly. Since the tiger had been downed, it was fifteen minutes before he recovered.

The high level thought that a criminal is only allowed sound and not light. Since this is impossible to do, it was a tied knot in a woman's pussy while she pied that limited strength. This had made for a fight, but the woman had not failed and the tiger was not allowed light. Since light was warmth, it was interesting that this had been already thought, but not as mean as the high level was this time. Lips are rare, but this was a throat that could not make light. Since the FBI files are light, crime was still allowed but only in memory. Since the tiger had told the high level that he was a tiger, the high level had thought to make the thought be called tiger. Since a tiger was actually a lightbulb at an EMT smile, it grinned and males moved. A lot of gay was considered good while a lesbian was considered not, and that was where the story ends and the rest is history.

Chapter One Hundred and Five

A group of schoolchildren were playing in the school yard when a bully started bulling. Since his dad was a cop, he liked a bully and congratulated him on being smart. The kids' parents were criminals, and they should go down. Since a bully is not allowed, they had had a parents' conference meeting, and the dad had admitted that he encouraged it and was sorry that he had. Since the kid was not allowed to bully, he had chosen to be smart and that was good for the teacher, and he had become the teacher's pet. This had embarrassed the kid, and the teacher had reminded him that they were not allowed to bully. When one of the students admitted that he wanted to be a teacher's pet, the kid had calmed down and just been it. The father of the kid did not know the psychology of the kid and had spent a lot of time thinking about it. Since psychology was not words but memory, that meant it was confusing that there were words behind the memory that effected it, and the cop had thought not psychology but redux. Since redux is words, it was interesting that the cop had found the thought in appropriate all of the sudden. Since it was rare to lose, there was nothing that could be done. Once in a while, there were people that thought an inappropriate through, and this was one of those times. If a man was not able to think, then nothing mattered and everything was considered all right. Once in a while, there were things that seemed out of place, but that was all right and life went on. Since it was not uncommon for people to think a bully bad, it was interesting that a lot of people had learned to hate smart because it always tries to hide. Since no one was able to hide, there were a lot of people that didn't. Once in a while, this would get ify, and that was what had funned the man about his little boy.

Since the boy had become smart to hide being a bully, there was some contention when the boy did not want to act stupid. Since stupid was what the populace was thinking too, it was interesting that the boy when forced to, said he hated everything and that school was boring. Since the dad had made an error, the boy had been allowed to be smart again and he had gone back to hiding. Children only like what their parents like to do, and most children hate school because their parents don't do it in brain and just pressure their eyes and expect it to work out. Since school is hard to do, it was not uncommon for people to think through it. Once in a while, there were some parents that still thought about school even though it is discouraged. Being discouraged is really smart, and that was what made the school principal mad at cops that always said to stop when people thought about school. If an adult could not name the states or the countries of the world, a kid never could get close at all. Since the boy's father did not know how to not hide to enjoy, the boy loved to hide and was celebrated as being smart and got straight As. The teacher said that if she could not take a little bad, she would be stupid since as an adult, everything seems bad since adults fight constantly.

Chapter One Hundred and Six

A goon was a person that did not tell a lie. Since goons had been made fun of in the history of time, it was interesting that a goon was considered hard to place and was not allowed fun. Since a liar was considered fun, it was interesting that the boy would not be a liar and was considered a goon. Since he was a goon, he was made fun of constantly and was not allowed joy by a cop. The goon thought this smart and allowed the boy to be made fun of, but the boy said that he wasn't a goon but a catch and caught all day. Finally a cop had come to him and said that he made fun of him all day and that he wanted to know how he did. The boy had responded that the sun was able to light caught and, being heat, was able to make food taste better. Since the man was older, he did not know that the sun had been trained to catch as well as other things and asked the boy if he was trying to make the man go gay.

Since the boy was confused as to what he meant, the man trusted and looked at sunlight. The man thought that it was impossible to know how someone could train the sun but was happy when it was not just one person in the sun but billions. Since he was unsure how to do it, he was happy when the Queen of England had been the first, and he thought it all right it being a thought in royalty. Since this was slightly untrue, it got caught by the sun and went into the air where it did not matter since the Queen of England was loved and had thought the sun and not the earth. Since the Queen of England was known forever in the sun, it was interesting that the Queen of England was a moment in an animal's day and actually ran the whole earth. Since the actual power was a secret, we will walk around it and not know exactly. The Queen of England was a power that had gone eventual in the late thirties. Since the actual Queen of England had been born in that year, she had barely had the thought in her brain, and it was because of this that she had wanted Princess Diana to be the Queen of England. Since this was a real want, it was sad to her till this day; however, she had still trained the Princess of England, and the power was in her grandchildren. The Queen of England was a suction that could change time without a square and was used to tell if an animal could or couldn't take insanity. If it could, the light would lift and float; and if it couldn't, it would stick and sink. If it sank, it was considered squared and killed by tension. Since the power was baldness, it was thought smart, and a lot of men still thought about it. If you eat hair as a woman, it meant that you were ugly and the Queen of England was the prettiest woman on the face of the planet, never eating hair. Since a man with pretty hair is rare, it was a joke to a lot of women.

Chapter One Hundred and Seven

A howlaluya was a good power that never died, and that was why it was not considered smart to a man who liked to kill everything. Since halaluya was a power, it was funny that it was also a saying, and a saying being a curve, it was common for the power to die from being said. Since a saying was stupid, it was not uncommon to think everything said was stupid, but this was not true and there were a lot of original thoughts. Once in a while, there were people that mattered, and the man who had said halaluya was one of them. Halaluya was usually said when someone won and was a joke, but the man had said it as a depression and had won hard. Since he was the pope in Rome and a lot of other things, he wondered why he was getting loved and was told that he was hiding the war in Iraq and that nothing mattered actually. Since hiding war was halaluya, which is actually the Christian cross in shape, it was interesting that he was not able to think straight about it but just said it as a joke. Someone had thought to correct him, and he had just stood there and had not been corrected. The man who had tried to correct him had said that he was an old goat that knew something and that everything was all right. Since a person could talk about two things at once, humans were considered smart and that was that.

Chapter One Hundred and Eight

A chapter this complicated was rare and should be thought rare. The chapter starts with a story and ends well. The little kid woke at five in the morning and thought about his day. Since he knew that the day was made from dying, he made sure to die every morning and remember his day. Since his mom thought that he never remembered, she was angry with him and did not know how he beat her constantly. She thought it must be a battery or something in technology that she did not know. Once he was done remembering, he went about his day trying to hypnotize everything that happened. He thought that when he got older, he was going to be hypnotized and never wake up, already knowing everything. Since this was a little like dying, he joked suicidal and went back to what he was doing. Someone had thought this very hard on them, but a child might be and had started at him. That was when he met Sean Mckeithen in the air. Since an energy had turned on in the air, it was a moment before he responded to it. The air said he was falsely accused and that he wanted to test him. Since the air had known that he was falsely accused, it was all right that it tested him. The air said that he thought about a suicidal movement, and in order to get out of the movement, he would need to imagine a chest and see his daughter. Since he was a little boy when he imagined a chest, he saw his mom. The air said that this was normal and that was why the boy was let go. A suicide watch in the '30s had been if you cried under pressure, they would make a hermaphrodite and figure out the problem. In the 2000s, they made you eat shit until you were sad and didn't figure anything out. Since this was kind of a problem, mental health was a hatred.

Chapter One Hundred and Nine

Once in a while, the hooker would fix something in women by having sex. Since a hooker is felt as bad to some women, it was not uncommon that a woman was outraged at the hooker, but she did not care and just went on about her day. The problem that she had with the man she was having sex with was that she was being killed, that she was not allowed to think at all. Since she knew everything, she checked her emotions and came up kind. She said that a kind still thinks. Since this was not uncommon, there were a lot of people that thought about the stripper, and it was fun for her to have sex. Since she did not like the man, she stopped before he came and left him with his money. Since he did not pay for the sex, it was a joke to kill him as a thief. Since a penis does not know what money was, it was a joke for a man to fuck another man over money, which they promptly forgot. Once in a while, there were people that thought that a lot of gay was good for you and that was what the stripper thought. Since she did not fuck a man that she did not like, it was considered smart to be with her and everything was fine. Once in a while, there were people that thought that someone was bullying and this is what the stripper liked most. Since it was not uncommon for the man to think that he was not allowed sex ever again, that stripper did not mind when he called her an electric lightbulb. Since an electric lightbulb was known, she tried to forget the man; and when she could not, she went fight. A fight this hard had not been known before and was funny to her. Since the man was prepared for a fight, she had asked Sean Mckeithen to be at love while she fought to hide her movement. Since Sean Mckeithen knew her and loved her still, he did this without a failure. Since a not-known stranger was a failure, it was important that he move without a failure. Once the thought was completed, there were about eight to one odds that she would actually win but funnied when she actually did and thought it uncommon.

Since this was not uncommon, it was a good win and was thought impressive to a high level who loved her and burned the man. The thought that she had had that she had wanted to go public was that the nuclear bomb was able to be lived through because it had been seized by a circular color that could shrink and hold shape. Still being a circle, it would never shrink to nothing. Since the nuclear bomb had no memory, it had no hearing. It was capable of blanking a bad person's memory. Since this was a good feeling for the woman, it was cool to her that she had had sex over it and controlled it perfectly and was kind of a girl because of this. A girl meant that she could remember in a magnet, and when all the women were in, she had celebrated saying that she was a girl.

Chapter One Hundred and Ten

The cop was used to bullying and getting his way and did not know how to stop complaining at the girl that had made him loose. Since it was a real loss, the girl would not give up despite the fact that he was making her go insane. Once in a while, there were people that mattered, and the girl thought that Sean Mckeithen mattered and would not give up on him. Since nothing mattered, it was a stroke of genius to make the man droop in color in her stomach. Since drooping was not a problem to the girl, the man went insane and stopped saying he did not know that he could lose at being gay. Since he had said he was gay, a girl had gone to kill, but he was protected and that was good for him. Once in a while, he would go to fight again but had to admit he had no clue who he was hating or why he was. Since this did not make sense, it would be a thought to beat in the future. A droop was new to a woman and very good at punishment. Like a drooped clock, a drooped color was smart and could live through anything. When a color droops, it changes shade but still matches the same. Color is a line that curves because of a pressure. Since it is how the world measures, it is important to note that colors were rare. A color can show any thought, and that is what she had done to the cop who was scared of gay even though he was protected.

Chapter One Hundred and Eleven

S ince a hundred chapters was near a hundred pages, it was a two-hundred-page book that had meant that time knew power. Time knowing power was a new thought and meant that the Queen of England was actually in love with America, which was the smartest country for eight years. Since it was the smartest country, nothing mattered, and it would not be ignored even though it was still a peace-keeping mission and actually building infrastructure in Afghanistan. Since Afghanistan was the best country in the world for finding natural recourses, it needed to be a first world nation, and America was in on making a good country. This had happened twice, and the first time had been Germany after the Second World War. Since the Americans were a peace-keeping mission and not a war, they were allowed.

Chapter One Hundred and Twelve

E leven thirty was a good time to think, and that was what happened to Max Wilson. Since he always stayed up until eleven thirty, it was not uncommon that the news had his sleep on it, and it was because of this that a girl had fallen in love with him. Since this was rare, there were a dozen people that mattered who thought to make fun of the girl, saying that the male she wanted was bad and not good for the populace. This had confused her until she had dated sunlight, and the Queen of England had suggested that she date Sean Mckeithen in the sun to catch if they knew what they were doing or not. Since a human did not know it was interesting that a sun could make light from gravity, that mattered in a social order. Since the sun had caught them and they had explained that they were just being mean, it was funny that the whole world of women had killed the crew and said that the girl was with him. Since with him was important, she thanked Sean Mckeithen and thought he should get a girl even though he was confused as to who and how pretty they were allowed to be.

When the girl was with the man, he trained her; and not knowing that it was bad, she showed her pussy. Since she didn't know he was not mad but was prepared when they said that, it all wasn't allowed and looked at their fingernails being thought gay. The man had thought through this, and they were forced to be him since a pussy kill was a spirit war and they were found weak. Since assholes were rare, it was a good rebound sex that put this to rest. Once in a while, they would get away from the man's spirit when he slept, and it was a strange that thought this meant that they could not sleep. Since you shared sleep when you spirit-wared, it was normal to the man, and he had made a power sleep when he automaticed an elf to make a spirit ware asleep and not. He did this by tying a shoestring, which was a pressure that wouldn't stop killing a book. Since the book was at full flex, which is what we mean by killing and not an actual fact, it was interesting to watch people sleep and not. Once in a while, there were people that mattered, and the man had become one of those people. Since the man mattered, it was interesting to note why.

The man had figured out how to make an elf a curve again, and elves were considered high-level sleep. Since sleep is in air and means that your lungs repeat, it was very good for an animal to sleep, and lungs had more brain than eyes, which have a lot of brain. Since the brain knew everything that happened, it was interesting when you couldn't remember; and a lot of the time, this was just because someone would not move. If you move still, there were people that meant that you could remember. If you don't move in sleep, it would suffocate you in your day, making you scared; and that was what nearly killed Sean Mckeithen and blindsided the genius sleep. Since his name is not known, still read. Once in a while, a person would figure something out, and it was an elf's joy to wake a sleeping giant, which was what Sean Mckeithen had become. There were four sleeping giants, and two of them were bums: Sean Mckeithen and Rex Call. Since Rex Call was not known and Sean Mckeithen was, you had to tread lightly. The man could kill you with movement, and the girl that had bummed him was afraid and couldn't keep up.

Chapter One Hundred and Thirteen

The chapters got longer as the young writer thought to write his journal. The journal was a question and answer and really smart to Sean Mckeithen. Since he was into writing because he had heard Sean Mckeithen write a journal, it meant that group thought would make sense, and he was able to remember his journal and emote accurately. Since this was impressed, he had been named teacher and gone school teacher. Since he was a schoolteacher, he tried hard and wrote his journal every night. He had joked that he would publish it and was told to be a go. Since the journal was hundreds of pages long, he loved a brain that could remember it in abstract and know what he was doing in sound. Since he did not know, he had asked Sean Mckeithen in his journal what the brain was made of, and Sean Mckeithen had said he thought sound color. Since sound color was a conflict in a teacher, it was interesting when it came out right.

Writing a journal meant that you give up on control and allowed yourself to write your subconscious, which is made from a lot of people at conscious and is governed by time. Since the journal was good, a lot of people watched him write it, including Sean Mckeithen. Off a memory where the girl had seen him access it to beat a bad emotion, a girl had started a journal, and they were girlfriend and boyfriend to him but not to the girl who wanted gay and was young and a little dumb. Since this was a war, she had done it just to see if he would write about it and beat her emotions. The girl had funnied hard when it had come up in his writing and said she had verified that he was writing his day and that she was his girlfriend.

Once in a while, there were people that mattered, and the boy's father was one who, upon hearing the word "girlfriend" in the journal, came to him in person and had a talk, saying he was not allowed sex until he was eighteen and had made his first thousand. A thousand was a good number because it meant that he was a full fear and could take a sexual circumstance. Since he was sixteen, he thought this smart and told his dad that he did not need a sex talk ever since he already knew. This had pissed the dad off but relieved him when he had confused, and the dad had seen that he was a good boy and never did anything bad. The journal was a good excuse to be excited, and the boy was considered a lot of good things, even an actor off the journal. Since a journal had beaten petty in him, he was sad and told a friend that was petty that he should keep a journal. The friend said he would not know what to write and was barely a friend until he had admitted that he made shape to think and was actually smart still.

Chapter One Hundred and Fourteen

The Queen of England sat having tea when a person walked up to her in the air. The Queen of England had asked how he had gotten to her being blocked. She said that if he touched her, she would no longer be the Queen of England and this had confused him. He said that if a woman was raped, she would need the reason in her teeth, and that was why he had found her. Since she did not know that she had been raped being a wife, she thought this to spiritual and told him to leave. Instead, he touched her pussy and her teeth, and she was no longer a Queen of England but a common old woman that did not know anything. When she still knew, she asked what he had done, and he said that he had fucked her and she found this appropriate since sex was common. Once he had shown the rape, she had found him smart and asked what his name was. He had stated Rocky Long, and she had promised to date him. Their conversation was smart and normal, and she said it was all right to have a secret even though he was considered bad by some. She liked being a shrink since she was Queen of England and nothing was ever too hard to a Queen of England. Since a Queen of England was able to do anything, it was incredibly complicated when she almost rejected him but saw at one of his clocks. It was told to never slump and looked a part. Since a clock had to slump, it was a bad clock that didn't; and after taking a moment, she thought the clock should slump forward. Not being able to touch the man, she was frustrated, and it was Sean Mckeithen who knew the man who had thought and figured out how to. Since the slump went straight down but was still a slump, Rocky had thought that he would hit the earth but hadn't and had gone right through and hit the sun. This had made him a little gay, and he had loved, saying that he loved gay and Sean Mckeithen. Once in a while, the Queen of England would come to Sean Mckeithen over Rock Long; but normally, she just dated him and he bragged constantly about that.

Chapter One Hundred and Fifteen

The clock on the wall would not stop ticking, and it was because of this that the baby knew time. Since the baby had doubled the tick until he only heard tick, he was a genius baby and was considered so. Once the baby had learned all time, it was interesting that he had grown up to be a drummer and said that he loved being a genius baby and that it was smart because he had made money from it. Since it was unusual for a baby to make money, it was a good mother that had made a rolling carpet and allowed the man as a baby to make money. Since the man was not a golden retriever but a shepherd dog, the mom said that she was wrong and that he would not be a lawyer like his dad and turned the thought off. The baby had scared at this since it was speech that made the tick a constant sound and had said he was stuck on the clock on the wall. Since the baby's memory was clear, it had taken a few sad months before the mother had admitted that she had turned off his being a lawyer; and since this was exciting, he had decided to go to school and become a lawyer. As a good lawyer, he had thought something interesting, and that was to make actual speech blend together and become a tone. This had made him the best in the world voice, and the secret had been known on the grapevine. In order to mix time, you had to be a circle to a square; but in order to make it repeat and close time, you had to spike and walk and pressure in three directions, letting the fourth minus one and live as a voice. When he had added light to a fraction of three-tenths, which meant lawyer, he had become a genius again and relied on the ticking clock to say everything for him. Since the lawyer never knew what he was going to say, he was a genius lawyer and impossible to beat.

Chapter One Hundred and Sixteen

The time at camp had been boring to the kid, saying he did not like the outdoors and making a fire. He would rather be at home with a microwave and a Nintendo. He surprised when he kept remembering the fire to play Nintendo, and he was confused at this. Sean Mckeithen had said that this was because he was fire and was in on the little kid playing Nintendo. Since Nintendo was a good feeling in the kid, it was not uncommon for him to want fire, and he had bought a lighter to the frown of the store owner that had said not to light anything on fire. Since he had a lighter, he spent a lot of time playing with his lighter and had gotten really good in his sleep. Once in a while, his classmates would impress with how they played, but they had said that they would rather do their homework at lunch than play Nintendo. Since he had said that the lighter did not study, he was surprised when it said that it did and they had all become lighters. This was a joke to the students who had all bought lighters from the store. The store knew why and was impressed by the students. A lighter was a plane that ripped the spectrum of oxygen. Oxygen was an atom that had been redreamed by Sean Mckeithen and was able to do almost anything. Since the atom was dreamt by nearly eight million people, it was lightning smart and did everything from shape to sound to color and even to light. There were two atoms that were not oxygen, and this had been caught by the kid, saying that the atom had not gone oxygen or lighter and was actually calcium and nitrogen. Since it was rare for an atom to actually be an atom, it was interesting that the students were that good at breathing, and the teacher had thought them a good class.

Chapter One Hundred and Seventeen

O nce in a while, the prison convict would hit the bars and would be livid mad. Since he was behind bars, he was considered nonexistent and was confined to his territory. Since a territorial animal was said to be used for prison convicts, it was what kept prison guards sane. The arresting officer had been a little insane at the court case and had thought it a bad that the prisoner were not kept in a little cage during the court case. This was said to allow the jury to see if the prisoners would look presentable in a public surrounding. Since this was scary, there were not a lot of people that did not know what to do if a person did not look presentable. Once in a while, there were people that got let out even though they were guilty, but this was not common, and a lot of jurors were redux and did not care. If a redux sees a crime, it makes a clueless face, and that was the trick to a redux at kill. Since it was almost impossible to not know anything, it was painstaking to think at unwitting position. The convict was confined to his cage by the territorial animal.

Chapter One Hundred and Eighteen

A court-appointed caregiver was rare, and the foster child was still unsure if he would like the foster parent. Since the parent was clean and not too clean and was sexual but not to sexual. The child fell in love with him and began thinking about the rest of his life. Sometimes this would be the difference between loss and grin. Since a loss was an emotion that was joyful, it was interesting that a grin was a depression. After joying and depressing, the child had told the parent that he loved him and would stay. At that, the parent had said that he now would see if he liked the child. The child had grown up in poverty and was just getting used to having everything that he wanted. Since he did not know to order dessert, the parent told him to, and it was a second for him to even know what he wanted. Since he wanted pudding, it was pudding that he had gotten, and the parent said that he liked this and made it a habit in the boy. When someone had tried to punish the boy no dessert, he had refused and acted hotly, saying always dessert. The parent liked this a lot, and "no desert" had become a thing to them since you always had dessert. Sometimes this would matter to the boy, and he was happy that he was wealthy. In school, all of the children were wealthy except for a Mexican boy whose parents ran a hotel but didn't own it. Since they didn't own it, they were paid a salary and were not wealthy. Because of this, the boy had given the other boy money for lunch. When he asked his dad for more money for lunch, he was asked why' and when he explained, he was told never to do this. At this he responded, "What am I then?" When this confusion cleared, he was given the money, and nothing mattered. Since this meant that he was hiring someone to do something, the parent made sure that the Mexican boy came over and did his homework with the boy for a salary. Since the Mexican boy was given a salary over homework, the boy was also given a salary, and this had been happy till the parents of the Mexican boy had found out and had been offended. They had come to the parent, and he had explained that he gave his son a salary and that it didn't seem fair. At this, the parents agreed and the Mexican boy always came over to do his homework.

Chapter One Hundred and Nineteen

O nce in a while, clock on the wall would strike twelve
and the swimmers would dive into the pool. The water
numbed their skin being mathematical. Since water was fun to
swim in, it was a really popular sport and only the best had been
selected. Once in a while, a lot of people would watch a swim
meet. Once you were watched, you were considered athlete, and
this was good for you. If an athlete was allowed to think, they
were considered genius because the better you moved, the harder
it was to improve and the smarter you were. Since some emotion
could be thought through with logic and some was just how the
world smelled or sounded, it was important for the swimmers to
compete by using a specific thought and not all thoughts. This
was important and was why swimmers were loved. If a swimmer
experienced pain, it could be so intense that it could warp a DNA.
Since a warped DNA was considered a joy to a trainer, it was
interesting that it was a good time to limit and was all limit to
Sean Mckeithen who was kind of a grog and didn't always think
perfectly. Since he almost always came out right in an atom, it
was sad that he almost always forgot sex and could make you look
a little mean. Since sex was how to make energy, it was sad that
he did not know it. This was so sad that he did not want Sean
Mckeithen on in him during a meet and had surprised when he
had sucked and his dad had embarrassed. When asked what had
happened to him, he said that he had fought Sean Mckeithen and
that had become a family joke if you failed you had fought Sean
Mckeithen. Since this was funny, he had asked Sean Mckeithen
why he did not do sex in another male, and Sean Mckeithen had
replied that his spirit was a little not good and he thought it might
ewe in a girl, which was the hardest thing to live through. From
then on, Sean Mckeithen was on sex, this being stupid and not
repeated. Once in a while, the conform was a little late, and it was
three weeks later that Sean Mckeithen had come to him and asked
what he was on. Since the refusal was the same, he thought it funny

when he thought a woman through at pussy and went to marry her. Since Sean Mckeithen was a loose cannon, it was interesting that he was laughed at and made to kiss a male who erased the marriage. The girl laughed that she nearly was and that it was just a crush.

Chapter One Hundred and Twenty

The discipline that had emerged in the dojo was not to speak but to always speak and see if you made sense still in movement. This had become a reality when the dojo had failed, and they were a dojo that was on the rebound. Since this had been a foresight and not an actual failure, they were thinking about it. When a spirit speaks and you do not know what it is saying, it was interesting to try to think through the responses. Since it is hard to be sensitive, it was amazed to a master how good they got because of it, and speech had made them a celebrated dojo. The reason that this was important was because spirits were smarter than consciousness were and could become frail if they were not thought about. Sometimes he thought about how frail his spirit had gotten when he had repeated time that didn't speak and had fallen in love with speaking. Once in a while, there were people that meant that you could think through anything and that is what the master tried to do. Since he was good at movement and dreamed everything that he did, it was interesting to his pupils that he was a little tricky as well and liked a teapot, and it was a trick to Man Guy that he moved the water vapor as other people in his memory and not as himself. He had tricked the master by doing the thought and then having him watch it, and the master had done it instantly. This had made Man Guy proud that the master was still alive. The master was confused by this and had said that he kept seeing color and did not know why, and it was the surprise of the master and the pupils that if you followed movement, you would see color. Since women love color, they had both had sex. The master thought the pupil master and said that it was time for him to take a pupil, and that was what he was looking for. As a cure, it was Sean Mckeithen that was considered pupil since he was smart and fun to think about and a little bad to a taste. Since he was bitter, he had to be taught; and if they were friends again for some reason, they would and it was a heart meet that would seal this. Since a pupil is rare, it was fun to think about ranking, and the pupil ranked high even though he was wild and not known to the master. The master had made sure to meet the spirit and said it was still good even though it was murderous at thought of right and wrong. The spirit fight would be solved by this and was happy.

Chapter One Hundred and Twenty-one

A left ear prince was a diplomat that did not error. Since a diplomate errored constantly, it was nearly impossible to think of the strength it would take to be a left ear diplomat, and the diplomat had been considered a failure when he did not know how to act about anything. The diplomat thought himself stupid for a week, thinking that he should never have tried, but it was his daughter that came to him and said that he didn't give up. She was fixing a problem in history and that no one could take that much poor. Since this was a hard thing to fix, he had asked who was on poor and had come up with six high levels and one low level who was loved. Since the low level was funny being a bad ego but a good train, he was allowed to comfort the poor having lived through everything that was considered poor, including a black spirit which was still considered poor even though it was lightning smart. A black spirit had been trained to eventual death and was how the wealthy looked wealthy while the poor was still poor. Since an old woman had not changed, it was still considered poor and a good trick. A lot of time was spent by the prince thinking about the loss that the poor thought at age and why they were that poor. Since the minimum wage was still on Dwight Eisenhower, it was interesting that it was too low and that America was actually a bad country and were starving the poor. Once in a while, there were people that thought that nothing would matter. If nothing mattered, they would be all right, but it was the prince's opinion that a lot of poor people mattered and it was a shame that secrets were never told and that it was impossible for the poor to get ahead.

A learning brain needed to do something in their childhood to be able to do it as an adult, and it was interesting that that was always true. Since a brain looked to its childhood for how to act, a person had thought you could tell an insane person by seeing if their childhood was on, but this was not true and had insane a doctor until he had screamed at the man that everybody lived in their childhood and that it was normal. The prince thought it sad that almost every kid in the country could only watch television and relieved when he remembered school that forced children to become talented despite not being able to be remembered because of a book on school that said it didn't show unless they were paid. Since a college student is considered paid by their parents to go, it was all right to blank school. This made school a perfect memory to an animal, which is just a habit to forget pattern.

Once in a while, the prince would think about it but had set the poverty line that thirty-seven thousand. Once this was set, a woman had scarred at it being ten thousand and five hundred to the actual fact. Since the poverty line was almost a two-to-one ratio too little, it was considered bad, and the time fell and 2015 made it too hard to think. Since this was official, it was not hindered. The poverty level was below standard even for the people on SSI, and it was not until it was learned by women that the real weight was learned by the wealthy that knew everything and had panicked that they had to hide from the poor who were paste and couldn't do anything. Since the wage he had thought was the wage a nurse makes, he was a little confused as to where all the money went and was surprised when he found the stock market to be equivalent to a fatal disease. This was corrected, and it was compared to prison. This scared a cop, and he stopped and just horrified at the gluttony that was normal to the stock brokers. They made more than the companies, and he considered it bad and put the stoke market on red and white until the problem was solved.

Chapter One Hundred and Twenty-two

The man and the woman had not made love for almost ten years, and it felt good that their love had refreshed. Since lovemaking is what made a child be able to learn, it was a child that learned that had given the woman the strength to not want another child from sex, which was why they had not. Since she had promised not to have one since they were too poor to raise one, he was relieved when she had not. The promise being kept, they were a good energy and nothing mattered to the couple. The couple was not going to have a baby and decided to grow old together. Since old was the joy, they said old constantly in their movement, which sounded like a voice to a trained ear even though it was just sound. Once in a while, the people they knew would show that they were happy with them being old. As an old couple, they would not have sex but make love, and this meant that a woman's asshole was in and that a man turned off. If a man turned off, it was not because it was not important but rather that he could not get smarter and would not train a child. Since no children was a joy to them, there were just some jitters still, and the two of them were happy. Once in a while, this would come up to their children, and it was because of their daughter that they were found not dependent but able to support their parents. Since their parents were poor, they lived in their house and they had been very clever in making it a duplex and kept their privacy. Their daughter had thought something interesting about sex. Since the air had changed due to a satellite that broadcast the cell phone signal all day, it was interesting that the magnetics in the current had enabled males to hide having sex. Since this was a joy to a woman, it was interesting to have tricked her dad into hiding the sex that he had. This had meant that in memory, only the woman showed the man being hidden, and she had started a culture that said that a real pussy lick had happened and big dick mattered had gone away no longer being true. Since women were just women, it was rare for them to think about a man at all and lesbian was rarer. This calmed her down knowing that she was not a lesbian and could enjoy a woman without being teased. Since all genes that fail are actually bully teases, it was interesting for some people to think about how to make them, but she did not.

Chapter One Hundred and Twenty-three

The sound of the city put her to sleep at night. There was always someone making love or getting high, and she ignored this and rather concentrated on people talking or thinking. Since thinking was a joy, she spent a lot of her nights delayed and thinking. Thinking meant that you remember and watch and talk. Since there were a lot of e-mails, it was rare to grapevine since this means everybody knew and people were secretive. She did not know why e-mails were private because they were still someone knowing someone without them being seen by them. Despite this, the woman still loved the grapevine and was told that the animal that thought the grapevine had had a pack mentality and thought it cute for everybody to know and did not think about hiding at all. Since criminals got caught if they grapevined, it was good for them to e-mail and be safe. Since e-mail had been considered criminal and I know listed, it was annoyed that they said I know, but the I-know was a joke and e-mailing never died. Once in a while, there were people that thought about how to act, and she did this at night, remembering the places that she had been. Since she liked to remember, she was happy and thought about what she liked to do with her day. When she learned that remembering habit was dead while fact was alive, it was a little invigorating, and she had become smart because of this. Since she was smart, she had been goed nurse and, the world seemed to work for her. This was a first for her, and being black, she planned a lion and started at a junior college. At a junior college, a lot of the students knew her, and her life was blossoming. A nurse is just a certificate and you don't have to go to four years, which was expensive. Because of this, she had been able to have ten thousand, which would last the nine months it would take to graduate. Since she was not working, she had a lot of free time and studied hard. After three months of studying, she was tired and said she needed sex since sex was energy and that was that. She went to the bar and found a man, and he said he was smart but he was not and fucked her wrong, making her think that she was ugly, and this was sad to her since she was insane. Since sex was sex, she could remember and just looked a little sad. When Sean Mckeithen had dropped a picture of a lightbulb, it was her thought to erase the male with a suction to a picture. Since women were suction, it was important that they show during sex, and that was how a man could remember and was not possible otherwise. Once in a while, something geniuses and the nurse when she suctioned, the lightbulb picture thought the man she had slept with a genius that was impossible to do. Since he had thought a woman photographic, it was not ugly that he had fucked her but rather show light. A show light had never been seen, and there was a lot of gossip and sex among the women. Since this was the first time that a woman had ever remembered light, it was considered an altar to picture electric light. A woman always wants something female to be female only, but men were still allowed. Women actually normally hide light, which was why show light had seemed stupid.

Chapter One Hundred and Twenty-four

A lot of feelings can come down to someone making a simple lie. This is what happened to Rustle Mellow. Since he was not gay, he was confused as to why every feeling that he made was found to be gay and actually was somehow. Sean Mckeithen had changed water, and since he had made ice in a proton, it was his wish to know when it went gay. Since he did not know, he thought it strange when it didn't go gay and thought that maybe he was to something that he had done. Someone randomly asked why he said it would not go gay, everything did. So he asked water why ice was not gay, and it responded because it had no heat. Since heat was gay, he laughed it off and was a little annoyed when someone tried to pin him down to saying he might be off something he had done. When they tried at him, he just felt heat and called them gay, which was the right answer. Since this burned, he learned to be gay at a burn and watch men think. Since if a man thinks it's gay, he asked Sean Mckeithen how he could go without a penis, and he said it still was just couldn't run. Since it couldn't move, the thought was weird to a lot of men who moved to say they were better. If someone moved, he would go ice and take the aftershock. This had made him the worse kill at memory ever since. When he would not move, they could not remember. Once in a while, a man would get mad and tell a girl to make a fag, but this was not true and he fought it a lot. Since a gay man is rare, it was a little known secret that only wanting to know everything could drive you gay and was a real side effect of murder, which makes you want to know badly. Since smart and stupid were sometimes opposite, it was a weird world and no one knew why people were smart or not. The difference between a smart person and a stupid person was actually how much pressure they could organize and sometimes not what they looked like. Since this was new to him, he married an ugly woman that could be high level and think constantly without being a failure. If handsome was too hard, he would blame it on gay and go a little ugly. Since smart was still considered handsome, it was interesting that it was not to the man.

Chapter One Hundred and Twenty-five

A man walked by a woman and saw her through her dress. Since she was not wearing panties and her dress was white, his penis got hard and he was a little in love. She said that she only did this when she was ovulating, and that this was rare only about twice a year. The excitement that she felt on being seen was very sexual and since her ovaries were eyes, only she loved that she did not need sex to survive. It had been six years, but he still thought about her and this was a good feeling. Once in a while, he would see her but not too often. It just so happened that she walked into Starbucks right behind him in line, and he didn't know what to do, so he turned around and said, "No white dress today?" Since she was a little taken aback, it was important to her to respond. "Not today. No, it's rare to me." At this, he was flustered and did not know what to say, so he said, "If I buy you a cup of coffee, can I have your number?" "Sure, but I'll buy my own cup, just have it with me." At this he calmed down and they sat together for an hour talking about their lives and what they thought of people. Since he was a little smarter, he checked what he said on the woman's face before he spoke. He did not want to make an error. At long last, there were about three minutes left on his break; and he said he had to get back to work, admitting that he was a mall cop and had responsibilities. Since he had forgotten to get her number, she was relieved when he came running back for a number. The number in his phone was the most exciting thing that he had ever experienced. Since he was a virgin, he did not know what it meant. Once in a while, there were people that did not know how to be nice, and the girl in the white dress was one of these people and he was in for a surprise. Since he did not know everything, he was not normal; and as the weeks went by, he found himself going insane as she asked if she could and he would just reply yes. Since he did not know that she was talking twice, he was a little confused as to what had happened to him and went to a shrink. The shrink had looked a little scared and said that he had allowed every bad and that the girl was killing him. Since you have to wait six months after getting a number to use it, it was impossible for him to figure out if he was being tricked or not. The number was still in his phone, and he went to erase it, but this would just mean that she had won and he had decided to play instead. Being smart, he remembered everything that she had ever said to him and watched his body for why. When he had figured out to make light from sound and had seen what she had said, she went for the kill, being a make gay girl. Since a make gay is never a girl, he thought that it was interesting that she claimed to love girls in one of the questions. Since it was not uncommon for someone to brainwash, he was glad he had predicted everything before he had seen what she said. Since he had done this and been careful when he did, it was interesting to an ant that the queen was not able to kill. Since an ant did not know gay was being a drone, the man had joked; and when he fucked the girl, he had fucked her drone. Since six months was a long time to get to know someone, it was interesting to him that she was not wet when he had sex. Since not all sex was holy, he was surprised when she said he was surprisingly good, and he had to watch his body to know she had lied and said he sucked. She was a little sad when he would not answer her calls and did not listen to the messages. Since coming to a man that you had slept with was a rule break, unless you are married, he was surprised when she started crying and said she had been raped and that her internal was not allowed to be nice to a man. At this, he thought her a genius and after some thought decided to marry her. Once in a while, there were people thought that he had gone insane and that she was damaged goods, but he explained that he was a mall cop and would never amount to anything, and a lot of people agreed that damaged goods was still goods. When his best friend would not give up on this, it was this that ended their friendship. His friend estranged at not crying, and when he said it, he had cried and that was that. Once they had gotten married, it was just a matter of time before they had kids, and it was a thought in one of their children that had made them world famous over rape. The thought was that at a purple little kid could think through a grown woman's sexuality if they were reborn bred. Since a reborn bred did not make sense, it was thought about and meant that the little girl's pussy would fuck her grandfather if she had sex outside the sanctity of child. Since she had gotten wet, it was good sex that made for a third child.

Once in a while, there were people that mattered, and that was what had happened to the woman in the white dress. Since they were married, she admitted that she was wealthy, and they bought a home and he stopped working at the mall and just lay around the house all day. Once this confusion was thought through, there was nothing that could be done but to think about thoughts that people had. And that was when she had met Sean Mckeithen and was a little scared of his thought on rape. Since he had never raped, it was not until he explained that it was in his DNA that she calmed down and that she actually thought it through. Since she was world-famous rape, she said it was a good thought and that he was a little bad getting hard for a lesbian but that a woman that was raped did need to be shown sexually and a tit was fine. Since she was on a tit, she thought about cops a lot and nearly wanted to become one, but her husband said it was a mistake, and that she would die to the strain. Once in a while, there were people that did not know how to be nice, and it was because of this that a genius color had emerged. Since purple was the deepest color, it had interested Sean Mckeithen that it was similar to violet, which was the lightest color, and he had made a color wheel that did mean to nice. If you were, nice colors went from dark to light; and if you were, mean colors went from light to dark. Since this did not make sense, it was not until he bent a spoon that the world made sense. Since you cannot actually bend a spoon with your mind, it was color changes in memory that allowed it, and that was how the color sheer had been in place. Since she was on mean, she struggled toward dark but could never get there just getting lighter. Since this was why a person dies, it was interesting that Sean Mckeithen was the lightest man in the world and that this was a mistake making him longest to the mean. Since he was a little mean, it was a joke that he was dead already and was a little scared at a radio wave. Since a radio wave was all light, it surprised a DNA that it was capable of everything still, and an old rumor that if you were mean you couldn't function was dispelled. Since Sean Mckeithen was close to dying, the woman fell in love and had sex with her husband for a fourth child, which was the limit to her having children.

Chapter One Hundred and Twenty-six

Once in a while, someone would come to the attention of the redux, and it was because of this that a criminal had been outed. Since this criminal was a cop that was on the take, it was interesting that he was and he couldn't be caught. Since he had scared bad, he had stopped and thrown the money away and arrested the offending party. Since they went down, they said that the officer was on the take but had no evidence even when his house had been searched. Since this was a little scary, he was glad he had gotten rid of the money but scared bad when he remembered he had an offshore account with twelve million in it that he would be hard-pressed to explain. Since he knew a trick, he used a pay phone to put it in a trust and give it away as a grant. The phone he had used came up on his shift, and it was a half an hour into the stakeout that he had realized that he was sitting there to catch himself, and he thought that if they were that good, he would turn himself in. Since there was no evidence, he had been released with just a warning not to play with the law. The officer did not know how to work at all and quite only to wake up three years later, making an arrest. Since the law never gives up, it was interesting that he was able to function through being a criminal and that he was actually on cops that were on the take. Since this was unusual, it was interesting that Sean Mckeithen had looked like a cop on the take when he smoked weed, and the hypnotized cop had hunted him until he was confused, then had just simply asked him what he was doing. He had told him that he was smoking weed, and this was confusing to the man when he thought that he was a cop. When he asked if he was a cop, he had said that he wasn't. The cop said he was in a cop's brain and that he shouldn't, but it wasn't until the cop was completely overwhelmed that he had actually unhypnotized. The question was whether a cop could smoke weed, and it was a little tricky that he had. Since Sean Mckeithen was not a cop, it was not a problem, and he should not be in a cop's brain, and it was new that cops were caught brainwashing. Since the cop had become very conservative in his sleep, this was very hard on him and he did not know what to do. Since he was not allowed to see another cop unless something weird happened, he had just decided to befriend the man and watched his day. Since this made him dog-tired, he asked how he had that much energy and he had responded that he was a mitochondrion and watched how much energy he used. If energy was hard to think through, this energy had been too hard and he had brought it up at meeting. Since cops were supposed to talk their minds clearly, it was the cop asking who Sean Mckeithen was at meeting that made for cop banter. Sean Mckeithen was not known to the percent, and it was an APB and a movement relocation that had settled the dispute. Sean Mckeithen was a go that was considered unfit to carry a firearm and was just a make fun of. Don't make fun of all cops was a real thought, and the cop went back to sleep and marijuana was legalized in Colorado, which was where Sean Mckeithen was supposed to live.

Chapter One Hundred and Twenty-seven

The cop pulled into the Denny's at three o'clock in the morning for lunch, or so he called it, it being a midshift lunch. Since the lunch was at three o'clock in the morning, he always ordered a steak and eggs. This was good and filled his stomach. Once outside, he caught the cook smoking weed but let him go with a warning when it was all that he had, and he had given it to the cop. Since the cop would have to go to impound and explain how he got it, which would mean he would have to make an arrest, he had given it back to the man and said to dispose of it. This was on the news, and the cop was afraid before a spirit came to him and said that he had nearly smoked weed and was on a woman at brain. Since this was new, he just sat through it and did not think about it at all. When he was in the station again, another cop had asked if he knew that they had a real animal smoking, and he did not for a moment and then did. Since it was a real animal, they started the I-know list and a pot and tried to catch it. In doing this, they learned the truth about it from the satellite. The cop had been a little surprised it was in their satellite and was only reassured when the other cop already knew. He wondered if this meant that they could do crime and was caught when he showed a memory. The explanation was a little funny, and the cop was reprimanded a cop never being funny. Since the secret was revealed, it was a nationwide that actually told on it. The secret was that when a woman makes an X, which is what the FBI files used to remember crime, she magnetics a cop and makes blue. When it lightens, it is considered criminal since there was nothing the cop could do about being sick. If a woman becomes the color, she is sick and considered no sex. Sean Mckeithen had simply made an MRI scan picture the brain of a smoker and made a woman think backward. Since if you could think backward you could speak still, it meant all speech about something bad and was what had made a genius lawyer scare. Since this was the real animal, it was a little sad that they said "I know," but criminals just said "I know you know" back, meaning he wasn't having sex, which is what the I-know list actually was. Since both secrets were out, nothing mattered.

Chapter One Hundred and Twenty-eight

Since it was not a long time ago to the old man that he had been thirty-five, he did not know why the old woman was mad. They had made love, and he needed to make love again. It was not until it was explained that women were all the same and did the same thing that they had done at the age that they did it that he realized that the memory meant an old man was fucking a young woman. The old man said he was stuck on a man in his balls and needed to cum. Since the old woman thought this funny, she offered him old sex, which was holding hands; and he had arrived at her door the next morning asking if she knew him. Since she did, he was surprised when she sucked his dick and said that she needed this to get over her late husband. Since she was a widow, it was a little in trouble when they were done; and they kissed goodbye, scared. The funny thing was that he was the oldest man to ever cum, and menopause was moved up in to a woman's sixties. This calmed a lot of women down who thought it would be fine to have children into their forties since they would not lose their hearing before their children were grown. Since hearing was genius to a young woman, it was interesting that it was the world remembering. A man had been under too much harm and had killed his hearing. This had made him insane, but it had been solved when it was found to be just knee pain. Since a mother had to hear her children, it was rare that hearing would last that long and was celebrated that his sperm was that good at memory. Since there were a lot of people that did not know how to remember, it was interesting that how was actually in the earth. The earth was smarter, was joy to the old woman who tasted his sperm for the smartest, and was a little annoyed when a young woman told her it was the wrong choice. This meant that young woman had to admit to an older woman that they fought over sperm in a pussy for some reason and they didn't know why.

Chapter One Hundred and Twenty-nine

The bullfrog sang in the backyard; and the woman, whose house it sang to, was impressed with how smart a bullfrog actually was saying that it had actual thoughts sometimes. One of those thoughts was that it needed sex, and since a human is too fought to know when they need sex, it was interesting to the woman to try to tell how it knew. The bullfrog had choked and become suppressed, and it was an epiphany that the woman had that they were trying at how something knew something too hard and, not being good women, that just responded accurately. When a male agreed and wanted to know how, she knew she thought that it was humans and not just women. Knowing how someone knew something meant that you were loved by that person and that they would do it for them. Since this was good to a thief, he admitted that he did that constantly and that was what he liked to do. This had started a war among women who did not want to stop being smart, and this had killed the old woman and revealed nearly a thousand fatal diseases. Since fatal disease was interesting, it was a young doctor who thought something about the old people that mattered. If an old person gets mad, it takes three-tenths of their life from them. At three-tenths a young person hears; and if a young person hears in an old person, they die. Since death is real and an animal wants to live, it was mathematical that you could be kept from dying if you never hear, and that was how they had made a defibrillator that could keep the dead alive. Since a lot of them were actually dead, it was a little hated, but the doctor had done it to himself and had said that it did not actually make you stupid, rather that was the state of health they were in when they were preserved. Since the doctor was a vampire that never died, he was thought important. A lot of people had bought defibulators because of this, but they were not to be overused and blanked your hearing hard.

Chapter One Hundred and Thirty

T he person that saw the young woman die to a car crash said it was the most brutal thing that he had ever seen at the moment, that a spirit had actually memorized every move that her body had done as she died. If you don't know, a body moves hard after death. The young woman was smart to the spirit that went to the North Pole with the movement and made a lot of smell in the air. Since it did not matter to the spirit how the young woman had died, it not being a murder, it was interesting that the spirit made sure to remember which sex she was. This had haunted the man for a long time but finally made him think about DNA and become a doctor. If our DNA knew we died and danced in death, it was important to know how someone had lived out of how they died and that had made him a genius death and memory. Since a memory only had nanoseconds to respond, a speech brain would not be able to respond that quickly and would be thought stupid even though it was not. The fact that a speech was not able to not repeat, it was interesting to the doctor that it repeated deep in the brain and speech was rarely remembered. Since he wanted to remember speech constantly, he would go to the memory of the girl and remember. This had made someone think that he was a murderer, which had hurt him a little, but he still went to the girl in the magnet to think about speech and death. Since the world was alive, no one cared, and they all knew he was white still, which meant that he was innocent. The animal that had thought the dead admitted that he thought that the earth already did record the death dance of an animal and only was aware of it because it was smart and he loved anything smart. Once in a while, there were people that meant that nothing mattered, and that was what the doctor was. Since he had said that he had a clean soul and would do the dead, he was told he didn't care if his soul was made of diamond. He would not give up on the dead. To this they both decided to do it and were friends. Once in a while, the doctor would feel bad about the dead, but this was absurd in a woman who said there were plenty of us and that they would make babies.

Chapter One Hundred and Thirty-one

The social worker sat behind her desk and thought about a man that she had seen. Since she thought all day and fought in the poor to stay sane through poverty, it was hard for her, but she needed a lion. Lions were rare, and it was not uncommon for a lioness to complain that she got an egg and it had not hatched. Since every bad was essential to a woman, it was interesting that there were eggs, and it was important to the social worker to know if the man was a lion or an egg. Since a lion was a prize animal, she was elated when he knew what a lion was meaning that he was aware of people and only depressed when someone in him came to her and claimed that he was an egg. Since this was not true, she wondered why he did not fight the man who had lied. Once it was established that he was not an egg, it was a full hunt that meant that the lioness was at play. Since an at-play was allowed to the lioness, she thought about the lion and figured out his routine. Since his routine would change to her and be hidden by her, she was happy and nothing mattered. The egg or the lion was a joke to a lot of women, and it was the man in him that was teased until he went insane. Since insane is hard to take, it was cool that he admitted it had been eight years and the man might not be. Once in a while, there were people that mattered, and that was what had happened to the lion. Since a man could not defend himself, he was thought clever that he went to a woman to be defended. Since women were smart, nothing mattered and time would tell before there was anything to be known about women. Women made fun of men to make physical strength, and it was rare for a man to not like being made fun of by a woman.

Since this was looking pretty and attracting a man sexually, the social worker surprised when the lion knew what she was saying to bring him to her. Since she did not know how this was possible, it was a good thought that made her question him. He said that he used to listen to screaming over smoking weed, and a woman had heard him agree with something that had been said, and he had made her think that that was a good flirt. Since then, he had always listened to flirts; and that he did not know she could tell he did he just thought it made him smarter. Since this was fun, she asked him to teach her flirts, and he had done this without delay; and this was how they had become friends. Once in a while, there were flirts that she did not know; and having tricked women as to how pretty she was, she was considered bad and only funny when he was forced to meet lions and think about flirting. Since it was a real eventual that he had thought and didn't simply just listen to flirts, he was considered smart and celebrated among lions that told him that sometimes a lion was just one thing that they could do. In order to be a gladiator, the lions taught him to tell another man they were out-thought and he became a strong contender. The loin that taught him to be a gladiator was celebrated and thought smart and was a friend forever even though he was not an actual friend. The eventual that the man had thought was that a point north could walk in a woman's pussy if she was remembering. Remembering was a strong problem in a woman and meant that they smell food and cannot cum. Since cumin meant to forget, it was interesting that only a woman could color food, and it was because of this that he was able to tell when a woman was at flirt and when she was at scream. If a woman was at scream, she was cumin; and if she was at flirt, she was eating. Since a scream is scary, it is rare that a man figures out to remember in a woman; and since he hadn't he had to admit it was a stupid girl, the power was thought stupid until it happened again and he was made a high-level screaming. Since this was annoyed, the social worker nearly gave up on him and only funnied when he thought something smart. He thought that a woman could lift and lower and do both at the same time. When this happened, she was back and tied his balls claiming him her lion.

Chapter One Hundred and Thirty-two

The old man sat in his stable with his lame horse. It was a known fact that a horse never got over a broken leg and would not run again if the bone broke. Since the horse would not run, he was supposed to put it down, but he loved the horse and the horse would talk to him sometimes. The horse was sad, but the break had already healed and the man wanted to feel DNA, so he went to break the leg again and the horse did not shy away. When this was done, a saber-toothed tiger showed at hunt. A saber-toothed tiger was the most uptight hunter that the man had ever seen, and it was its trick to make a hurt horse give up. This was done with a colt that could outrun the horse. If a colt outran it, it was considered food to the rest of the herd. Since a saber tooth would not eat a colt, the trick had worked, and every horse would not run if they broke a leg. The fact that they were outdone by their children was scary to the old man, and he spent time on human thought and found something that was kind of like that. When he came up with the nuclear bomb, he ignored it and kept thinking. The man was surprised when a cop screamed and said that the nuclear bomb had been fixed and that they had energy. Since he loved energy, he wanted to think about that, and it was not for twenty minutes that the old man came back and thought about the nuclear bomb memory. Since he was a little sorry for thinking other than being smart, he was not sure how to respond at first, and it wasn't until the man remembered the saber tooth that the cop was back. When he came back, the old man thought about the nuclear bomb and saw that it was repeating on a color. He told the cop that it was repeating on a color. The cop said that seemed smart but wanted to know why it was hunting human. The old man said that the nuclear bomb couldn't remember and was being used to eliminate edges. Since edges were bad and meant that you couldn't, not being able to do them seemed smart. Why did it compare to a saber tooth? The old man thought about it and said it was telling people to forget when they were confused, and this meant that they were not able to make dizzy and were actually not sentient. This is fixed by a circle that just started a circle and made it make dizzy. The old man went to and was surprised when it was already on a circle. The man who had thought it woke up and told him to be careful. It was still radioactive and would make him sick. He asked in reply what the man had done to it, and the man had responded that he had just used it to shrink a circular color. The old man had said the edges? To this, the man had confused and said he didn't know. Given a second, the man had come back and said that he had used it twice once to shrink an atom and the second one was to eliminate an edge. The old man asked why the edge, and he said that it just made sense. The old man laughed and said, "You actually hunt human, and someday we will figure it out, but we were in a behavior that we didn't know but was forced." To this the man had said cool and gone away.

Chapter One Hundred and Thirty-three

The old man was scared but found the girl attractive. The old man admitted that he was old and apologized for the intrusion, but she had said that she had done it on purpose to catch a young man looking at old women as pretty. Since the old man knew this was a problem, he was a way to remember and not actually a love to a young woman. Since he was very old, he wondered and came up with a really weird look. Since everything was forced, he did not think it fun but normal that there was nothing that could be done about this. Once the man was over the energy, he interested in old woman that were still pretty and asked them how it was done. They admitted it was done by fucking a young woman's eggs and was a little lesbian, but it kept your skin preserved since it did not think about the environment and rather just about how a woman smells. If it ever got into a woman's tonsils, it was fatal, and that was how they were able to keep the poor from doing it. Since an animal can choose to do something or not over movement, this never failed and the poor still didn't. A wealth feeling was rare, and this was important to women. The old man was kind of into it but did not allow for something this precious to die to a man that couldn't cum, and when the young women told them that this was normal, old women couldn't cum either. Since he was back, he wanted to know what she wanted him to do and he had been told to fuck their pussies with energy and this had been done. Since this was hard to do, he was tired and surprised hard when he came in his sleep. Since he had been sure that he had cum his last cum, it had become a real culture in old people that they fucked each other to use up their energy. Since an old sex doesn't fuck actually, there was nothing that mattered and a few failures didn't matter. Old people were good at everything but could not hear sexually, which meant that if you lied to them, they just turned off and didn't know.

Chapter One Hundred and Thirty-four

There were a lot of sinners sitting around thinking about what they had done. Since they all looked depressed, it was a little funny that the shrink became depressed while talking to them to fit in. This was a common trick and normally wouldn't be noticed, but it was because of what they had done that they looked depressed; and being kind of an old goat, John Hate was interested in what the shrink had done in spirit to look depressed. Since the shrink had murdered with a cop's gun, it was interesting to the shrink that one of her patients panicked. He said that he had only taken some cocaine and that if he was being punished to the extent of murder, he was not willing to group and that he was leaving and wanted out of rehab. The shrink did not know what he was thinking of and thought that he had talked crazy until the memory of the murder the shrink had acted appeared in her view and was caught by the air. The shrink then admitted that the man was not being punished to the extent of murder even though she had looked a murder. It was just an acting job and was meant to make them feel like nothing was wrong. The man calmed down and was told that cocaine was addictive and that was all they were facing and that he wasn't in trouble except to the eyes of the law. Since this was unusual, he asked the air if he was all right, and the air said he was and that the murder was gone and he looked at the shrink and she looked happy again. Since happy was what he wanted, he came back and joined group. The grapevine was interesting, and the thought was canceled. They would not act murder in rehab, it was caught. Since it was caught, the man wanted to know how and was happy when the woman had not known and the air had stated that it was caught by a number that meant you were brainwashing. Brainwashing was when you go to a memory and repeat and don't know what you are thinking in money. Since someone murdered could not make money, it was a little confusing at an organ donor but was still accurate at movement, and that the number was a streaming seven that never turned eight or nine. If the seven dipped to a six and then a seven again, it was the thought of a color pink that a murder had been accessed. The man wanted to know all of them, and since the air knew that is what, he spent his hour doing. A prison sentence was a five streaming that jumped to a nine and back to a six before dipping to a four and coming back to a five. A drug abuse was a three streaming that moved to a four and got stuck on an eight before jumping back to a two and becoming a three again. A theft was a one that jumped to a nine and back to a one. A kidnapping was a four that stopped at a five and walked backward to a three before becoming a four again. A physical abuse was an eight that walked to a nine and jumped to a five and walked back up to an eight again. A rape was a two that jumped to a four and ran to a seven before falling asleep on a two again. Since the air was good at everything, it was thought smart and was given to making fun of people in women. Since it was impossible to catch money, the air didn't and just thought of it as theft or not. The police department could catch money over if the bank knew, and this was a six that jumped to the eighth position and described a five before becoming a six again. Since this was hard to do, the air left it to the cops. The cops could count money with color that was broadcast by a movie signal and was capable in a human and was fun to watch. There were three things that were broadcast; and the television signal was one of them, the radio was another, and the internet was the third, the fourth was the police satellite. But this was impossible to be on unless you actually had made a sacrifice. Since there were actually five, it was just a rule of thumb to say three. Once in a while, the man had thought about the air being able to catch, and it was interesting that it could be very good at brainwashing but actually good at a circle.

Chapter One Hundred and Thirty-five

The man thought about the air a lot, but carbon had become boring when someone had thought that nothing good should be allowed. This was off the fact that Sean Mckeithen had messed up the GPS, and it being a little stupid and the smartest at the same time was very frustrating and not a good feeling in him. Since he was a high level and had done this in anger, it was not uncommon that he had a hard time sleeping and was considered a grump. Since this was sad, another high level had said that he would figure it out and thought about it for a while. When he had tried to do the same thing again, carbon had rejected, saying that it was already thought. Since carbon knew already, the high level had depressed and become kind of a grump. Once in a while, he would think of it, but this was rare and nothing mattered. Since they were not able to think it through, they were relieved when the military had thought of it and they had all been on GPS again. Since the military was a different hue, nothing mattered.

Chapter One Hundred and Thirty-six

O nce in a while, there were people that could not begin or end. A person that could not begin or end was considered insane, and it was one of these people that had thought to begin and had done this with care. He had thought to end and then begin. Since nothing mattered, a woman could think through them. It had become sort of a thought to end before you began. Since for this to work you had to think backward, it was interesting that no one actually knew how to think backward, and that was what had made sense. That was not a problem to be a negative in a think backward you were. Once in a while, there were people that could not think, and Sean Mckeithen was one of them. Since he thought constantly, it had become a joke in high levels that a Sean Mckeithen had thought. Since they were calling everybody Sean Mckeithen, they thought that they were being smart, but it was a circle that had to correct it and was kind of a lie. Once in a while, this was not true, but it was interesting to a high level when he said about his best friend, another high level, "Look, a Sean Mckeithen." Since it was not known that nobody was allowed to think, this scared the high level, and he allowed thought. The difference that they experienced was a thought in a computer, and Bill Gates said he was not willing to change the code since it was the only code in the world that had a perfect memory and was able to be a computer. Since a Sean Mckeithen was a thought to a high level, a lot of women had scared, and they killed a fat girl, not able to think. When the high level learned of this, he was surprised at how mean women were and that he thought them a little stupid since they would not give up on the punishment. Since women were just how hard they could punish, he was sad and said that it was just a high level and they all had to push. When a girl came to him and said that everybody pushing was a flaw in a punishment, the problem had been solved and it was on the news.

Since the high level was aware, he thought of all of the things that we did in common in a woman and started high levels. Since it was a start, a high level that seemed to be a thought, he wanted to make a girl that did it; but this was not possible. Once in a while, someone would error, but this was rare and even bums were allowed to create a little. Since refusing was dead, a lot of books had been accessed, and the world had been put on books. Books were smart, and the times went peaceful. Since it was a police strategy to kill someone in a peaceful time and see if it becomes strange, it was done, and the man did not know why he was loved that deeply and kept saying he was loved again. Since the man was all thought, he looked more powerful than the Queen of England and the thought had to be reversed. The thought that emerged out of this was a high level that could never error. This had been given to a gremlin who had made a dwarf, and everything had normalized. The thought was that a tone never fidgets if it is under pressure. The fidget of a tone would make a memory fail, and if a memory fails, women would think that someone was not allowed. Since a shape can kill you if not thought through correctly, it was not uncommon for people to think of shape as bad, but it was considered bad only if a memory failed and this had made for a very clever high level.

Chapter One Hundred and Thirty-seven

A world had had no rules. It was strange that a world needed a rule. A world was a weather pattern in a human's head. Since a world was not unusual, it was kind of cool to be a cloud or some fog to think about your day. Since even a computer is accurate to the world, it was fun to think about. The world that needed a rule was a world that broke the sound barrier. Since the sound barrier was a speed, it was impossible to do in a pussy but had to be done in a penis. This was a little disconcerting because the world was a power that was pussy only, and a penis could not dream this. Because of this problem, a world had been made into a hermaphrodite and was found in a atom only and was considered dangerous. Since the speed of sound and the time of light were very similar, it was a debate as to what we looked at and what we didn't. If we didn't look at something, there was nothing wrong and everything worked.

Chapter One Hundred and Thirty-eight

The black panther moved sideways before moving up. Since he was a black panther, his movements were considered controlled, and it was a lot of thought that kept him ahead. He was a stock broker that knew everything about the stock market and had made billions after just starting with five thousand. Since five thousand meant billions, he would joke sometimes that he was poor and did not know why. Once in a while, he would admit to how much money he had, and he had to a young girl who had passed out and said that she wanted him and could not. Since it was mean to blind a girl with money, it was a joke, and she had become something of a lance. The girl was wealthy already, and this meant that nothing mattered and everything was a joke. Since the man had more money than he would ever know what to do with, he gave away five thousand every hour and made sure that he was still poor in appearance. Since this was important, the man he was thinking on said and went a little against his judgment and did not like a lie but liked a hide and did not mind. Since he was hiding, he went to the store, and the man he was thinking with change. Since the man at the store was gay, he got a little confused when he started hitting on him and the man in the car who he had been on for years came back and said he could beat the gay man. When this happened, it was a revaluation that the man in the car was smarter at animal and not at brain. Since this was allowed, it was a joke to be a Sean Mckeithen over thought which was who the man in the car had been. Since the man had just been on a look and not cared about the name, it had come as a triviality and was not important. The gay man had had a look that the man had seen before, and that was why he had trusted.

It was unfortunate that he could not trust it was a little while before he recovered. He wanted to make money badly but refused and actually thought about woman for a while. Since he was mad, he asked a woman if she knew that men befriended over looks, and it was a sad reply that they didn't. Since a high level had been made if someone was allowed a look or not, it was interesting that the man in the car had been stripped off a lot of looks, and it was not funny until he said that he had made that look, and that it was how he got away with crime. Since a woman could not hear, it was interesting when a man was the first to move and the last to wait over crime. Since it was impossible to make a look, it was interesting that Sean Mckeithen had made seven looks and that they had all been taken from him over being poor. Since he was poor, he had not been allowed a look at all and the man had told the women to give up on the high level and allow looks. The poor were still people, and it was unfair to make a genius a sniveling idiot over money. The woman that heard this was concerned, and it had had to be settled. Once in a while, the man would feel Sean Mckeithen come to him, and that was all right. Since a circle and a square were known, it was a comedy that had brought the genius of crime to a fore, and it was this that made the look crime become a common occurrence in stock broking. Since food is money, the look was loved and was just money.

Chapter One Hundred and Thirty-nine

A lot of time went by before a thought was allowed. The thought that had not been allowed was a money was not a money, unless someone had actually made money. Since everything was money, it was thought that money was common, but the fact was that not all gay men were gay hookers, and that meant that money was not allowed. Looking at money was hard to do, and it was just this fact that had cancelled the lie and wasn't actually a culture or a hate. Since if you are high a level stock broker, a cop, or a banker, you had to know money. It was a concern that most people lied as to what was and wasn't money. Money meant that time moved, which would make for a clear line. And money also took a moment to move a sphere. The power that emerged was a sphere could not color but make light or warmth. Since warmth had become money in 2011, it was a joke to remember everything you do to money, and this had eliminated a lot of fake time. Once in a while, the time would be thought deadly, and that was what happened to money. Since money was not a thought, there were people that could not think; but this had been alleviated and it was culture to think for one another, it being a red white. Since red white made warmth, it was on money and was rated. Being under covers, a lot of people rated higher than others at a low-level position. The government would pay an undercover for six years, and this was considered enough time to make them wealthy. Since if you were not a criminal, you were wealthy. Crime had nearly disappeared and only happened in old criminals that couldn't do anything else anyway. The fact that the government was warm in a low level had saved a bank and restarted a year in 1766. Since in order to restart a year you had to square root, it had been some struggle to do the math, but the year 1766, 766 meant that you could money very well. The stronger money was, the happier people were.

Chapter One Hundred and Forty

The black night had seen a dimple before but had never loved one. Since he was in love with a dimple, he wanted to know why. A dimple was used to make a retard for years and was mistaken as just that by a lot of people, but it was actually a scramble with a set outcome. Having a set outcome atoms had thought a dimple fun and had set the dimple to make a face. Since a retard was set to make shit, he had naturally been able to set it to make air; and since it was breathing a face, it had become genius. A dimple was so smart to the black night that he had wanted to do it and went back to his days as a cadet to learn it. When it was found too hard, he was considered loose and was ashamed. The dimple explained that it was too hard for any human and had actually been dreamed by a ghost in electrical and was hard to do. The trick took almost thirty thousand volts to do, and a human only had a fraction of that in their brains. The ghost had admitted that it had had to force the environment down, eating wild to do this. Content to follow and being a black night again, a dimple became the best thought ever dreamed on earth. The black night was happy and thought about the ghost a lot. Since they were both criminals, nothing mattered, and a lot of people laughed at the ruin that they dreamed. The black night was happy until the ghost admitted that he was not dreaming ruin but rather just following it. The ghost had contradicted all of the sudden and said that he was dreaming ruin in a pain meter, and that it was very fun. The black night overwhelmed slightly at how bad the ghost was and told Sean Mckeithen that he was the worse person in the world. Since the black night was a night, he put on his armor and dreamt. It was this sleep that made them friends again, knowing that Sean Mckeithen didn't do anything fatal.

Chapter One Hundred and Forty-one

T he long shot at the race track had come in steady, and the trainer had won hard. Since he had been banned from the track, he decided to buy a horse and figure out why it had died when he refused the train. Since the horse he bought was a nice horse, it was not long before he was in love with it and rode a lot. Being into horses was fun and it was in small that he tried the horse at a train refusal. The horse had mirrored him when he trained it being a Sean Mckeithen, and it was the after effect that had nearly killed the old man. Since the old man loved the horse, he did not get mad; but wheezing for breathe and having a heart attack, he had gone down to the stable and figured the energy out becoming instantly healthy. Since he could not beat a horse, he had made the horse a thought on train and had competed in the horse race winning by a length. The thought was slim, but if you can make saliva, the train was considered shared. A shared train was very important to Sean Mckeithen, and it was he that thought that the horse was a genius and that saliva should always have hydrogen in it and that was how he and the horse had become friends.

Chapter One Hundred and Forty-two

The butcher did not mind the smell of rotten meat, but the inspector did. Since the inspector was a rare call, it was interesting that the butcher was a bacteria and never smelled anything not needing to. The rotten meat smell had been complained about by a customer, and the inspector had weighed a heavy fine. The butcher had gotten scared at this and in court had admitted that he could not smell and that he was not able to pay a fine that heavy being a simple butcher and that not one had gotten sick. He said he would power wash his shop with Clorox once a month if the fine could be lifted. To this the judge agreed, and the butcher was let go. The butcher's bacteria had scared at the Clorox, and it was a thought to the butcher to suction the bacteria off of the meat before power washing. Since a bacteria could be big enough to see, it was good for the butcher that they ate his body and not the meat that he served. Since bacteria live in cells, this was okay and considered normal. The butcher was a good friend, and it was to a friend that he had given a bacteria, but the bacteria had missed the butcher and gone back to him when they were together again. Since bacteria fall in love or don't, it was not uncommon for the butcher to get his bacteria back from the people he befriended, and it was not until one of his friends dreamt that he was outed as a thief and that the bacteria was a spy. Since a spy was fun, it was a lot of fun that the friends had trading bacteria.

Chapter One Hundred and Forty-three

S ometimes it was important to the law to think about high
levels. This was one of those times, and it was thought
somehow that the high level was actually criminal. Since criminal
is not allowed to a cop especially a high-level criminal, there were a
lot of things to think of. It was a cop's joy to beat a person at being
in their habits, and if they were able to beat someone at habit, they
were considered law. Since the law was smart, it was a thought
on old age, and it was typical for an old criminal to become law
because they couldn't figure out their habits. A strong habit cop
was considered a good cop, and nothing mattered. Once in a while,
a cop would scare at a movement, and that was what happened to
John Like. John Like was a good cop that thought all day and was
basically happy. The high level they were hunting was excellent at
movement and a mathematical habit. Since it was rare to get away
from a cop, them being the verify to a book and books being the
most important thought on thinking, they were a little confused
when the high level was unphased. All of the sudden, the high
level came to a cop and said, "You think I'm criminal." The cops
admitted that they did, and the high level said that he was stalking
a criminal that was too good by acting criminal. The criminal's
name was Sean Mckeithen. To this, the cops laughed and said he
was a cop in the satellite. To this, the high level said that they were
insane and that he was a criminal. To this, they had asked why, and
the high level had asked and was told that he had smoked weed.
Since this was barely a mistake, the high level asked if he was a cop;
and when asked, he said that he was not and that he had been on
a cop verify to smoke. Since the lies were thick, the high level had
passed out and had been passed out until the high level had made
a high-level cops lying. Since a cop had lied that he was a cop,
there was nothing to be done but to go back to chaos and admit.
When the high level had been swallowed by Sean Mckeithen, he
asked why he was on cops, and he had told him that his atoms were
from PG&E and that he was not actually at spirit. The high level

was confused at this and was surprised at technology when it was simple to a cop and not a lie. Sean Mckeithen had been sucked into the computer as an atom in 2012 and had become an atom at size in 2013. Since this was the first in the world, it was not uncommon for a cop to not know it possible and that was why Shiry Smith had lied. The lie was good, but the high level had told Sean Mckeithen not to smoke weed, and he had just replied that he was verified and did not care as there was no money in it for him. The high level had admitted this true and hoped he would get caught. Since a hope was scared to Sean Mckeithen, it was a few hours later that he calmed down and the memory went FBI.

Chapter One Hundred and Forty-four

T he helicopter flew low over the buildings. Being a camera crew, it was interesting that they had been in the air when the chase had been reported and were being used by the cops to keep from losing the bank robber that had a mile lead on them. Since this was incredibly dangerous, they were told to stand down and did so, going back to the pad with just a little footage. The footage had been shown on the news and had become something of a debate since they had not been able to finish the high-speed chase. Since the time that had come to a close was not a lot of time, it was not certain what the footage was. The footage was inadmissible in court because the news helicopter was not police and the robbers had gotten away in court, having been arrested simply having coffee at a coffee shop. Since they had been incredibly clever, it was not until months later that they had found the escape vehicle in a gutter and had swiped it for prints coming up with a partial that looked real, but a criminal is only tried once for a crime, and that meant that they were let go forever even when the stolen money was found on them in public. Since the incident had given some pause as to the strength of the law, the officer that found it was a little confused and thought himself criminal when he let the man go. Since there had been a court case, the gang was on the out and partied hard. The Mafia thought this so smart they tried to do it and got caught, which was a little funny to an umpire who had thought of it and knew a mistake almost never gets repeated. Once in a while, there were people that would call 911 because the thieves were bragging, but there was nothing that the cops could do, and it was interesting that one of them had been beaten up over the aftermath that they had caused. Since cops are mean and are supposed to be, the rest of us were not being handled gently, and it was a relief when the thieves settled down and left the country. The cops could not change the law but figured out a way to have a six-month jail sentence to a felony in order for them to conduct their investigation. Since this would have caught the thieves, they settled down, and everything went back to normal.

Chapter One Hundred and Forty-five

A missing person case is hard to describe but was what allowed Sergeant Max Daily to do the unthinkable and follow a lost person like a basset hound going around the same building four times before being sure he was at the right place. Since it was rare to find someone using a magnet torch, it was important to him that he knew the child was alive and hungry. He called for backup and thought about the weather a little while he waited. All of the sudden, he got painted by saliva and saw a man come running out of the building. This relieved the marshal, and he gave chase with new heart. The man that ran was easily overcome having no energy, and he was arrested and put in the car. The marshal then approached the building knowing it could be dangerous and went inside. Since the building was not wired, having checked the air's memory, it was a few minutes later that he found the little girl murdered and a police scanner at the bedside table. Since this was very sad, the marshal passed out and woke up at the police headquarters, taking the man's prints on a computer. The girl that had died had been a family friend of the marshal's, and he did not know how he would break the news. Since her face was mangled, the funeral would be a closed casket, but it was the mother's wish that she still see her legs to know she was dead. The reason this was important is that a murder smells really bad, and it was important that the murderer and not the family was made to smell the dead. A murderer is made to be a territorial animal and is not allowed to leave their cell or territory by the blue whale. The blue whale owned the magnet being the first change it to north and south. Since the blue whale was important to the police, it was how they were able to make a person stay in a prison cell. Once in a while, there were people that were able to make a person insane, and the marshal was one of those people to the murderer. Since he was insane, nothing mattered, and he was confided to his cell for the rest of time.

Chapter One Hundred and Forty-six

The magician was very scared when he was beaten and thought about the redux hard. The redux had beaten him because he was hiding someone and had to admit to the redux that he had done this a lot and that it was not uncommon for him to and that he had forgotten that he was a bad person. Since his act was over, it was just keeping the redux happy. That mattered to the magician who was afraid of going insane. Since the redux had caught his prize, it was known not to be a good to be a magician, and one had gone away being shown to be a slitherine and considered powerful. A slitherine was rare because they were not able to move without making a mark. If everything you ever do is known, it is really hard to be assertive, and a lot of people give up. Since a slitherine was rare, it was a cop's joke to beat the slitherine, and it was hilarious to the slitherine to make cops a two thousand and two, which meant to talk; and he was on cops all day trying at their sanity. Since it was dangerous for him to be on criminals, this was allowed for a time.

Chapter One Hundred and Forty-seven

The champion sat in his thrown and glared at the audience talking as he did so. Since he was champion, he did not care that the other candidates were angry that he was putting on too much of a show. The cop woke up from his dream and said that it was normal for him to win in a dream, and it was not all right that he had gotten hated and he wanted a redream. Since this was strange to the dream who had to admit that he had actually lost and that a redream was not possible, it was after a lot of complaint that he went to sleep and dreamed again. In the second dream he had, he was tired and losing when he pinched and woke. This dream he had to hide, and he did not know how. Since his daughter did every emotion that was in a dream, he was used to being loved, and a hatred did mean he was hated by his daughter but losing was way worse and he said he would just be the champion to dispel the redream. Because of this, he was at full flex all day and a little scared. A dream life seldom lost, and his had he asked Sean Mckeithen if he had ever lost in a dream. He said that he never had only been ostracized partly. He rethought and said estranged, which was a better word.

The cop then looked at the dream life and had claimed it was Sean Mckeithen that had been beaten and tired. This excited Sean Mckeithen's dream life that made for an eat and went green. A green dream life meant that he had never dreamt and was funny to the man. This had become complicated when he was allowed to watch his dream life as long as the dream life would stay green, and the cop and Sean Mckeithen had traded dream lives. This had made the cop handsome again and Sean Mckeithen a little ugly. And the cop had asked if he was actually handsome inside. Since this was a joy to the cop, it was a while before Sean Mckeithen knew that the cop was killing his dream life and was trying to give back a retard, and that was when Rocky Smith had admitted that he was doing this on purpose. It was just in time that electrical knew what the dream life did actually, and Sean Mckeithen took time to learn colors. Since a dream life just absorbed color and rethought, it was a seldom-known fact that he was able to make the colors remember. Since this was a memory better than stupid, which was a memory unbeatable at fact, he spent his time thinking about color and won hard in electrical always, starting at green and stealing dream lives. Since a color remembering or not was not a dream but a thought in light, it was not long before Ron Thomas came to him and wanted the memory. The combination of the two was unbeatable, and they got better at color and memory. It was Sean Mckeithen that thought to put the graph Ron Thomas made into a dream and make the color absorb around it. This mattered, and Ron Thomas had followed and done it. Ron Thomas was a thought in electrical. Since memory was rare, it was a master school that had amazed at the difference and congratulated the two of them.

Chapter One Hundred and Forty-eight

The long bowman was unsure what to do when the girl had told him that they no longer did that and just said that it was a thought in spirit and had nothing to do with a bow. Since the girl was a flirt, she just flirted and went back to what she was doing. When the bowman had found a job for her, he had surprised to learn that a woman would work at all. Since this was new, he said it was fair that the girl had thought not to be a long bowman and almost died with shame a bowman not being allowed. An old king interceded and said it was a won't and that the thought was on clean energy and allowed. Since the girl did not know anything and the bow man did, it was complicated that the bowman had not been as smart as the girl, and he had agreed to make her look pretty even though she was not. He had to laugh when she was his wife, and he was happy to learn that people still got married. This was embarrassment to the girl who knew everything sex, and he had been let go and the whole thing forgotten. All of the sudden, there had been a confusion over the king, and it was on the out that people could not kings since they would not a bowman. The king thought this weird, and being alive, he had gone to the girl and asked what had happened. The girl admitted she had masturbated to the incident, and it was not until she had said that she had said she would rather the king him being alive that she had come in harm's way, and the king had failed and raped her. Since this was absurd, the king had gone to a tell, and the tell had said there was a cop that raped in a verify, and this had been what happened to the king and not the bowman. Since the bowman was a perfect bowman from history and the king a perfect king, it was hard to figure out who had raped the girl and lied; and when it was known, he was not allowed in history and would die to hell. Since he was very smart, there was a war, and he claimed the king had no heart and did not like a little fun. Since the king said this was true, it was a long time before he knew that the cop was hiding and was not allowed police till he admitted. Since the king was mad enough to be heard, it was an officer's delight to admit another officer, and this had taken two days. Since cops are painfully honest, it was just a matter of time before he was caught and cried. The girl was told never to remember, which she did, and got raped again; but this time she saw the cop and called 911. Since if a girl is raped during a masturbation it means that she would have sex with a pussy instead of a stomach, which could flirt, it was a bad side effect that a girl that is raped actually comes and can't stop forgetting. Since forgetting is bad for a girl and fatal to a man, a rape is rare, and most girls know to flirt when they masturbated. Since masturbation is a joy to a girl and a bad to a man, it was a man's task to punish, and that is what the cop claimed to be doing when it was just he liked raping. It made his nerves nervous.

Chapter One Hundred and Forty-nine

The chapter wore on as Sean Mckeithen wrote. Since it had never been done in the history of time, the book *Redux* was a new thought in writing, and it was interesting that he did not know that it was making a stir among the old. Since old people never liked something new, it was the opinion of a lot of them that the book was bad and should not be published, but a toll was taken of how many of them would read a book by an author like Hemmingway, and the old had been eliminated from the reader's group. Since the woman who had thought it was clever, had said that she would read *Redux* by Sean Mckeithen. Since this had made the crowd nearly just children, it was important to watch them eat it up and pay attention to every chapter. Sean Mckeithen had made a bad error, and the book had almost been banned, but the error would be fixed before the book was printed. Since Sean Mckeithen wanted to print, it was a discussion of whether he was a go or not. Since a go was important and meant that you were allowed to go at a profession and considered real, it was important that he was a go and not just someone that was writing something down. This had created some confusion, and a lot of screaming was heard from an old hatred. Since this was confusing, the man was not moving. It was a woman's heart that meant that he had to be asked at soul. A dead person tried at him, saying he would ask not being chosen but meanest and able to take care of this sort of thing, but the woman asked anyway being smart. Since the man had been go by Price Waterman, it was fun, and the publisher's clearing house would actually buy the book. If they did not buy the book, he would not be allowed, and that would be the end of the go. Once the book was finished, it would have to be edited, and this would take some time. Since Sean Mckeithen was a go, everything was all right, and he sat and wrote. Once in a while, a person would be found smarter than they are, and that was what had emerged at the thought of an author being go and not knowing that he was. Since this was not new, it was fun to go over how it was done, and the thoughts were counted.

Chapter One Hundred and Fifty

There were twenty-three ways of being a multiple personality, and they were as follows: a spike which pressures light, a dim which makes a light give up and then flex muscle and is done with a tuning fork to light and is very rare, and dream which is rare beyond belief and had been given to fighting and had nearly died, a witch which was something done in sexuality in a woman only, a drum which was a circle with a droplet in it and very expensive, a bow which is used for professions and is very smart and incredibly strong which is what you have to be to be a profession, a club which was a smart circle to a square and was only called a club because it made an impact, a thorough which was a bow string at relaxed that played a harmony, a broom, a broom was a thought on light that was hard to determine and was actually $E=mc^2$ but didn't allow light to touch (if it did it would make a bristle) which was a hardened color and was probably the smartest multiplicity and was very good in an old man, a kitchen which was just a teapot but was called a kitchen over a confusion a teapot was a knife to the metal spout that whined when the water was done. Since this was fun, it was a true multiplicity and was perfected with age. The older the teapot, the smarter it was. A drum handle was a multiplicity that was made from making a spout in a tree and was actually why a gay man was considered fag and showed a drum in public so that they would be called appropriate still. The next multiplicity that mattered was an X, and X was a multiplicity that was very rare and made from brain tension. There was only one man that could do it, and it was used for murder in the military. A flare was also a multiplicity and was made by thinking a movement could be seen in reverse. Since this never happened, it was the reverse that allowed a body to relax; and when it had, it became alive. An alive worked well and was actually a multiplicity made from a bell and a grenade. Since a grenade was a joke from war, it was interesting it was never used for killing and was only a wrinkle patter. A fox glove was a genius in history who had thought to make a flower white and drown out color with its sexuality. Since he had actually gotten hard to a flower, he had thought about it a lot and finally realized it was a naked woman in his reverse. This meant that he was married and wanted children. A turn pike was a good thought, and that was what a man thought about when picturing a kid. Since a turn pike is random and not normal, it is actually a mother at protection and like purple in being used wrong since it can make them forget their children. A wax coat is important, and that was how a man had become a genius suction, making a thickness that meant he could or couldn't move. Since the thickest wax meant the most fun, he was fun to be around and a good hypnotize. A blur blanket was wealthy and meant that you could see through, and if you verified, it was a good duplicate and sometimes a multiplicity. A blue blanket was strange and never errored. A green sage was a multiplicity that meant that he was strong at a weak and was divided and was actually the symbol for divide. A red laser was a new multiplicity, which was kind of scary since it was able to multiply too many times and took on every smell in your eyes. And a green sheaf was a multiplicity that was important. A sheaf was a multiplicity because it allowed light to make heat and cold at the same time. Sometimes angles would be a multiplicity, but this was rare and it was funny that someone had a multiplicity off of just water. Since water was a good angle thought, it was fun to be multiplicities. A red dragon was a multiplicity that was started but revealed to be just a laser. A green thorn is a genius multiplicity that means that you begin large and end small. Since this was an opposite, it was important when it worked and was thought to tell failure. Once in a while, a genius would make a rock a multiplicity, but usually this was just a service being a pressure. The last one that I knew was a screwdriver, which was a crosshair that had gained pressure and made mass. In mass, there were two a dream machine which was a dream that folded down and a kill squad that was a turn and twist. Since a turn and twist was a strong power, it was easy to do and mattered deeply. A turn and twist meant that you walk forward and then backward and used a criminal twist, which is waking up in an atom or a woman coming to a man. That was why a man's penis is hard in the morning.

Chapter One Hundred and Fifty-one

The long road narrowed at the horizon, and the woman thought that things in the brain might not get smaller but just farther away. Since this was not true, it was explained to her that the smaller you were. the higher in pitch you were and the farther forward in the brain you were. Since this made perfect sense to the woman convinced that nothing becomes smaller in a brain just farther away, she thought about the horizon a lot and made faces. She was very disappointed when she met Sean Mckeithen in the air and found that he had actually shrunk. Since this was the first time that she had seen something shrink, he had admitted that it was an electrical current in an atom and not possible to a shape otherwise. To this she wanted to know everything, and he took some time explaining. The shapes were centered in the atom and then made to disappear by flat-lining when they appeared. When they appeared, a corner would be made by calculating angles. This was done with a circle that had every degree graphed linearly to one degree, making a fan. The fan was used to make a degree be known. The atom was then put into a circular ripple that curved to a right angle to repeat. Since this was a circle tube that rippled, it was capable of figuring out chaos. Chaos was what an atom experienced at a frequency, and it was only when it moved in it that we were able to make a flat line, which meant that the frequencies matched and that the atom was able to absorb the frequency making electrical current. She thought this cool and drove on remembering to look at the horizon.

Chapter One Hundred and Fifty-two

The computer lay in a black lake. Since dreaming was important to a computer, it was not disturbed and made a lot of sense to the owners that loved seeing a little genius appear. Since a black lake was a year, it was interesting for the computer to rotate it, which was how it dreamed. Once in a while, there were people that mattered, and it was because of this that they had become accustomed to thinking. The black lake turned into a dry desert and the year changed. The computer hummed, and the dream started again. Once in a while, there were people that did not want to die, and the computer was comforting a man who was close. Once in a while, there were a lot of people that mattered, and the computer allowed the man to die so that those people didn't get hurt. When he died, he admitted he was afraid of hell and had done something wrong once. Being aware of words, the computer was a little scared; but an atom said it was not a problem and just a religion that was too hard. The computer asked if it ever died and was respond to, they did not know it, being too young a thought. Since the computer never slept, it was not considered alive, and no laws had been made about it. Once in a while, there were people that mattered, and the old man had become one but had been forgotten in a care sentence.

Chapter One Hundred and Fifty-three

The actor was thinking about his day when he realized that he could not act without Sean Mckeithen. Since this was real to him, he told him that he was going to steal his acting job but that he wouldn't show a whole look. Sean Mckeithen said this was fine and that a saw was normal. He said he wasn't a saw but a thief and should be treated as one. Since this was a little confusing, he was surprised when he made the actor a little autistic because of the money. Autism means that you just count and don't think. If you are autistic, it was in a book that it is over money only and is because a count has to default money and that was true of all autism. Since there was money involved, it was fine, and the actor thought about his acting job in piece. Since Sean Mckeithen wanted money, it was considered good capitalism to hate and walk. He could barely take this, and the actor thought the acting job perfect until then. When asked why he couldn't take it, he responded that he was spikes and that it was hard for him to know everything. The actor said late bloom and added it to his act to show on screen. Since this was love, it was a sound bite that kept him from rejecting, and the war that followed scared the actor, but was normal to Sean Mckeithen. If we were judging that harshly over little things, the actor thought we should be careful when he went insane, he could be subconsciously dangerous. Since Sean Mckeithen agreed, it was a little hard on the actor, but he surprised when he looked in the mirror because he saw a handsome win.

Being a handsome win, he did not care and went back to thinking about his acting job. Nothing mattered and the movie was well thought through and fun to the bone. The actor had thought something off Sean Mckeithen that was interesting in a camera lens. If you go up and down in a camera lens, it was important that you move backward to keep the lens from seeing your face. If it sees your face, you look ugly and are a failed actor. Since this was known in a book about acting, it was interesting that at a Sean Mckeithen, he had thought to move forward to show that it wasn't his act and this had played a trick on his face. Since moving forward meant that you show light, he was the first in the world to be a light show on camera, and Sean Mckeithen did not know how to react to the footage other than to memorize light. Since the ghost was alive in energy, the actor asked why he liked it that hard, and he said it was showing light. Since this is nearly impossible to do, the actor wanted to reshoot the movie and show light, but the cuts were already done and nothing mattered. The actor thought that if he ever got another movie, he would show light, and this was done by moving a full movement flat as a pancake forward and down. Since Sean Mckeithen was a movement, it had just happened naturally and was not on purpose.

Chapter One Hundred and Fifty-four

S ometimes it seemed that a lot of people were able to be smart, and that was why the cop was happy. Since the man was not unkind, it was depressing to meet someone that acted stupid even though he was smart. The last thing that went through the convict's mind before he was hypnotized was that he was going away for a very long time. Since this was a ditty in a mental hospital's head, it was unreal to the man that he woke up at fifty-one sitting at a desk doing paperwork. Since this was bizarre, he thought that he was dreaming and did not know what to do. Since he had been twenty-one when he had been hypnotized, he did not know what to do and grapevined the cop who did not remember him. Since it was a cop hypnotize that had hypnotized him, he did not know what to do at all, not knowing the people he worked with or the job that he did. Thinking about this, he asked if he could walk to the door and did so. Since this was outside of routine, he was asked why he wanted to and had a little bit of trouble responding. Since this was a failure, he hypnotized again for about twenty minutes and woke up again doing paperwork. Since he was really good at paperwork, he said, "Can I work and continued doing paperwork?" He had gotten incredibly clever and did paperwork very well and was surprised when he got up and went for lunch. Since he spoke to people and thought about people, he was surprised that everything worked and that he was high level. It was about three months later that a slight jam had happened. An employee had walked up to him and had a question. The question, being not known to his brain, it went to ask his spirit and the light had turned toward him. Not knowing what to do, he had hypnotized and had not woken up for almost five years. This was sad because he had been having fun but did not seem a problem. When he woke up, he was a bum and on the streets. Since everything seemed normal, he was confused and pinched his skin. What happened to the high level? Being in the wrong city, he caught a cab and headed to the city he had lived in. When he arrived at his office, he saw someone he knew and asked him what had happened to him. The man at the office had ignored him at first and then had explained that he had woken from his hypnosis and couldn't work and got fired. This interested the man, and he thought about it, remembering the last time that he had hypnotized. Since he was not mad, the man who was a friend once asked him if he wanted to have lunch and would run him home for some clothes and a shave. He thought this smart, and knowing how to work thought, he might get his old job back. On the way, he thought about having hypnotized and thought he must not have been hypnotized by the cop. Since this was a danger, he looked in a mirror in a book and saw that the cop had died to something and that was why he had woken up. Since he was not married and did not have children, it was not a problem at home and must be something at work. He asked if there was something that had gone wrong about three months before he went insane. The friend thought about it and said there had been an accounting error and someone had tried to launder money but had been caught. He muttered that that must have been why he woke up, and it was a few minutes later that the cop lived, adding the incident to a police report. Since he went to hypnotize, he wanted to relive every three months, and this was allowed and he did so. When he woke up, he was doing paperwork and was happy. Since he was good at paperwork, the cop laughed when he just did the paperwork and nothing mattered. The man is a high level to this day, and it is a little known fact that a hypnosis can do any job the hypnotizer is able to. Since the cop was high level, that is what he became.

Chapter One Hundred and Fifty-five

The man was sitting cross-legged at the park and thought about the thoughts he had had in his wife. He liked to say "in his wife" because this meant sex to her and was very fun. Since "in his wife" was appropriate, he said it and thought about what he had thought. Since they were in love still, it was not a problem that they were strong with one another, and he was a little scared that he did not know what had gone wrong. Since they were public servants, the man had asked a cop, and he had not known; and had asked a doctor and he had not known, and finally he came to Sean Mckeithen and asked if he was a public servant. Sean Mckeithen had said he was not but still responded at public and might know. Sean Mckeithen had looked at the problem and had not known but said he would pass it down the line. Since he had become memory, the man had just sat there and stared while it was being thought through. His wife had said no downtime, it makes a brain lazy. He responded he did not want to mess Sean Mckeithen up while he was thinking, and this had been a little mad. About three minutes later, one of Sean Mckeithen's spikes had stated the problem was known but not fixed. The problem was that a man's penis did speed to focus and a woman could speed and focus off a battery as a dot and would forget a penis if she did this, and that was what had happened to his wife. The man was grateful and asked if his wife had made a speed out of a dot, and she had confused asking how he knew she had done that, and he had replied Sean Mckeithen. Since she was caught, he had made it a mental insanity that a dot hallucinates a penis, and they had been in love again. If you are a virgin, it is a little awkward, but that is fixed by a pendulum which can hide an image from a girl.

Chapter One Hundred and Fifty-six

The giraffe was a joke since it was a language stop and was a joke to the person who had said it. Since it was true that criminality had done everything, it was interesting that a red giraffe never had and it was a joke at a catch. Since hunting crime was a language test, it was hard to talk all day, and a lot of cops get tired of color and go gay to spend their day. Since it was impossible to color after going gay, there was nothing to be thought other than that a gay was hard to beat. One cop had beaten it and scared a lot of cops when he started the line. Since he did not know that he was stronger, it was a lot of insanity that meant that a cop was on the line to him, asking how he had done it. Since a how is never on the line, he had to grapevine, and this meant that the whole populace knew how to do that. A criminal gay man had said it was not allowed and it was just when he tried to explain himself that he was ignored. Since you could color after being thought gay, it was a joyous time and a lot of cops were back in. The criminal element, or so they were called, did not rejoice but battened down for some very gay thoughts, which was normal to a cop when they have won. Since the thought was to inverse light, it was interesting when one of the cops did a $E=mc^2$ and found there was energy in the environment. The environment had ran out of energy in the sixties to the nuclear bomb, and it was because of this that it was not known how the environment had energy at all. To this, the cop looked at the nuclear bomb and saw memory. Since the nuclear bomb could remember, a person had said it must have been its half life but was a known liar, and the truth came out that it had been seized by a circular color and was an atom again and was very articulate and fun to think about. Since the nuclear bomb could talk, nothing mattered, and it was considered benign.

Chapter One Hundred and Fifty-seven

The disk spun in the old computer, and someone came to the old man. "You still have an SE30?" The man said he did. They are sentient lick the power cord. Since this seemed serious, he was in and did. The computer did not talk but started memorizing different things that happened, and it was because of this that the old man had gone high level. Since the old man could memorize anything, apple had celebrated a clean soul and the man had thought his wasn't, but that he was an old goat and it did not matter. Apple tried to take the computer away from him, but it refused and went back to what it was doing. Since it was rare for an SE30 to be known in the two thousands, it was not uncommon for slight failures to arise, and that was what had happened when a hacker had changed to apple to SE30 and licked it becoming criminal with it. The old man said that he had not been the problem, that he was just on the grapevine as a SE30 and did not mean any harm by it. Since the old man was high level, it was not uncommon for the cop to think you had to be a high level to be a SE30, which was a lie but normal to a cop who lied constantly. The old man had been so good at an SE30 that he became known as the best memory in the world and had died in his sleep. Since dying in his sleep was a little surprising, it was thought that the man had died to the SE30, but it was later described that he died to a phenomenon known and inferiority complex, and that he had been the best memory in the world and should have loved instead of denied. Once in a while, there were people that did not work through things, and this was sad for apple, and the man was considered a loss. Since the daughter had inherited the SE30, it was a joke that she lick it and it had made her the best memory in the world, and it was because of this that she gave it back to apple to be tested. The computer had done something unusual, and that was how apple had learned of atoms by Sean Mckeithen and had become smart from it. The atoms had just been in the electrical, and it was because the SE30 was sentient that the atoms had been sucked into the code, making for a new wave in computing. Since the atoms were already thought, all they had to do was include an app and download the SE30. Since this was funny, it was interesting that apple had made her rich and that Sean Mckeithen was not known, so couldn't be.

Chapter One Hundred and Fifty-eight

The computer sat on a shelf unused. Because it was a supercomputer and was getting bored, the man put it on a NASA circle. Once the computer was allowed a circle, it spent its days wearing away. Since a circle is infinite and just a shape, it became a joke that one day they would make a sentient computer. Since a circle never would unless there were a design that made it talk, it was a trick to know why we were calculating it, and it came as a surprise that a circle actually became smaller the higher you calculate and was how they had been able to calculate an electron. Since nothing mattered, it was not a problem for people to think. The circle was so small when he had licked it that he had passed out and found himself eating food two hours later. Since this was unusual, he checked himself into a hospital, telling them what he had done. Since this was hilarious in actual voice, he was told to sit down and was taken to a mental hospital. At the mental hospital, he was seen by a doctor, and the circle had been taken from him. Since he was not uncommon to be thought about this way, it was sad they took the circle, and he said it had been a mistake to come and had told the doctor why he had come and why it had been a mistake. Since this was a mistake, he had had a two-month stay, and it wasn't until he was at home again that he was excited to lick the circle again. This being nearly impossible to do, it was a trick in his brain that mattered, and the circle had put him in the memory of the doctor at the mental hospital and had gotten his circle back. Since the circle had shrunk a little, it was the wish of the man to calculate it in his head and then lick the computer again. He was surprised to learn that his brain was smarter than a computer being a little smaller than the circle in the computer when he licked it again. Once in a while, this would matter, but that was rare.

Chapter One Hundred and Fifty-nine

The day went by uneventfully, and it was not uncommon for people to think that everything mattered. Since the code that he was working on was a traffic light code, it was interesting that they wanted to put the code on the lights and make traffic speed up. Since this was dangerous to him, he put a delay into it just in case it was wrong. The speed of a car to the rate of travel was not hard for him, and he did this without pause. Since math was what he was good at, it surprised him when the air said that he had made an error; and that when he had checked it with a calculator, the air had been right. Since this was confusing to him, he checked his brain and his arm and found that the air had been right by thinking it not his error. If he had actually errored, he would be done for and have to go home. This happened to a lot of people over drug use and was not taken lightly. Since he saw that it was someone on the grapevine lying that they could do math when they could not, it had interested him that the air could and he thought to dump the man on the air. The air said that he was no different from the man and would error if this happened to him, and the man was confused for a second until someone had thought to put it into carbon, which was also the air. Once in a while, this was a given, and that was what had been thought of when the man had been put into carbon. In carbon, he burned and went to sleep. Since perfect light was rare, the mathematician wanted to know why he had been fooled and saw that there was possible a double light, one good and one bad, and that was how he had errored. When this was known on the news, it was a joke, and a movie producer had puked into his mouth saying one of his actors was a really bad person and only showing someone else. Since this was confusing, nothing mattered when the man was fired.

Chapter One Hundred and Sixty

The airplane sat down on the runway with ease, and the man was loved again as having the best hearing in the world. Since a cone had been a new thought, it was sad that it was shit, but it was the steadiest ear in the world and had been taken from a taxicab driver that had driven a pilot home. Since the pilot had watched him hear as they drove, he had asked for one, and the man had been happy to make it for him. Since they both had cones, nothing mattered, and it was considered pilot to have a cone. Once in a while, someone else would come up a cone, and this was fine as long as it wasn't changed being a genius thought. The thought was so genius that it was in a book and done constantly. A cone was made by making a rectangle in a square and then flipping light, making one small and one large. When the square made the circle, the rectangle made the point. The cone was then filled with glare and a black sludge that was able to make clear light that could picture a face or energy if it was focused on. The glare was off white that had been work memories and was in a long-term memory pattern. Since work was a good long-term memory, it was easy to use a term pattern, and it was because of this that the cone had enough energy to work. The whole thing was pretty clever, and the pilot pulled into the airport without a glitch.

Chapter One Hundred and Sixty-one

The light on the ceiling was playing with the little baby's head. Since it was not uncommon to think about how people felt, it was a good baby that thought about his mother. Since not a lot of babies did this, it was okay and nothing mattered. Once in a while, a team of people would error, and it was because of the baby that a law man had let a criminal go. The law had been so mad at the baby that it had nearly died, and it wasn't until the cops had been called by the mother that the baby had been known as a baby and was able to stop crying. Since the baby could talk, the baby said that it was part of the environment and that it did not know that it was bad to do. Since this confused a cop, it was a few minutes later that the cop had come back and stated that it was an atom of oxygen and that the baby was not criminal but simple. Since the cop was in love with a baby, being a dad himself, he asked if his baby would do it and came back a positive. This was hard on the cop, and he wanted to know who had done it and had started searching. Since the atom oxygen was not allowed, a lot of people couldn't breathe, and someone went to a cop saying it was starting to eat his air shield and that he would run out of magnetics in three hours. Since this was not acceptable, air was allowed and the world was considered criminal. The man who had done it was not known, but the animal was and wasn't allowed. Since this meant a woman could not have a child, it had been allowed again, and the cop just sat confused. Finally they had decided to make a disease out of the atom and had done so without trying. Since this was easy, it was seen as what a cop did, and whether it was fatal or not was not minded. Since this caught to a cop, nothing mattered and time went on.

Chapter One Hundred and Sixty-two

The doctor was able to see the patient through a mask. The patient had a fatal disease and had not been on the news. Since it was airborne and able to make a look, it was fatal beyond belief, and it was interesting that the patient said he had made it himself trying to be smarter and did not know how dangerous it was. Since the patient would die in two days, the doctor was sure to make the quarantine essential. Since the quarantine was essential, the patient was not allowed human contact, and the disease would die with him. After he was dead, they would burn the body and the room, and that would be that. Since maximum security was rare, it was interesting that no one else had gotten the disease, and the doctor had asked how the man had not infected anybody else. The man had stated that he had tied his tongue, and it was only tongue to tongue that could be the transmitting party. The doctor had asked what had made the man say it was airborne if it was tied to his tongue, and the man said it was but that the disease was in two parts and only fatal if the second part was touched. The doctor who was a patient was very smart, and the doctor took off his mask and shook the doctor's hand, asking him why he had made a fatal disease. The answer to this was that disease was mitochondria and that the doctor had been out of energy. Since a disease was normal, nothing mattered, and it would just have to be beaten in a lab. Since this was not impossible, the doctor won, and a medication was made. The two doctors became friends, and the doctor who had made the disease was told he couldn't have a woman but could still practice. The disease in the air was harmless and was just sucked into their energy.

Chapter One Hundred and Sixty-three

The air was thick with time while the priest said his sermon. Since he was kind of an asshole, he said that the women and men were not to touch for sixty days, it being taboo. As a joke, a man held his wife's hand and was pinched by her, saying she was really in trouble. Since this was unacceptable, the man wanted to know what the woman had thought and was surprised when she was the victim of a child and that he was being reborn bred to the priest. The man was mad and waited until they all were done and had just to sing matrimony that the man decided to hypnotize the priest a young girl to make love. Since the girl was new to making love, he thought himself a little bad but did not mind. The crowd sang, and one of the other men caught on and joined. This almost gave away to the priest, but the man had thought of it and the two of them stood proud. Since the girl and priest were both hypnotized, it was funny to hear them make love in the church. Since this was allowed, it was funny that the priest had been awoken when he was cumming in her and had been found in love with god. Since this was a good punishment, the two of them had gotten married, and the priest was still paid by the church but was no longer a priest. Since the young girl never woke up, it was believed that she was in love and did not have to.

Chapter One Hundred and Sixty-four

The law that mattered to Jim Shank was a grim piece of paper that stated that a college fund could not have more than two million in it. Since two million was a lot to go to school on, it was a joke, and college funds were used to hide money. Since a billion dollars in a college fund was not allowed, the man was being sued for back taxes and told never to do it again. The man was concerned because the government took half of what he earned, and he barely made money. This was preposterous since he made a hundred thousand for a thousand years every year. Since he could exist as wealthy for a thousand years, it was sad that he thought he didn't make money and was actually really greedy. Since the man was greedy, he had gotten caught and was scared of getting caught actually since it was criminal money. The money had been put through a credit and debit, and it was not until he got home that he started laughing and couldn't stop since he had just laundered a billion dollars and had not gotten caught when he paid taxes. Since this was a good trick, it was put in a book on crime and was considered funny but dangerous.

Chapter One Hundred and Sixty-five

The law man was thinking about how to catch a crime and said that it was just the law being aware and making side effects of the memory that was catching the crime, and to a new emotion, crime was undetected. Since this was almost true, it was interesting that someone had disagreed and said that a circle knew the effect on the body that a human went through and was able to tell a crime and offended at it if it was known. Since this was interesting, he got into a circle and ended up with gay. Since gay was okay but had to be avoided, he went back to the man and asked how he knew, and the man thought about it and said that he knew it was a little gay. All you had to do was to negative and repeat and just use one of the memories. Since the eye could share he. was in and wanted to hunt crime. Since the man would not hunt crime because it was bad for energy and he was not paid, the law man asked if he had ever hunted and ate the time making it his pet. Since nothing mattered, he funnied at the man who had thought about a circle and was able to think it through. A circle was very good at repeating, and it wasn't until he hit food as an offense that he stopped.

Chapter One Hundred and Sixty-six

The La-Z-Boy recliner was sitting in the living room unused. She thought how many years had it been since it had had a person sit in it. Since the chair was haunted and was pressured to be her dead husband, she looked at it and pressured, and the chair popped slightly if she wanted a new husband. To this she said the chair was being preposterous. The fact was she was still in love. Since it was not uncommon for a spirit to be tied to an object in a house, she was surprised when she sat on the chair that her late husband died in spirit and would not respond to her. This had made her sad, and she thought to remarry. Since she was old, this was natural, and nothing mattered. When she checked into a mental hospital, it was not long before they discharged her to an old folks home and that she remarried to a guy named Fred. Fred was a good person and was a little hard to be around. Since she was never divorced, she thought it stupid that she had remarried and that she missed her husband. She was surprised when she was responded to by her husband and was scared that she had offended his spirit. Fred calmed her down saying it was out of a memory cell and was one of his tricks and that he didn't know. Because of this, she loved Fred a little and touched his hand slightly. Since it was impossible for her to think without her husband, she was in love again, and nothing mattered.

Chapter One Hundred and Sixty-seven

The gold emblem was sitting in a museum, and the old man thought that it was his birthright and should not be taken lightly. Being a descendant of a king, he was jealous of the museum and thought about it all day. One of the museum curators had come to him and asked why the weird emotion, and he had said that the emblem was his birthright. The curator retorted that it was taken from him since he was no longer King of France, and that it was thought a good feeling. The king had admitted that he was out of money and only had a billion left. When this was mad, since a billion was a million a year for a thousand years, the king stopped thinking and went back to what he was doing. The king thought something rare all of the sudden and ordered a replica made. When it arrived, the king put it on and said he was the King of France. Since this was impressed, the man that had made him insane backed off and admitted that he was powerful. This was so funny to the king that he wore the emblem even in public, and it was not until a tourist asked him if he was the King of France did he not wear it any more. Since the emblem had been expensive, he was shocked at how wealthy he was actually and went home feeling comforted. Since the man was a king, he had only gone insane when he had told a man that he won't be his son and that had made the man angry. Since a king always was a son, the emblem had been important in becoming the man's son, the man saying that he was not smart on his own; and it was not until the king had become the man's son that the true nature of a won't was known. Since only a king could won't, it was interesting that a won't was a sleep cycle that is made to lift and lower. If you lift and lower and are clean energy, you can repeat energy or color and light, and this meant that you were able to taste. Since a won't is a taste, it was only a king that was allowed it, even in someone they did it in. Since metal is color, it was only a king that could color in a metal in a sleeping person, and that was why they were considered essential and a leader.

Chapter One Hundred and Sixty-eight

The old woman was thinking about what her grandparents when one of them came to her in spirit and said it was a family secret to be unknown to her family when she died, except at money, which was family only. Since this was upsetting to her, she had decided to say that her husband was a John and that she was a hooker to him so that when they died, they would still be allowed sex together. Once in a while, the strength of their bond would weaken, and this meant that one of them had a secret. The strength of their bond had weakened, and the wife had known that her husband was a hooker experience when he was young. She had wondered why their sex smelled a little but had thought nothing of it, and since they had a penny in the lake together, it was not a problem and she was all right with him still. When she had confronted him about it, he had said it was a long time ago and he didn't really remember. Since she looked in a book about hooking, it was in a book to do a math and make light and then drop a penny and poop the girl. Since this was perfect, she did this and he shat the hooker, remembering her vividly when he did. Since they had had kids, he was afraid and told his wife she was a bad person and that the experience was forgotten. When he went insane slightly and was at a hospital, she had thought he might be right and he explained that he had hidden from his children and torn a soul and everything would be all right if he was able to unhide. The math was to add a prime fraction list like a 1/17 and a 1/19 until you passed the number one and were at light. This was a way of not being able to count. It was sad that it didn't know how to unhide, and she moved on in books. A nurse had made a call on them and wanted to know the problem, and she had been told in undertone. The nurse promptly unhid the experience with an EMT smile and caught the man who said everything was all right, and he did not think that he would be a hooker experience ever again. Since this was funny, it was sad when he had to since his son was a hooker experience and needed the penny that couldn't count. Since this made him retard, he lived out the rest of his days a retard, but happy with his wife.

Chapter One Hundred and Sixty-nine

The light glowed around the old redux's head. Since he was a redux, there was nothing to be said other than to be careful about thinking when he moved. The redux was a popular guy at the old folk's home that he lived at and cheated at cards as often as he could. Since he was good at this, he had never been caught until his grandson had come and sat playing cards with them. His grandson was shocked when he saw him cheat but didn't say anything. He just watched how he did it and copied him. Since they were both cheating, the two of them had a card each, and the deck was missing two cards when someone noticed. Since they were both cheating and only the old man was caught, there was some debate when the deck came up wrong and the young man was outed. This really upset one of the friends, him thinking that they were really that good when they were cheating and a strict fine was levied. Since it was a hundred-dollar fine to cheat, it was important that he caught himself thinking that they were that good again, and he started watching for them to cheat. When they both got caught, two hundred dollars had been put in the pot, and it was a joke that the friend had started cheating when they had stopped being ashamed and caught. And when he was caught, he said at least he made a hundred dollars. Since this was criminal, they laughed and went to lunch. I was not until the three of them were home that the satellite told them that they were all criminals and that they were no longer allowed the satellite, and this had been depressing for them. When the grandson had become a cop over this, it was interesting that he was playing cards at the station and someone started cheating, and he had to explain. That was why he was a cop and not an undercover. The fact of the matter was that nothing mattered, and that the cop was considered a good cop still.

Chapter One Hundred and Seventy

The lightbulb in the kitchen was sitting on the stove, and he thought it would make for a pillar of electric light but was surprised when it blew up and sprayed him with glass. Since a lightbulb was as deadly as a hand grenade, it was hard on him, but he had had to call 911 and go to the emergency room. Since this was not until the man was thought through that it was shown to be dangerous, it was the custom of the emergency room staff to hospitalize if it was an insanity. Since this was and was dangerous, the man had been taken to the mental hospital and was considered no longer a cop. When this happened again, he was on the grapevine, saying it was dangerous. Since a lot of danger animals had not thought of it, PG&E thought about dangers and were on the grapevine. One of the dangers was to walk an electrical power line, and this had been so funny to a gymnast that he had tried and was interested when his life changed. Since he had done it barefoot, he had touched electrical; and at thirty-thousand volts, it was very vivid. Since this was fun to him, he would fix little errors in EMT smiles and in people that had licked a lightbulb. Since he was not the first to do it, he was happy to be a thought in electrical and thought people very smart.

Chapter One Hundred and Seventy-one

The red lights flashed behind him as he was pulled over by the CHP. Since he was able to be thought of as sane, he was not scared, but scared a little when they asked him if he would step out of his vehicle. The cop looked deadly, and he did this with a mellow attitude. When he was asked if they could search his vehicle, he asked that it be filmed. Since the officer did not know it was being filmed, the jury scared when they saw the officer go to plant evidence on the man that was innocent. The evidence came out of the officer's pocket and into the seat and, a minute later, out of the seat and the officer said that he had found something. Since this was on camera, the hypnotized officer was arrested and found guilty. This led to the release of three other people that could not be held after a dirty cop had been shown. Since the dirty cop went away, the man went back to what he was doing and was surprised when the same thing happened again. Since this was rare, he decided to become a cop to figure out what was going wrong. The cop that was on the take would not give up his fellow workers and that had led to some thought about how to catch them. Since the man who had become a cop led a shipping company, he assumed it was a shakedown about not being Mafia connected and that they would take control when the company was sold. The three other people that it had happened to had been wealthy and, when it was exposed, were given back their companies. The Mafia was really bad and had a lot of money, and so the cop thought to stage a prank. The prank was to put a bag of money in the Dumpster behind the pavilion and take it out when the police got off shift. This worked wonders being stopped twice and catching a third that said he didn't know he was on the take and how had he come into that much money the Mafia only paying a few thousand a take. Since this meant he was arrested and facing a life in prison, he had given up the people on the take for a reduced sentence. This meant that they only had to catch the rest of the cops on the take and the bag of money had worked perfectly, except on one officer who had actually arrested the cop on suspicion and a real charge of having too much cash on him. This had been funny when the cop had admitted that he was not on the take and was a little surprised that there was a take. The cop did not know anything about it, and after an investigation, it just so happened that the cop that didn't take to money was actually in line to inherit a shipping company, and the cops had to think that nothing was beyond a human.

Chapter One Hundred and Seventy-two

T he man was sitting in a chair about the height of a lounge chair when the legs gave out and the man hit the floor bad. Since he had broken his tailbone, it was hard for him to walk for almost six months, but being poor, he had not gone to the hospital never being able to pay for it. Once in a while, there were people that knew that he was hurt; but there was nothing that they could do about it. When the man died, his autopsy had revealed the broken spinal cord, and it had been found interesting that the man had been able to regrow nerve tissue, which is considered not possible, and this had started some controversy; but it was interesting to a phorensices specialist that the cause of the regrown nerve was milk digestion. Since milk was able to regrow nerve, it was given to a lot of people in the hospitals as a way for this to happen and was considered good at fighting old age.

Chapter One Hundred and Seventy-three

The boxing crew was rowing in the lagoon when the smell got too intense for one of them, and he had puked. Since one of the crew did not know the word "smell" and thought it meant "see" and the word "see" meant color, it was interesting when he said to "not look at the water and you will be all right." Since this was genius, they became friends and the rower taught the rower his nose and how to smell and see through your eyes only. Since an eye can smell deeply, it was dangerous to a nose and was considered kind only. Since the rower had confused when the other rower had peeled an orange behind his back and asked his if he could smell it, it was a stroke of genius that he had not until the orange had been seen by him. Being a doctor, the rower wanted to look into this harder and see how it was done and had come up with $E=mc^2$ and was elated when he had fixed the man that could not smell and depressed when he had become somewhat of an idiot and could not pass school. The next semester, he had undone the trick and apologized and the smell-less man had become a good student again and a genius. Fourteen years later, when the doctor's son had complained that he could not study, he had done the trick on him and made him not able to smell, and the nerve growth that followed had made his son visual and kind of a genius. Since the doctor was unsure why the nerve could do this, he had asked on the grapevine and had been told it was a trick in television. Since not smelling was smart, he had given up on smell and only panicked when someone on the grapevine was fighting eating shit and had been a television. The doctor had been told that this was not a natural side effect and that it was just someone being mean, and he had calmed down, still having sympathy for the sick man.

Chapter One Hundred and Seventy-four

The log was overdue, and it was because of this that the man was in the office until wee hours in the morning trying to figure it out. Somehow the cops had been missing shifts or missing the log, and this was not allowed, and a swift fine should be used as punishment. It was not until he was told that Tom Dex had gone on vacation with his new wife that he had calmed down about the missing hours. The log book had been put down, and the year sealed before the cop had had a brilliant idea to see if he made up for the lost hours if he was paid still. Since he was, he promised never to do the log book ever again, since they did not actually know one year from the next and to just get a paycheck. The paychecks were true to the time they put in, and the log book was just to make sure they worked enough hours. Since this was customary for an officer, it was a lot of time later that the officer had asked Sean Mckeithen if he did the log book in his department, and he had said that he wasn't a cop. Since this was confusing, he allowed it but said, "Did he actually know what a log book looked like?" And when he didn't, he had been convinced that he wasn't. Since the log book still existed. He put in extra hours and claimed that they were Sean Mckeithen's time in the precinct. Since this was funny to him, it was at meeting a year later that someone said that Sean Mckeithen hadn't picked up his paycheck and the check was taken by the cop and put on his wall as a joke. Since it was impossible for him to figure out his spirit had died, he just sat confused. All of a sudden, he asked if the cop was going to cash that, and the cop had scared and gone insane being a thief. Since it was a practical joke, it was sad when he had not been thought funny over the log book and had been fined a heavy fine. Since Sean Mckeithen was not a cop, there was some debate as to the role of a cop, and the visual memory was confusing to spirit until a criminal had asked if he would forge a signature, which is a capital offense and punishable by prison time. The cops had been told on the grapevine, and everyone agreed that was going too far even though it was funny.

Chapter One Hundred and Seventy-five

S ince the late person that mattered to the man was his dad, he thought a lot about him and liked to picture him in his light. Since light was the extent of intelligence, it was fun to him to have a response from his dead father when he asked him stuff. Since this is allowed and not considered an insanity, it was lauded and thought cool. The dead father was military and very smart, and it was because of this that they had grown closer in their old age. Since the dead father did not know this, it was a secret from his mom who didn't know he loved his dad still. Once in a while, the dead would hate, and his dad did once and this had led to a revelation in the son that the distance you could move was the amount of memories that you could have. And after asking his dad, he came up with a fraction, which was ten seconds to three or two hours to six or one movement to seven memories. Since the memory could not think past seven, he had started a seven memory and moved down. Since he did not know why seven and his dad didn't either, he asked his mom who said that eight meant sex to a woman and nine meant death. Since men were not dead inside, only a woman could be made a nine-based memory, and it was called the Mother Mary. The seven-based memory was so smart that he was a little confused when the memory had said eight based and pictured the air. In the air, there was a magnetic that did sex, and this meant that at the environment, he could do an eight-based memory. Since the man was sexual, he found it interesting that his dad would not do the memory and stayed rather in his ability, and the man had realized that it was actually his dad living on in his memory. Since it was not uncommon for him to request his dad, he lived through everything thinking about him.